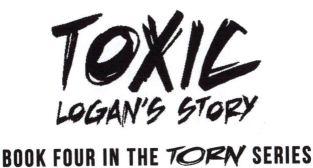

LOGAN'S STORY

BOOK FOUR IN THE *TORN* SERIES

NEW YORK TIMES AND *USA TODAY* BESTSELLING AUTHOR

K.A. ROBINSON

OTHER BOOKS BY

NEW YORK TIMES AND USA TODAY BESTSELLING AUTHOR
K.A. ROBINSON

THE TORN SERIES
TORN
TWISTED
TAINTED

THE TIES SERIES
SHATTERED TIES
TWISTED TIES

BREAKING ALEXANDRIA

This book is dedicated to anyone who has had their heart broken.
Never give up.
Love will find you.

Contents

Part Three: Logan

A Note to Readers

This book focuses on Logan and Jade from The Torn Series. It can be read as a stand-alone or with the previous three books in the series. Please note that due to the timeline in *Torn*, *Twisted*, and *Tainted*, the first few chapters will have several time jumps.

Happy reading!

PART 1   LOGAN

PROLOGUE

I stared at the room number on my schedule and then looked back at the classroom door in front of me. *312*. I was in the right place. I took a deep breath before opening the door and walking in.

Several students looked up to see who had entered. I ignored their stares as I focused on the teacher sitting behind her desk in front of the classroom.

She smiled as I approached. "Can I help you?"

"Uh…yeah, I'm a new student," I said nervously.

I had no idea why I was nervous. It wasn't like I hadn't moved to a new school before. My mom had moved us around a lot—so much so that I'd lost track of how many schools I'd been to. She'd promised me that this time would be different. This would be the last time we moved.

Yeah, right.

That was what she'd said every single time. I just hoped that my freshman year would be the year that she really meant it. I was tired of moving all the time, and now that I was in high school, it wouldn't be as easy to make friends.

I held out my schedule, and the teacher glanced at it.

"It's nice to meet you, Logan. I'm Mrs. Jenkins. Let me grab you a book."

She stood and walked to a door a few feet away from her desk. Once she disappeared inside, I glanced over my shoulder to see two-dozen students staring at me like I was the most interesting guy in the world. I sighed, hating how this happened every time. Being the new kid sucked, but what could I do?

The teacher reappeared and walked back over to me. "Here is your book. We're starting on chapter three today. Why don't you take a seat next to"—she glanced at the seating chart on the desk—"Chloe Richards. Chloe, will you raise your hand, please?"

I turned to face the classroom and saw a girl raise her hand. I walked toward her, ignoring everyone else as they continued to stare at me. I sat down next to her without even looking her way. I knew my new neighbor would be watching me like everyone else.

"Class, let's give Logan a warm welcome. Now, if you'll open your books to chapter three, we can begin," Mrs. Jenkins said.

Once Mrs. Jenkins turned away from us to start writing on the board, I glanced over at my neighbor. My mouth dropped open as I stared at her. *Damn.*

She glanced over at me and smiled before turning her attention back to the front of the room.

The girl was gorgeous. Her hair was a light blonde color, and her eyes were bright blue. I noticed she was wearing a shirt with some rock band on the front. She was tiny, but she had more curves than most girls our age. She looked like an angel.

She glanced over and caught me staring at her. She leaned close to me and whispered, "I'm Chloe."

I smiled at the sound of her voice. It was as sweet as the rest of her.

"Logan," I whispered back.

"Where are you from?" she asked.

Where am I from? I sighed and decided to go with the last state we'd moved from. "Missouri."

"Cool. I've lived here my entire life. I'll warn you now—there's nothing to do around here. It's boring as hell."

I smiled. *I don't think I'll be bored with you around.* "Good to know."

We both turned back to pay attention to what Mrs. Jenkins was saying.

A few minutes later, Chloe poked my arm. I gave her a questioning look.

"Do you think her hair is real or a wig?"

I snorted in laughter, but I quickly covered it with a cough when the students in front of us turned to look. "Uh…I don't know."

"I vote wig. There is no way she could get her natural hair that high on her head."

I glanced up at the teacher and then back to Chloe. "I think you're right."

"Finally! Someone agrees with me!" She snickered.

I spent the rest of class glancing in Chloe's direction. I couldn't get over how pretty she was. Sure, I was a teenage guy, so I noticed things like boobs and ass, but there was just something about this girl.

When the bell rang, she turned back to me. "Let me see your schedule."

I handed it to her, and she glanced over it.

"You have a couple of classes with me. Our next one is together, and we have lunch together, too. I always sit with my friend, Amber. You're welcome to sit with us if you want."

She smiled at me, and I knew right then and there that I was fucked. This girl was already under my skin, and I wanted her more than anything. I would make her mine.

"Sounds perfect," I said.

FOUR YEARS LATER—FALL

I deepened the kiss and started slowly sliding my hand under Chloe's shirt and up her stomach. She froze at the touch and pulled away.

"What's wrong, babe? If we're going too fast, just tell me. After the other day, I thought..." I looked at her with concern in my eyes.

I'd thought that we were in a good place, but her body language was telling me otherwise. We'd been together for a few months now. Plus, I'd known her for over four years, so I knew when something was wrong with her.

"Logan, remember how I wanted to talk to you the other day?"

I nodded, but I stayed silent as I tried to ignore the sinking feeling in my stomach. Something was seriously wrong.

"Well, I need to tell you something." She closed her eyes and took a deep breath before opening them to look at me again. "Something happened between Drake and me. Right after you and I got together a few months ago, I went over to his house to hang out and study for a couple of our classes. Neither of us intended for anything to happen, but we ended up having sex. I am so sorry I didn't tell you. I just couldn't stand the thought of hurting you. It was an accident."

I froze as I looked down at her. Drake was the local rock star and someone she'd become good friends with since we came to West Virginia University. While she had sworn that nothing was going on between the two of them before, I'd noticed how he was always watching her. My gut had warned me about him, but I'd refused to listen. Instead, I'd blindly trusted her, assuming that she would never lie to me.

"*An accident*? What? You just accidentally fell on his dick?" I yelled, losing my temper.

How could she do this to us?

We'd been doing so well together. I was happy. She was happy—or so I'd thought.

I took a deep breath, trying to calm myself. "Why are you telling me this now? Why wait all these months and then dump this on me?"

"I don't know. I guess I just couldn't take the guilt anymore. I don't want to keep lying to you." She stared into my eyes.

"I'm glad you told me, Chloe. I want you to be honest with me. I don't really know what to say, but I'm trying to understand here. You said this was right after we got together?"

She nodded.

"Okay…well, as long as it was just once, I am willing to look past it. I know how confused you were about us then."

I pulled her into a hug as she burst into tears.

"What's wrong, Chloe? I forgive you, baby girl. I forgive you."

She continued to sob, and then she managed to gasp out the words that would seal our fate, "It wasn't just then. It happened again a couple of weeks ago. I went to his house to try to work things out because we hadn't really talked since it happened, and things got carried away."

My body tensed as I tried to fight the rage building inside me. "You had sex with him two weeks ago? What the fuck, Chloe?" I dropped my arms from around her like I'd been burned, and I stood up. She was still crying as I continued yelling, "That son of a bitch! He knew you were mine, and he still went after you. Twice! Un-fucking-believable! I'm going to kill him!" I stormed across the room to the door and threw it open.

She jumped off the bed to come after me. "Logan! Logan, stop! Where are you going?"

I glanced over my shoulder at her, and I headed for the stairs. "I'm going to teach that bastard a lesson. I knew something was up between you two. I just never thought he would pull that. I never thought you would do this to me! How could you, Chloe?" I continued to yell as she chased me down the stairs.

All around us, students stopped dead in the hallway and stairs to stare at us as we passed.

"I'm so sorry, Logan, but please just stop."

She reached for my arm, but I threw her hand away.

"Stay away from me, Chloe, or God help me, I won't be responsible for my actions."

We had made it down the stairs and out into the parking lot. I quickly unlocked my car and jumped in. Chloe tried to open the passenger door, but I kept it locked as I put the car in drive. I left black marks as I screeched out of the parking lot. I glanced back in my rearview mirror to see her running for her own car and jumping in. I turned my attention back to the main road.

I drove straight to the bar where Drake's band often played, knowing he would be there on a Friday night. As soon as I shut off my car, I jumped out and ran toward the building. I heard Chloe calling my name as she chased me across the lot, but I ignored her as I went into the bar.

When I entered, Drake was up on stage, playing with the band. I headed straight for him with Chloe on my heels. Before she could stop me, I jumped up on the stage and punched Drake in the face. She screamed as Drake's head jerked back from the force of it. Blood started trickling down from his nose to his lips. The crowd started screaming, and the other band members quickly grabbed me as I lunged for Drake again.

"What the fuck?" Drake yelled as he glared at me.

9

He glanced up and went pale when he saw Chloe standing in front of the stage, crying and shaking.

"You stupid son of a bitch! Did you think I wouldn't find out that you've been fucking Chloe behind my back?"

I lunged again, and Adam, one of Drake's bandmates, was caught off guard, letting me go. Drake saw me coming and jumped back before landing a punch of his own in my stomach. I grunted and dropped to one knee before standing back up and going after him again.

"Come on, pretty boy, I'm standing right here. Come and get me," Drake taunted.

I threw another punch that Drake wasn't quick enough to dodge, and it landed in his rib cage. I threw myself at Drake while the pain distracted him, and we flew backward into the drums, sending them flying. I could hear Chloe screaming at both of us as we continued to throw punches before Adam and Eric pulled us apart.

Eric pried Drake off of me and held him tight as Adam twisted my arm behind my back and held me in a death grip. I struggled to get loose, but it was no use.

Jade—another one of Drake's bandmates, who had been standing on the end of the stage the entire time—put her fingers in her mouth and whistled. "That's it! Grow the fuck up, boys, or at least take it outside!"

I looked at Drake with pure hatred in my eyes. "How could you, Drake? I asked you that day at lunch if there was anything between the two of you before I went for her. You told me nothing was going on and that nothing would. You promised me that you would leave her alone, and look what happened. You fucked her not once but twice behind my back."

Drake glared right back at me. "Yeah, I did fuck her twice because once just wasn't enough for me, and I'd do it again if I could."

I tried to lunge for him, but Adam was prepared this time, and he held tight.

"All right, guys, both of you outside now," Adam growled as he held me back.

He marched me offstage and across the bar to the door. Eric followed closely behind, still holding on to Drake. With their arms wrapped around each other, Jade and Chloe followed behind them at a distance.

When I stepped out into the cool night air, I breathed deeply, trying to control my rage. *How did my life come to this?*

Chloe was everything to me, and she'd betrayed me. She might as well have stuck a knife in me. It wouldn't have hurt as bad as this.

Once we were far enough away from the bar doors, Eric and Adam released Drake and me, and they stepped back.

"All right, you want to kick the shit out of each other, be my guest. We're not going to stop you, but you guys need to get your shit together. Fighting over a girl is fucking ridiculous, and you know it. So, do what you want. Just get it out and over with before our drums suffer anymore," Eric growled.

He and Adam made their way over to where Jade and Chloe were standing.

Drake and I faced each other, both of us glaring at the other. We glanced down when Chloe stepped forward to stand between us.

"Listen to me, both of you. This is so stupid, like Eric said. This is all my fault, and the two of you beating the shit out of each other isn't going to fix anything. I fucked up, not you two. So, if you want to take your anger out on someone, take it out on me. I ruined everything." Tears ran down her face as she looked at both of us. "You both mean so much to me, and I will never forgive myself for what I have done to you."

She quickly turned away from us and headed across the parking lot to her car before either of us could say anything. We watched in silence as she pulled out of the lot and disappeared around the corner. Once she was out of sight, I turned my attention back to Drake.

"You destroyed everything!" I shouted at him.

"Fuck this. I'm going back inside. As much fun as it would be to watch you two idiots beat the shit out of each other, it's cold out here," Adam muttered.

He turned and walked back to the bar. Eric and Jade watched us for a second before turning and following him. I didn't miss the pity in Jade's eyes, but I ignored it. I didn't want anyone to feel pity for me.

"You think I don't know that, asshole?" Drake said as he glared at me. "I know this is my fault."

"Then, why did you do it?" I shouted.

"Because I love her!" he shouted back.

That stopped me in my tracks. Of all the responses I'd expected, that hadn't been one of them. Drake used women. He didn't love them.

"You what?" I asked incredulously.

"I love her. I've tried to ignore it—believe me, I've tried—but I can't. I love her, and I don't know what the fuck to do about it."

"You're incapable of love, Drake. I've watched you screw every woman in sight for months!"

"I haven't touched another woman since I figured out how I felt about Chloe. I wouldn't do that to her." He ran his hands through his hair. "Look, I think we need to talk and not in the middle of a parking lot. My house is right around the corner. Let's go there and figure shit out, okay?"

I stared at him, debating on whether to go with him or punch him again. Finally, I decided that talking was the only thing that would solve this whole mess even if punching him would make me feel better. "Fine. Let's go."

Neither of us said a word as we walked to his house. He hadn't been kidding when he said he lived right around the corner. I waited impatiently as he unlocked his front door, and then we walked inside. Once he flipped on the lights, we stepped into the living room and sat down across from each other.

"So, now what?" I finally asked after several minutes of silence.

"I don't fucking know. I *do* know that I want Chloe more than anything else in this world," he said as he stared at me.

"Yeah, well, so do I. I've loved her since the moment I laid eyes on her. It's taken me four years to get up the nerve to tell her how I feel, and then you come along and sweep her off her feet in a few months."

"I didn't mean for it to go down like this. I'm not a complete asshole. I just…I can't control myself around her."

"I've noticed," I growled as I clenched my hands into fists. "If I had known she was sleeping with you and me at the same time, I would have—"

"You would have what? Left her? Told her you hated her? Called her a slut?" he asked.

"I don't know what I would have done, okay? I've spent most of my teenage years in love with her. I don't know what to do."

He sighed and ran his hands through his hair. "This is so fucked-up! I actually care about a girl, and she's with someone else."

"We have to let her choose. That's all we can do," I said.

He looked up at me and smirked. "And the loser does what? Walks away and pretends that none of this happened?"

"I guess so. What other choice do we have?"

"I can't just walk away from her, Logan."

"You have to. And if she chooses you"—I took a deep breath—"I'll have to walk away. We're ripping her apart."

"You're right." Drake stood and kicked the chair he'd just been sitting in. "Why the fuck can't I let her go?"

"For the same reason I can't—you love her. Chloe is special."

He smiled, the first one I'd seen all night. "Yeah, she is."

I frowned as he stared off into space with that damn smile on his face. He pulled out his phone and started typing on it.

"What are you doing?" I asked.

"Texting her to see if she's okay. She was really upset when she left the bar."

"So, what do you want to do? Go talk to her now? Or wait until she calms down?" I asked.

"Let's wait. I doubt she'll speak to either of us right now," Drake said as he looked at me. "Look, I know you don't like me, and I sure as hell don't like you, but let's try to be civil with each other until this is sorted out. Once she chooses, we can go back to hating each other. I don't want to upset her more than she already is."

"Fine with me," I mumbled.

We spent the next hour texting Chloe, but she didn't respond to either of us. I started to worry, especially with her psychotic mother trying to contact her again.

"Maybe I should go check on her," I said as I stood and started walking to the door.

"You're not going over there without me. I don't know what you'll say to her. I'm coming with you."

I rolled my eyes. "Whatever. I just want to make sure she's okay."

I ignored him as we walked back to the bar where our cars were parked. I climbed in and drove back to the dorm, refusing to think about anything. I would deal with everything when I was in my room by myself. If I thought about it now, I'd lose my mind and probably hit Drake again.

I pulled into the dorm parking lot and shut off my car. I stared at the dorm in front of me, unable to move. I didn't want to face Chloe right now. I loved her more than anything, but I also hated her at the moment. We'd finally found happiness, and she had gone and screwed it all up. If she had stayed away from Drake, we would still be together in her room right now.

I opened my door when I saw Drake walking past my car. I followed as he walked into the dorm. I wasn't about to let him see her alone either. I couldn't handle that yet. We were both silent as we walked up the stairs and onto her floor. Once we reached the door, Drake knocked. A minute later, the door swung open, and Chloe was standing in front of us. Even though I was pissed, the mere sight of her took my breath away.

She smiled as soon as she saw us. "Hey, guys! How are you?" She giggled. "Actually, never mind. You're both pretty damn fine, like always."

She turned without another word and made her way back to her bed. She fell on top of it, and she glanced back at us, still smiling.

"What the hell is wrong with her?" I mumbled to Drake as I stepped into the room. "Are you all right, Chloe?" I asked, my voice louder.

"I'm great! I had a couple of shots, and now, I'm all set." She smiled brightly at us. "What are you guys doing here? Wait, you're together, and there's no blood!"

Both of us continued to stare at her.

I glanced around the room to see a bottle of vodka on her nightstand. *Shit, she's drunk.* That was what the warm welcome had been all about.

I leaned down beside her bed and looked into her glassy eyes. "Just how many shots have you had, love?"

"Only a couple." She motioned to the bottle on the nightstand. "See? It's still full. I just opened it tonight."

Drake glanced at the stand before looking back at her. "Uh…Chloe, the bottle is empty."

She stared at the bottle. Realizing that he was right, she slapped her hand across her face before laughing. "Whoops! Guess it's a good thing it was the cheap stuff. Otherwise, I'd seriously be drunk right now."

Drake and I exchanged looks with each other, both of our expressions filled with concern. She was past drunk and moving into wasted.

"Chloe, honey, you *are* drunk, excessively drunk actually," I said as I watched her.

She rolled her eyes. "Seriously, guys, I'm fine. Why are you here?"

Drake spoke up from his spot in front of the bed, "Look, Chloe, you're trashed, so I don't think right now is a good time to talk, like Logan and I planned. We'll come back tomorrow"—he glanced at the bottle again—"or the day after. I'm pretty sure you aren't going to be up to any talking tomorrow."

"I said, I'm fine!" she grumbled as she sat up.

Two seconds later, she grabbed the garbage can beside the bed and threw up violently into it. I jumped back a couple of feet as she continued to throw up. It seemed like hours had passed by before she was finished.

Jesus. I'd never seen her like this.

Finally, there seemed to be nothing left in her stomach, and she rolled back onto her bed, groaning. "Fuck. Maybe I am drunk."

Drake chuckled quietly. "No shit, Chloe."

She glared at him. "Just say what you came here to say, asshole."

"We came to tell you to decide who you want. Both of us want you, but who you want is what really matters. Whoever you don't choose will back off, no questions asked."

She looked back and forth between us. "What if I want both of you?"

And then, she passed out.

Fuck.

2

I couldn't sleep at all that night. Instead, I tossed and turned as I replayed the last few months over and over again in my mind. I tried to figure out what I had done wrong to push Chloe away. From the beginning, I'd known that Drake was interested in her, but I'd ignored it. I'd thought that she was smart enough not to fall for the asshole who slept with every woman he saw. Of course, I hadn't even considered the fact that he might actually care about her. I hadn't thought he was capable of caring about a woman.

I'd been overconfident and stupid. I'd thought that she was mine, and no one would take her away from me. We'd been through so much together. We'd been attached at the hip since I moved to West Virginia my freshman year. I'd stayed by her side through everything with her mom. When her mother, Andrea, had shown back up in Chloe's life to torment her, I was the one she would always come to. I was the one who would help her clean her cuts when her mother had beaten her. I was the one who would beg her to go to the police. And I was the one who would understand her decision when she had refused. She had been afraid that she would be put into foster care and never see me or her other best friend, Amber, again.

I was so angry with her, but I was hurt, too. I had trusted her completely, and she'd stabbed me in the back. The one person I'd thought would never hurt me was the one who had ripped my heart to pieces. Even if she chose me, I wasn't sure that things could ever go back to the way they had been before. And if she chose Drake...I would walk away. I would cut ties with her and start over again. The thought of leaving her behind had me clenching my fists in anger. Drake was the reason that my entire life was falling apart, and I hated the asshole with every fiber of my being.

I finally fell asleep just as the sun was starting to rise.

I hadn't been asleep for more than an hour or two when I heard a knock on my door. I rolled out of bed and slowly walked to the door, terrified of who I would find on the other side. I wasn't sure that I wanted to see anyone at this point.

I opened the door to see Chloe standing in the hallway. Her eyes were red and puffy from crying. Despite the circumstances, I longed to reach out and comfort her. I pushed the thought away. Without a word, I turned back into the room and sat on my bed. Chloe walked in and closed the door behind her.

I sighed before glancing up at her. "I lost, didn't I?"

She looked at the floor. "Not really. I'm so tired of hurting both of you, Logan. I love you both…just in different ways. I'm not choosing him, but I'm not choosing you either."

I tried to hide my emotions as I realized that I was losing her. It felt like someone had punched me in the chest. The pain I was feeling right now was unbearable.

I rose and crossed the room to stand in front of her. "I understand, and I accept your decision." It nearly killed me to say the words, but I forced them out.

Tears started falling from her eyes. "I'm so sorry, Logan. I ruined everything we ever had. I didn't just lose my boyfriend, but I also lost my best friend in all of this mess."

I pulled her into a tight hug, unable to watch her suffer. "You haven't lost me as a friend, Chloe, but I need some time before I can go back to the way things were. Just don't give up on our friendship. I promise, I won't leave you."

She hugged me back tightly. "I understand. Thanks, Logan."

She pulled away and made her way to the door. I watched as she opened it.

"When you're ready, you know where to find me," she said before leaving me.

I didn't move for several minutes. Instead, I stood there and stared at the door, willing her to come back and tell me that she changed her mind, that she chose me. In my heart, I knew that she wouldn't come back. I walked over to my bed and dropped down onto it. Once again, I wondered what I had done to end up like this. All my life, I'd tried to help people, and I'd been a good guy. And for what? So, I could watch the love of my life walk away from me.

Unable to stay in my room any longer, I changed into a pair of jeans and a plain T-shirt. I grabbed my jacket and then my keys off the desk, and I headed for the door. I had no idea where I was going, but I knew I needed to get out of this room.

The hallway and stairs of my dorm building were nearly empty as I made my way outside. I walked to my car and pulled out of the parking lot. I drove around town, debating on where to go. I circled around until I was almost back at my dorm. Then, I saw the bar where Drake played—Gold's Pub.

What the hell? I might as well drown my sorrows. I pulled into the parking lot, and I looked around to make sure that I didn't see Drake's car. Once I knew he wasn't at the bar, I stepped out of my car and walked inside.

It was still early, and only a few people were around. I walked to the far side of the bar and sat down.

Seconds later, the bartender appeared in front of me. "What can I get you, honey?" She smiled at me.

"Whiskey," I muttered.

"Coming right up." She turned and walked farther down the bar to grab a bottle. She returned with Jack Daniel's and a shot glass.

I watched as she poured the shot and handed it to me.

"Leave the bottle," I said after I took the shot.

She raised an eyebrow but said nothing. I poured myself another shot as she moved away to wait on someone else. All I wanted to do was get wasted. Then, maybe I could forget how much of a shitfest my life really was.

"Logan?" a voice asked from behind me.

I turned to see the drummer of Drake's band standing there. "Hey, Jade."

"Want some company?" she asked.

"Sure. Why not?"

She sat down beside me and motioned for the bartender to bring over another shot glass.

"So, how are things?" she asked as she poured herself a shot.

"Wonderful. My girlfriend cheated on me with a guy who has slept with half of Morgantown. I couldn't be happier."

She sighed. "I'm sorry for what happened to you, Logan."

"You have no reason to be sorry. You didn't cheat on me."

"I know. I just feel bad for what happened to you. If it makes you feel any better, I know Chloe and Drake never meant for this to happen. They both tried to stay away from each other."

I snorted. "Right. I'm sure they did."

She glanced over at me as I poured another shot.

"They did. I know you don't like Drake, but I've been friends with him for a long time. He's a good guy. If he didn't love Chloe, he never would have gotten between the two of you. And I know Chloe cares a lot about you. She never wanted to hurt you."

"Then, she should have been honest with me!" I shouted as I slammed the shot glass down on the bar. "That's all she had to do. Instead, she kept things from me, and look where we are now."

"I know. I'm not trying to defend them, honest. What they did to you was wrong, and now, all three of you are paying the price. I just wanted you to know that you're not alone. I know it all seems really screwed-up right now." She stood and placed her hand on my shoulder. "Call me if you need someone to talk to, okay?"

I nodded, not bothering to look up at her. I didn't need anyone.

3

I spent the next few days avoiding everyone. I couldn't stomach the pity in their eyes or their comforting words. I even avoided Amber until she got pissed off enough to beat my damn door down and demand an explanation. After I told her what happened, she went on a rampage and declared Chloe enemy number one. I told her to be nice. While I was angry with Chloe, I didn't want to tear her and Amber apart. She wasn't happy, but she agreed not to go beat the crap out of Chloe on my behalf. I considered that a victory. Amber wasn't one to hide her feelings.

Jade showed up at my door one night with a bottle of Jack Daniel's and two shot glasses. I almost closed the door in her face, but she pushed through before I could stop her. I wasn't in the mood to talk to anyone.

"What do you want, Jade?" I asked as I rubbed my eyes. I was exhausted, and my bed was calling my name.

"I know what you're doing, and I'm not going to let you do it," she stated as she dropped down into the chair next to my desk. She set the Jack Daniel's and shot glasses on the top of the desk.

"What am I doing?"

"Avoiding everyone and hiding."

"I am not," I muttered as I closed my door.

"Yes, you are."

"So, what if I am? Maybe I don't want to deal with people right now."

"That's fine. You don't have to deal with people, just me." She poured a shot and handed it to me. "Drink up."

"What are you really doing here, Jade?" I asked as I took the glass.

She poured a shot for herself. "I'm keeping you company. I don't want you to sit up here by yourself and mope. It isn't healthy."

"And getting drunk with someone I barely know is better?" I countered.

She laughed. "Good point, but I'm still not leaving. I don't want you to be alone."

"Why do you even care?" I gulped down my shot and handed the glass back to her.

She hesitated for a minute. "I don't know, but I do, so you're stuck with me. I'm going to cheer you up."

I laughed. "There's nothing you can do to cheer me up."

"Then, we'll sit here and stare at each other until you decide being miserable isn't worth it."

I sighed as she poured another shot and handed it to me. "Fine. Stay. Stare at me. I don't care."

We were both silent as we each took two more shots of whiskey. I sat down on my bed and waited for her to say something again. I knew next to nothing about Jade. The only thing I *did* know about her was the fact that she played drums in Drake's band.

Drake. Even his name pissed me off at this point. I forced myself not to think about him before I started shouting obscenities while Jade was around. It wasn't her fault that her friend was a girlfriend-stealing asshole.

"So...tell me about yourself, Logan," Jade finally said.

I looked up at her and grinned. "Really? You want to get to know each other?"

She shrugged. "Sure. Why not? You could use a friend. I can be that friend, but I'd like to know more about you."

"More? What do you already know?"

She gave me a weak smile. "Well, let's see. I know you like Jack Daniel's. I also know you're from Charleston since Chloe told me you went to high school together. You work at a garage…and you have the prettiest blue eyes I've ever seen. That's about it."

"It's like you can see into my soul," I joked, ignoring the comment about my eyes.

I wasn't stupid. Jade hung out with Adam, Eric, and Drake. There was no way that I could compete with those guys. Rockers were more her speed, not some country kid like me. I looked up to see her watching me closely. She really was pretty. I'd never noticed before because I was with Chloe.

Comparing the two was laughable. Two girls couldn't be more different. Where Chloe was all light with her pale skin, blonde hair, and light blue eyes, Jade was all dark. I'd seen a few different colors in her hair, but right now, it was black with pink streaks. Her eyes were a warm chocolate, and her skin was tan. Surprisingly enough, I didn't see any visible tattoos on her body, unlike the other members of her band. She had a small stud in her nose, but she didn't have any other piercings, not even in her ears.

"You're not going to tell me anything, are you?" she finally asked.

"What do you want to know?"

"Anything you want to tell me." She smiled.

"Fine. Let's see. I moved around with my mom for most of my childhood. By the time I was fourteen, we'd lived in sixteen different states. She finally settled down in Charleston, but I don't know why. I didn't ask. I was just glad to be in one place for more than a few months. I don't know much about my dad besides the fact that she kept moving to avoid him. I think she was scared of him."

I stopped talking, surprised that I'd told her that much about me. No one knew about my dad, except for Amber and Chloe. I didn't even know the asshole's name. For some reason, I'd never asked my mom. I didn't want to know anything about the asshole who had terrified my mother so much that we had to run from state to state for over a decade.

She frowned. "I know a lot about asshole father figures."

I stayed silent, waiting for her to continue. When she didn't, I asked, "Care to elaborate on that?"

"What? Oh, yeah. Sorry. I just meant that I could relate. My stepdad was the perfect example of an arrogant prick. I hate him. He put me through hell before I finally left home."

"Did you grow up in Morgantown?"

She shook her head. "No, I'm from Tennessee. I ran away from home when I was seventeen. I planned to go to New York City, but I met Eric on my way there. He offered me a place to stay, and we ended up forming the band with Adam and then Drake. The guys are more of a family to me than my mom and step-prick ever were. I do miss my little sister though."

I raised an eyebrow. "You have a sister?"

"Yeah, she's four years younger than I am. I probably wouldn't recognize her if I saw her. She wasn't quite fourteen when I left."

"Are you the same age as us?" I asked, referring to Chloe, Drake, and me.

"Nah, I'm three and a half years older than you guys. I'm twenty-one. Eric and Adam are my age. Drake is the baby of the group. My sister is only a year younger than you guys though."

We were both silent, lost in our thoughts. It was strange to know more about Jade. I'd always thought she was nice, but I never really paid much attention to her. She was just one of Chloe's friends, nothing more. Now, I could see that there was a lot about Jade that I didn't know.

"Anyway, tell me more about you. What is your major?"

I grinned. "Accounting with a minor in graphic design. I'm good with numbers and computers. I'm not sure if I want to be an accountant or a web designer."

She shuddered. "I'd rather stick my tongue on a hot oven than deal with numbers all day. If the band ever makes it big, I'll be sure to call you to handle our finances. I sure as hell don't want to do it."

I laughed. "It's not that bad if you think about it. Number equations always have an answer, regardless of the variable. There's always a way to solve it."

She shook her head. "I'll stick to the drums."

"You've never been to college?"

She hesitated. "I didn't even graduate high school, Logan. If it wasn't for Eric, I'd be on the streets."

That surprised me. Jade seemed like an intelligent person.

I couldn't wrap my head around the fact that she didn't even have a high school diploma. "Why did you quit?"

"I ran away from home. It would have been easy for step-prick to track me down if I enrolled in another high school or even a GED program."

"What about after you turned eighteen? You didn't need to hide then. He couldn't drag you back since you were a legal adult." I said.

"I focus all my attention on the band. If I'm not doing that, I'm working. I have a few kids in the area that I give weekly drum lessons to for extra cash. It isn't a ton, but it helps Eric with the rent. I don't have time to go to school."

I nodded, but I still didn't get how she could put the band ahead of her education. My mother had beaten it into my head that I had to go as far as I could with my education. She wanted me to have so much more than she had.

"I think we've had enough heart-to-heart conversation for one night. I'll leave you alone to mope." She stood up and walked to the door.

I was surprised by her sudden departure, but I nodded. "Thanks for stopping by, Jade. I appreciate it."

She smiled. "You're welcome, Logan. I know you're hurting right now, but you're not alone. I hope you know that."

She was gone before I had the chance to respond. I stared at the door, wondering what the hell had just happened.

After that night, something shifted between Jade and me. At least, it did for me. For the first time ever, I saw her as more than just Chloe's friend or a member of Drake's band. I saw her as my friend. She stopped by my dorm room a few more times, but we never talked about our pasts again. Instead, we would argue about music, bullshit about our day, or go over my classwork together.

Just as I'd suspected, Jade was smart, really smart. I never brought up her lack of education, but it bothered me. I really did hope that the band took off, but there was a good chance that it wouldn't, and she'd be left with nothing. In this world, she would need a high school diploma to find work—period. I spent some time researching how she could get her GED, but I never mentioned it up to her. I didn't want to piss her off or offend her. So, I stashed the information away as I debated on the best way to bring it up.

I saw Chloe several times on campus, but I couldn't bring myself to speak to her. She looked as miserable as I felt, but I wasn't ready. She'd hurt me, broken me. It would take time to heal from that. I even saw Drake once or twice. While I hated him, I no longer felt the rage I had in the beginning. I didn't have it in me. I hated the fact that I couldn't be angry with either of them. I *wanted* to be angry. Instead, all I felt was disappointment and sadness. I'd thought that I made Chloe happy, but it was obvious that I hadn't. I lacked whatever it was that drew her to Drake.

I kept replaying my relationship with Chloe over and over, trying to figure out what I had done to screw it up. To me, every moment had felt perfect. It was obvious that I was missing something. I was lacking, and the worst part was that I would never know what I had done wrong. Even if I could forgive Chloe, I knew I would never have the courage to ask her what I had done to ruin everything, what I had done to make her love another man.

Maybe it was the whole bad-boy thing. I knew girls liked that. Drake played that role perfectly. The women, the band, the tattoos, and the piercings—I knew those were things that women loved. I'd just never expected Chloe to be one of those women, and I'd never expected the womanizer in Drake to love Chloe back.

I hated the fact that I was hurting Chloe by ignoring her and by keeping her away from Drake. I would watch both of them, and I could tell they weren't together. If I told her that it was okay for her to be with Drake, I knew she would go running to him, begging him to take her back after she let both of us go. I wasn't sure that I could stomach that.

I started going to the gym more, and I picked up extra shifts at work just so I had something to do. I'd made friends with a few guys at work, and I even went out with them a few times, but it didn't feel the same as it had when I was with Chloe and Amber. As days turned to weeks, I knew I needed to man up and get over myself. I needed to forgive Chloe, so both of us could all start living our lives again instead of hanging in this miserable limbo.

Knocking on Chloe's door was one of the most selfish and selfless things I'd ever done. It was selfish because I was sick of being miserable, and it was also selfless because I knew that once I told her I forgave her, she would eventually find her way back to Drake. It was inevitable. I'd been a blind fool before, and deep down, even I'd known what would happen.

I'd tried calling her a few times, but her phone always went straight to voice mail. I'd hoped that I could take the coward's way out and not have to come face-to-face with her when I all but gave her my permission to go back to Drake, but I'd had no such luck. I was going to have to grow a pair and act like an adult.

I almost laughed at the startled gasp Rachel, Chloe's roommate, gave when she answered the door. It was obvious that she hadn't expected me. I glanced behind her to see Chloe staring at me with a look of shock on her face. She was holding a bag, but it slipped from her fingers. Feathers flew everywhere as the bag hit the ground.

I chuckled as I stared at the mess. "Do I even want to ask?"

"Pillow fight," she whispered as she continued to stare at me.

"Mind if I come in to talk?" I asked quietly.

Rachel held the door open the rest of the way, and I walked in. I stopped when I was standing in front of Chloe. I glanced back to see Rachel still standing by the doorway, looking like a deer caught in the headlights of an oncoming semi.

"I'm...yeah...I'm going to go. Call me when you're done." She gave Chloe a hopeful smile as she grabbed her keys, and then she made a hasty retreat out the door.

Chloe and I were silent as we stared at each other. She looked away and quickly bent down to start scooping the escaped feathers back into the bag. I took a deep breath before I knelt beside her and started helping.

"How have you been?" I asked once we finished searching for feathers.

"Fine. You?" She stood up quickly and set the bag by the door, trying to avoid all eye contact with me.

"Not so good. I've missed you a lot, Chloe. I don't like how things are between us."

She shifted her weight from one foot to the other.

"I tried calling you first to see if it was okay for me to come by, but it went straight to voice mail. I wasn't sure if you were avoiding me or if you had shut off your phone."

She shook her head as she walked over to pick up her phone. "It's off. I would never ignore you, Logan. I've missed you, too."

My forehead crinkled in confusion. "Why is your phone off? What if someone needed to get a hold of you?"

She snorted in a very unladylike manor. I couldn't help but give her a small grin. It was so Chloe.

"Like who? Besides Rachel and Jade, no one has been speaking to me."

Jade? She hadn't mentioned spending time with Chloe. Then again, why would she? She knew that I hated when she would mention Chloe or Drake. I made a mental note to ask her about it later.

"Has anyone been giving you a hard time since…everything happened?"

She shook her head as she set her phone back down. "No, everyone has left me alone, even Amber."

I frowned, unhappy that Amber hadn't listened to me. She'd let me come between her and Chloe.

"I see. I'll talk to Amber tomorrow. She doesn't need to ignore you because of me. You've been friends far too long to let me get in the way. That doesn't answer my question though. If no one was bothering you, why did you shut off your phone?"

She gave me a weak smile as she sat down on her bed. "Um…my mom has been calling me a lot lately. I shut it off, so I wouldn't have to hear it ring all night."

My body went rigid. Her mom was a psychotic bitch who thrived on making Chloe's life miserable.

"She's still bothering you?"

She nodded. "Yeah, but it's not a big deal. I just ignore it."

I sat down next to her. I was about to hug her, but I stopped myself at the last second. For the first time since we had become friends, hugging her felt wrong. "Why didn't you tell me? Have you been talking to her?"

She scooted across the bed a bit to get away from me. I winced, but she didn't seem to notice.

Jesus, how did we come to this?

"No, I haven't spoken with her since that day I called you. Drake got on the phone with her then, and I think he scared her off for a while, but she's back with a vengeance."

I couldn't help but stiffen at the mention of Drake.

"And I never told you because it's only been happening for the last week or so, and we haven't exactly been on speaking terms. I couldn't just run to you about it like I did before."

I took a deep breath before turning to look at her. "Chloe, you can always come to me about this stuff, no matter what's happening between us. Just because things ended the way they did doesn't mean that I don't care about you anymore. You're still my best friend and always will be. That's actually what I came here to talk to you about tonight. I miss you, Chloe. I know that there's nothing left between us romantically, but I don't want to lose you completely. You've always been such a big part of my life. These past few weeks have been hell without you."

Tears broke free from her eyes and started rolling down her cheeks. She threw herself into my arms and hugged me as tightly as her tiny body could manage. My gut clenched at the contact. God, I'd missed her, but it hurt like hell to hold her, knowing she wasn't mine anymore.

"Oh, Logan! I've missed you so much. You have no idea. After everything, I was so sure you'd never speak to me again. I thought I'd lost you!"

She sobbed into my chest as I rubbed her back.

"I told you, I just needed time, Chloe. I could never leave you for long. You're too important to me. I felt like I had a hole in my chest."

She pulled back to look at me. "I have, too. My world is not the same without you in it."

We sat together on her bed and just talked for hours. She finally came clean and told me everything that had happened from the beginning. I listened quietly as she spilled every regret, every loss, every happy moment. When she finished, we were both shaken and tearful.

"I wish you would have told me everything from the beginning, Chloe. Things could have been so much different for all of us." *Maybe it wouldn't have broken me if I had known.* I didn't tell her that though.

She obviously had enough guilt to deal with right now without me adding anything extra to it.

She nodded as she wiped her tears away. "I know that now, but I figured it out too late. I was too deep in with you, and I didn't want to hurt you."

"I know you didn't, baby girl, but you did. What's in the past is exactly where it needs to be—behind us. From this point on, we'll start over, no more looking back at our mistakes. We'll only look to the future. I'm not about to lose you again." *I'm willing to let you go even if that means he'll have you. I love you that much, Chloe.*

She hugged me tightly as a smile spread across her face. "I'm never going to let you go again. We're Logan and Chloe—partners in crime until the end."

It was well after midnight when I finally left Chloe's room and went back to mine. I dropped down onto my bed and closed my eyes. I felt relieved now that I'd told Chloe that things were okay between us, but it still hurt like hell to think of everything. I didn't want to be alone. Without really thinking about it, I texted Jade.

Me: Hey. What are you up to?

She replied a few minutes later.

Jade: Just finished practicing with the guys. You?

Me: Just got back from talking with Chloe.

Jade: How did that go?

Me: As expected.

Jade: I'll be over in a few. I'll bring our good friend Jack.

I smiled at her text. Jade was good for me. She made me smile. It was nice to have a friend who wouldn't judge me for what had happened. She wouldn't react, unlike Amber had. Jade was just…there.

Twenty minutes later, Jade knocked on my door. As soon as I opened it, she walked in and dropped down onto my roommate's bed. He'd stayed in the room once, maybe twice, since the beginning of school. I wasn't complaining though. It was like having a room to myself.

She poured two shots and handed one to me.

I grinned as I took it. "You know, I feel like we're on the verge of becoming alcoholics with the way we drink when we're together."

She laughed before taking her shot. "Don't be a pussy. I could drink Jack every day if I wanted to."

I rolled my eyes as I dropped down onto my bed. "So, I talked to Chloe."

"How did it go? Did you go at it like animals?"

It was my turn to laugh. *I wish.* "Not quite. We talked."

"And?" She pushed for more.

"And we're okay. I told her that I forgive her for what happened."

"Do you?"

I sighed. "Yes and no. I don't know if I'll ever really forgive her. I loved her completely, Jade, and she threw it back in my face. How the hell am I supposed to have a relationship after this? I mean, when I'm with someone in the future, I'm going to wonder if she's sneaking around behind my back with someone better."

"Better?" Jade asked, sounding half-confused and half-pissed.

"Yeah, better. It's obvious that Drake is better than I am, or she never would have gone to him."

"You're an idiot, Logan. Drake isn't better than you. It's just that…sometimes, people are just drawn to each other. I know you don't want to hear this, but I've seen the way Drake and Chloe look at each other. They love each other."

I winced.

"I know it hurts to hear that, but I won't lie to you. They love each other. Sometimes, people are just meant to be. It doesn't mean that Drake is a better guy than you. It just means that he's the one she's supposed to be with."

"So, where does that leave me?" I asked sadly.

"In your dorm room, drinking Jack with an awesome drummer chick."

I laughed. *Leave it to Jade to make me smile.* "So, what about you?"

"What about me?"

"You know all of my nasty history. How's your love life?"

She rolled her eyes. "I have no love life. I haven't had one for a long time."

"How come?"

She hesitated for a second. I watched as she filled her glass before taking another shot.

"I loved someone once, but it wasn't meant to be."

"Wasn't meant to be?" I raised an eyebrow at her.

"I...I thought I loved him, but he wasn't right for me. I told you before about my controlling step-prick, right?"

I nodded.

"Well, Mikey was there for me when I was living at home. He made me forget all about my home life. I thought I loved him, but I'm not sure if I really did. He was more of an escape than anything. The longer we were together, the more controlling he became. It didn't take me long to realize that I was walking headfirst into a relationship with someone exactly like my stepdad. I didn't want that, so I ran away without even saying good-bye to Mikey. I couldn't. He would have either stopped me or tried to come with me."

"You've been gone for...what? Four years now?" I asked.

She nodded. "Yep."

"And he's never tried to find you?" I asked incredulously. If Chloe were to disappear, I would do everything in my power to find her.

"If he tried, I don't know about it. I mean, I left a note in my little sister's room, so my mom and stepdad would know that I hadn't been kidnapped or anything. I'm sure they told Mikey I left. That probably went over real well with him. I didn't leave any kind of trail. I don't have anything in my name, not even a cell phone. Everything is in Eric's name, and they don't know about him. I doubt Mikey could find me even if he wanted to."

"I...wow, I don't even know what to say, Jade. I can't imagine just leaving home and not talking to anyone for so long."

"It's not so bad. Like I said, the guys are my family now. The only person I truly miss is my sister. Once she turns eighteen, I plan on hunting her down. If I tried to see her now, I doubt my mom and stepdad would let me. My stepdad is an ass for sure, but in some ways, my mom is worse."

"If your stepdad was as bad as you say, weren't you worried about leaving your sister alone with him?" I asked.

She gave me a weak smile. "She's only my half-sister. She's his actual kid, so he wasn't mean to her. He hated me because my mom had fucked around on him and ended up with me. They hated me for something I had no say in."

I frowned. "And I thought my life was screwed-up. I'm sorry you had to go through all of that, Jade. It's bullshit."

"Don't feel sorry for me. I'm happy now, happier than I ever was there. One day, when the band makes it big, I'm going to go back home and rub it in all their faces. I'm going to tell both of them how much I hate them."

Neither of us spoke for a long time after that. Instead, we drank shot after shot, both of us trying to forget. I was sure Jade was lost in memories of her old life, and I was torn between thinking about everything with Chloe and worrying about Jade.

Chloe's mom had always terrified me. I'd seen Chloe come to school with bruises and cuts more times than I could count. I couldn't help but wonder if Jade had gone through something similar. I wasn't sure if I wanted to know.

Regardless of how these women had grown up, it was obvious that they were incredibly strong. I knew that they had to be damaged mentally from the abuse they dealt with, but they had rarely shown it, especially Jade. I'd known her for a few months now, and I'd always thought of her as a strong person. She had to be since she dealt with Eric, Adam, and Drake day and night.

Before I realized what had happened, I was drunk—not the stumbling-around-and-puking kind of drunk but a happy drunk. With the exception of the last few weeks, I rarely drank. I'd seen how Chloe's mom was when she was drunk, and I wanted no part in something that did that kind of damage to a person. But this wasn't that kind of drunk. Instead, I felt weightless and relaxed. While I knew things weren't even close to being back to normal, for the first time since everything had happened, I had hope that I would be happy again. I knew it was just the alcohol talking, but I didn't mind. I liked it. Between school and Chloe, I was always stressed. It was nice to just let loose for the night and chill.

It dawned on me that I looked forward to these nights with Jade more than I'd realized. I looked up to see her absentmindedly running her finger around the rim of her shot glass. Without either of us realizing it, she was quickly becoming my go-to friend. She was becoming important to me, and I'd be damned if that didn't scare me. I never got close to anyone with the exception of Chloe and Amber. I wasn't sure how I felt about my realization that Jade was important to me. Being close to her left me open and vulnerable. Over the past month, I'd had enough of feeling vulnerable.

I stared at her, taking all of her in. She reminded me so much of Chloe with her rocker-chick style, but they were so different. Both of them were beautiful in their own way. I couldn't believe that I hadn't noticed just how beautiful Jade was before now. She had just the right amount of feminism and ball-busting attitude that it made for a deadly combination.

I racked my brain, trying to remember if I'd ever seen her with a guy. I couldn't think of a time when I had. I'd seen Adam and Drake leave the bar with a one-night stand tons of times. Hell, even quiet Eric had picked girls up occasionally. Jade never did—at least, not that I'd noticed, and I'd been to tons of their shows.

"Why are you staring at me like that?" Jade asked, pulling me from my thoughts.

I'd been looking at her for God only knew how long. I grinned sheepishly as I dropped my eyes to the floor.

"You're beautiful," I stated without really thinking about it.

When she didn't say anything, I looked up to see her watching me.

Finally, she grinned. "If you're starting to spout off shit like that, you've had too much Jack tonight, my friend."

I gave her a questioning look. "What do you mean?"

"You've spent the last few months with *Chloe,* Logan."

"So?"

"Chloe's gorgeous."

"What's your point?" I asked, getting annoyed fast. *Why can't she just take the damn compliment like a normal person?*

"I'm not even close to Chloe. After being with her, there's no way you can think I'm pretty."

I studied her, waiting for sarcastic Jade to break free. Instead, I saw the truth in her eyes. She really thought that she wasn't pretty. She wasn't just fishing for compliments.

I stood and walked over to where she was sitting. I crouched down on the floor in front of her. "Jade, you and Chloe look absolutely nothing alike, but that doesn't mean you're not beautiful. You are."

Her eyes widened, and she quickly looked away. "Well, thanks then."

I reached forward and grabbed her face to pull her back toward me. "Who told you that you weren't beautiful?"

She shrugged, still refusing to meet my eyes.

I sighed as I studied her. "Let me guess. Step-prick?"

Again, she shrugged.

"Damn it, Jade. You should know better than to listen to an asshole like him."

Maybe it was the alcohol, or maybe I wanted to make her see that I meant what I'd said, but I leaned forward until we were only inches apart. Our breaths mingled together as she finally looked at me.

"You're fucking gorgeous. One of these days, you're going to find a guy who's smart enough to realize that. Don't let the assholes in your past make you doubt yourself, Jade."

Her gaze dropped to my lips for a split second before returning to my eyes. "What are you doing, Logan?"

"I...I don't know," I told her truthfully.

All I knew was that her lips were inches away from mine, and I was thinking about doing something stupid. No, I wasn't thinking about it. I *was* doing it. I leaned forward those last few inches and pressed my lips against hers. She sucked in a shocked breath as I kissed her softly. After a moment of hesitation, she started to kiss me back. I took my time, leisurely exploring her mouth with my tongue. A tiny moan escaped her as she raised her hands and ran them through my blond hair. Fire shot through my veins as she tugged on my hair. My hands slowly slid down her body until I was gripping her hips tightly to pull her tighter against me.

She broke the kiss unexpectedly and shoved me away. "Stop, Logan!"

I froze, unsure of what had just happened or what to say. "Jade, I—"

"Don't. Just...don't." She scooted farther up the bed to get away from me. She sighed and ran her hand over her face. "Look, we've both been drinking. That shouldn't have happened. Let's just pretend that it didn't."

I nodded. "I'm sorry. I didn't mean to do that."

"It's fine. I know you're hurting and looking for a distraction, but I won't be your rebound, Logan. I'm your friend, and that's it, okay?"

I nodded as she stood up.

"I should probably go."

I didn't bother to answer. She was gone before I could even process what I'd just done.

You fucked up. Good job, asshole.

I couldn't believe that I'd kissed Jade. I was better than that. She was better than that.

I shook my head as I walked over to my bed and dropped down onto it. That couldn't happen again. I wouldn't use her like that. She was my friend, for Christ's sake! I only hoped that she still would be after that monumental fuck-up.

But the worst part was that I'd enjoyed kissing her.

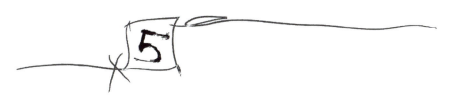

EIGHTEEN MONTHS LATER

I moaned before opening my eyes. I lowered my gaze to where some chick—I thought she'd told me her name was Nicole—was sucking my dick. She raised her eyes to look at me as her head continued to bob. Without thinking, I reached down and grabbed her hair to push her closer to me. She took the hint and took me deeper as she continued to suck on me.

I leaned back against the wall as I felt myself building. A minute later, I exploded. Lucky for her, I always wore a condom, regardless of whether or not the girls had said they were clean. I couldn't be too careful nowadays, especially with girls who would suck me in the restroom of a run-down bar an hour after meeting me.

She released me and stood, and I peeled off the condom and threw it in the trash. I shoved my dick back into my pants and zipped them up. She frowned for a second before leaning into me. I almost winced when she ran her fingernails down my chest, but I caught myself at the last second.

"Are you done already? I thought you might return the favor," she whispered huskily.

"What? You want me to fuck you?"

She nodded, and I laughed.

"Sorry, babe, I'm not about to stick my dick in someone who's willing to blow me in this disgusting restroom."

Her mouth fell open in shock first, but then she became angry. "Fuck you, asshole. You're the one who asked for a blow job!"

I shrugged. "Didn't mean you had to say yes."

I walked out of the restroom and headed for the door. I forgot about the girl as soon as I'd stopped looking at her. It was a shame really that she had done that for me. She was a pretty girl. I could see that even though she covered her features under way too much makeup. If she wasn't such a slut, she would find guys who were interested in more than what she could do with her mouth or her pussy.

I walked out of the bar and headed for my car. I had almost an hour drive ahead of me before I would make it home. I would try to go to bars that were far away from my house in Morgantown. I didn't want Amber or Chloe to know what I did on the nights I wasn't home—not that Chloe would find out now anyway. She'd left with Drake three months ago to live thousands of miles away in L.A. A major label had picked up his band almost a year ago, and he'd moved out there to record. I knew they would be huge one day. They already had a large fan base, and their first tour was set to start in just a couple of weeks.

My thoughts drifted to the girl back at the bar as I drove home. She had been just one of many who I'd met and screwed around with all in one night. I'd been doing this for almost a year and the way these girls behaved still surprised me. It shouldn't have though. I knew that all women were sluts—well, not all, but the majority were.

Jade. I squeezed my eyes shut. *Don't go there, brother.* Jade was a subject I never wanted to think about.

Women are easy. I would just have to flash them my dimples and let them rub their breasts against my arm while I bought them a few drinks, and they would be mine. It was always as easy as that. They wouldn't care to know anything about me—where I worked, if I went to school, what my favorite book was. No, all they would care about was how fast they could get my dick inside them.

Chloe. She'd done this to me. I couldn't help but feel resentment toward the one person I'd loved. If I were being honest with myself, I still loved her. But I also hated her, too. After she had ripped my heart out, I'd changed completely. I'd stopped trying to be the nice guy, the gentleman. Time and time again, she'd proved that wasn't what she wanted.

Not two weeks after our heart-to-heart when I'd told her I forgave her for what she had done to me, she'd gone back to Drake. I'd had to stomach seeing them together constantly, watching her kiss and hold him when it should have been me. I'd said nothing. I'd done nothing. Instead, I'd sat back and watched as he took everything I wanted. They'd barely made it six months before he fucked up. The fucker had been hiding a cocaine addiction for God only knew how long. Since Chloe's mother had been an addict as well, the betrayal had hit Chloe especially hard. To add insult to injury, the dumb fuck had gotten caught only a few weeks after Chloe's mother committed suicide.

As horrible as it sounded, I had been glad when Chloe's mother died. She'd tormented and abused Chloe her entire life. Up until the moment she'd died, she'd been on the run for beating and almost drowning Chloe. Only a few minutes before parking her car on a railroad track where she'd met her untimely fate, she'd even called Chloe to tell her how fucking worthless she was.

Chloe had no idea that I still loved her or that I hated her. To her, I was still the same Logan I'd been when we first walked onto West Virginia University's campus. Now, I hid who I truly was from both her and Amber. Neither of them needed to know that I was a cold-hearted bastard. No, to them, I was still sweet and kind Logan. To the rest of the world though, I was what I'd hated most about Drake. I was a slut. I used women. And the best part was that I didn't give a damn.

I chuckled when I realized that Drake and I had switched positions in life. Now, he was the idiot who only had eyes for Chloe. He was whipped. I was the asshole who didn't care. I guessed I should thank him for that. If it wasn't for him, I'd still be wearing my heart on my sleeve.

When Drake had fucked up, Chloe had come running back to who she knew she could trust—Amber and me. We had taken care of her. We'd made sure that she ate, we'd tried to make her laugh, and to make her forget. I'd been an idiot at first, hoping that maybe she would see me as more since Drake was gone. Nope. Instead, she'd pined over the asshole for months. She'd acted skittish around me until I finally sat down and lied to her.

"Chloe, can we talk?" I asked as I walked into her new bedroom.

A week ago, Amber, Chloe, and I had just signed the papers to rent this house.

"Uh...sure. What's up?" she asked. Her unease was apparent.

I sat down on the edge of her bed and looked up at her. My temper flared when I saw how bloodshot her eyes were. She'd been crying over that asshole—again. He'd ripped her heart out, and she still cried over him.

"Look, I've noticed how uneasy you are around me. I wanted to let you know that you don't have to be."

She frowned. "I'm sorry, Logan. I don't mean to be. I'm just confused and upset right now. I need you, but I'm afraid something will happen, and I'll lose you. I couldn't handle that."

In other words, she was afraid that I would try to win her back, and when she told me to fuck off, I would leave—permanently.

"Chloe, I do love you."

She winced.

"But I don't love you like that anymore. I know now that we aren't supposed to be together like that. We're friends, and that's how it should be. You don't have to worry about me trying anything. I want nothing from you."

She smiled, and I could tell it was genuine.

"Thank you, Logan. I'll never forgive myself for what I did to you. You're my best friend, and I refuse to ever let you go."

She'd hugged me, thinking that everything was perfect between us. *What a fucking joke.* Things had been far from fine, and they never would be.

That was the first night when I had gone out on my own. I'd been careless that night, going to a bar close to the house, but Amber and Chloe had never found out about it. I'd picked up a blonde, and we had gone back to her house. I hadn't even known her name. After that, I'd started going out once or twice a week to pick up women. I never took them back to the house though. I always went to their places, and they never knew more about me than my first name.

Amber, Chloe, and I had fallen into an easy routine for almost six months. Then, just when Chloe had started to get back to normal, Drake had decided it was time to show back up again. He'd begged her to take him back, and she had. She was an idiot.

Once a fuck-up, always a fuck-up.

He would break her heart again. I had known it, and I had been sure he knew it, too, but I'd said nothing. Their relationship wasn't my problem. Chloe wasn't my problem. It was time I moved on with my own life and stopped worrying about her. She'd controlled my life for long enough.

I pulled up into my parking spot next to the house. That was one of the main reasons I'd wanted this house so much. In Morgantown, a college town, it was hard to find off-street parking. As many drunken idiots as there were around here, it was a relief to know I wouldn't wake up one morning to find a huge dent or worse on my car.

The house was dark with the exception of the living room. The TV was on as well as a small lamp, which meant Amber was actually home for once. Lately, she'd been gone more than I had been. I wasn't sure where she would go, but I had a good idea. I was pretty sure she would go out and do the same thing I was, but I wasn't sure why. That wasn't Amber, but neither of us were perfect.

Who am I to judge?

I walked into the living room to see Amber sitting on the couch.

She looked up and smiled. "Hey. I've been waiting up for you. Where did you go?" She shut off the TV.

I shrugged. "Just wanted to get out of the house for a little while. What's up?"

"Sit down. I want to talk to you." She patted the couch beside her.

"Okay..." I sat down and gave her a confused look. "I'm sitting. What do you want to talk about?"

"I'm not sure if you're going to be really happy or really pissed off when I tell you this."

"You're moving out, aren't you?" I asked, finally catching on.

She laughed. "Ha-ha. Nope. You're still stuck with me. It's about Chloe."

She's pregnant.

She finally dumped him.

He cheated on her, and she's coming home.

The first thought made me sick to my stomach, but the others actually made me happy. I was a sick individual.

"Drake called me earlier. He and Chloe want to get married, but she's apparently freaking out about planning a wedding. He wants me to get it all ready for them, and he'll bring her back here. It'll be a surprise for her. He gave me all the details—where he wants it, who to invite, and all that crap."

Married. I closed my eyes and willed my hands to stay at my sides instead of finding something to throw. *Married.* She would be tied to him forever. She wouldn't be my Chloe anymore. She would be Chloe *Allen.*

Fuck.

"When?" I spit out.

Amber shrugged, pretending not to notice the bite in my tone. "Whenever I have stuff ready. He only asked for a few things, so it'll take me, like, a few days tops to get it ready."

"Why are you helping him?"

She shrugged again. "Because he makes Chloe happy. He's screwed up before, but I really think he cares enough about her to do what's right. He'll take care of her, Logan. You know he will."

I shook my head. "How many times has he hurt her? He'll do it again."

"It's her life to live, Logan—not ours." She paused before continuing, "Are you upset because she's marrying him? Or because she's not marring you?"

I glared at her. "This has nothing to do with me, Amber."

"You still love her, Logan. I'm not stupid. You think you hide your emotions so well, but you don't."

"Whatever. I just don't want to see her get hurt again."

"Damn it, Logan! Talk to me! I'm your best friend, too, not just Chloe!" Amber shouted, surprising me.

"What do you want me to say, Amber? That I never got over her? That I'm pissed off because of what they did to me? That I think this marriage is a mistake?" I shouted right back.

"That's exactly what I want you to say. I want you to *talk* to me. Stop acting like nothing gets to you, and talk to me like you used to!"

"I don't want your pity, Amber."

She frowned. "I don't pity you, Logan. *I never have.* What Chloe did to you was stupid, but I've never looked down on you or pitied you for it. We all fuck up. We all get fucked. It happens. You just have to remember that those things shouldn't change who you are. You can't stop living because of what they did to you."

"I haven't stopped living. What on earth are you talking about?" I asked.

"When's the last time you went out on a date? Hell, when's the last time you got laid?"

I laughed. "You don't want me to answer that, Amber."

"Yes, I do! Talk to me. I want to help you!"

"I've had sex every week for the last year!" I spit out. I didn't even care anymore. I just wanted her to leave me alone.

Her eyes widened in shock. "You have a girlfriend, and you didn't tell me? Who is she?"

"I don't have a girlfriend. I haven't had one since Chloe. Let it go, Amber, please."

"You said you've had sex constantly. If not with a girlfriend, then who? Do you have a fuck buddy?" she asked.

"I have lots of fuck buddies, Amber." I sighed. "I'm done talking about this. Just let it go."

She studied me for a minute, unsure of what to say after my confession. "Fine, I'll let it go—for now."

My shoulders sagged in relief. "Thank you."

"You'll come to the wedding, won't you? Chloe will want you there."

I groaned. "Yes, I'll be there."

Whether I wanted to or not, I knew I would go. I'd do it for Chloe because I knew how bad it would make her feel if I wasn't there. Once again, I was worrying about how she would feel. Instead, I should have been listening to my gut telling me this was a bad idea.

Amber leaned over and hugged me. "Thank you, Logan. I know this is hard for you, but I promise that one day, you'll look back at the time you spent holding out for Chloe, and you'll laugh at yourself. There's a girl out there for you who will make you forget about Chloe completely."

I snorted as I hugged her back, but I said nothing. Instead, I gently pushed her away and stood up. She called my name, but I ignored her as I walked back to my room. As soon as I was inside, I closed the door and peeled off my shirt and then my pants. I dropped down onto the bed in only my boxers, and I closed my eyes, pretending that I wasn't shattering into a million pieces.

I just wanted to go fucking numb and stay that way.

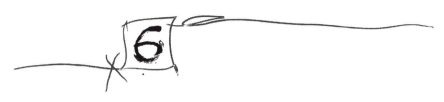

6

Amber hadn't been kidding when she said she would have the wedding ready to go within a few days. A week later, I was standing in the middle of a clearing overlooking Cheat Lake. I snorted at the irony. Of course they'd get married next to Cheat Lake. I was surprised I wasn't Drake's best man. That would complete the torment that this day was sure to be.

I'd been standing with Amber next to my car for over twenty minutes before anyone else showed up. Amber had beaten me here—*shocker*—but we were waiting for Chloe's cousin, Danny, and Drake's bandmates. I winced when I thought about the fact that I would have to see Jade today. This day really was one fucked-up mother. I couldn't wait for it to be over. All I wanted to do was drink. No, I didn't want to drink. I wanted to get drunk. That was saying something. Even when I went to the bars to find women, I would only have a drink or two.

"Can you at least pretend to smile?" Amber asked as she leaned on my car.

I flashed my teeth at her. "There. Happy?"

She laughed. "I asked you to smile, not act like you're going to go cannibal on my ass and eat me."

I rolled my eyes as her phone lit up and Adelitas Way's "Criticize" started playing. Her face lit up as bright as her phone, and I knew instantly who it was—Adam, one of Drake's bandmates. I knew she'd fucked around with him before everything went to shit between Chloe and me, but I had no idea if they were still messing around or not. It'd been almost a year since they last saw each other. I knew that because it'd been as long since I saw Jade—not that I was keeping track of the time though.

"Adam, Eric, and Jade are almost here. The preacher dude is following behind them," Amber said as she typed into her phone.

I almost groaned at the stupid smile on her face. Adam was as bad, if not worse, than Drake had been. The guy would fuck anything with a vagina. I'd seen him leave Gold's Pub with some seriously questionable chicks. Then again, I had been doing the same thing lately.

Eric was the only member of the band that I hadn't been able to get a feel for. Drake and Adam had played the man-whore parts well, but Eric was different. I'd seen him with girls once or twice, but he had been nothing like the other two. Where Adam was loud and full of shit most of the time, Eric was quiet, thoughtful even. I didn't know him at all, but I respected him.

Then, there was Jade. I sighed as I thought about her. I'd fucked up with her big time. I knew it, and she knew it. And I'd never even apologized for what I did to her. If I were being honest, I'd hoped that I wouldn't run into her again. I was a coward.

Amber and I both looked up as two cars pulled into the clearing. A man stepped out of the second one—the preacher I assumed—while Eric, Adam, and Jade climbed out of the first one. Amber was smiling like a lunatic as she ran up to them. She gave a small hello to Jade and Eric before leaping into Adam's arms. She began kissing him like a preacher wasn't standing ten feet away from them. I laughed at her sudden show of affection, but it died in my throat when I saw Jade was watching me.

She'd changed her hair—again. I couldn't keep up with her hair colors. She'd had it every color of the rainbow since I met her, but I had to admit that I liked how it was now the best. She'd left the strange-colored streaks out this time and dyed it a light brown. It fell around her shoulders in loose curls. Even curled, I could tell that it'd grown out quite a bit since the last time I saw her. She'd left off her dark eye shadow and liner today. The effect was devastatingly beautiful. Without the makeup to make her look like she could kick my ass, she looked angelic. Her skin glowed. She looked happy—at least, she did until she saw me. Then, a spark of anger appeared in her brown eyes.

Not thinking, I walked over to where she was standing. She watched me warily as I stopped in front of her.

"Hi," I whispered.

She raised her chin, letting me know that she was still pissed. "Logan."

We stood awkwardly, staring at each other, as I fought for a way to tell her I was sorry.

"Look, about what happened at Chloe's aunt's house—"

The anger in her brown eyes intensified. "Don't you dare," she whisper-shouted, "try to bring that up today. Just drop it!"

I nodded and looked away. I felt like she'd drop-kicked me in the stomach.

I'd screwed up with her so badly, both in my dorm room and at Chloe's aunt's house. I'd taken advantage of her when I never meant to.

We'd all been staying at Chloe's aunt's house—well, it was now her cousin's house since her aunt had died—and I'd offered my room to Jade since there weren't enough bedrooms for everyone. Things had been awkward at first, especially after I'd made a fool of myself when I kissed her in my dorm room. Since that night, we had barely spoken two words to each other. For some reason, I'd thought offering my room to her would make things right. Jade and I had shared the bed while we were there, both of us staying on our own side, which hadn't been hard to do since it was a California king. And it had worked until the night before the band and Chloe left.

Something in me had snapped. Since that night in my dorm, I'd noticed more and more how beautiful Jade was, but I'd never acted on it. I'd been ashamed of kissing her while I was drunk, and I'd had my head so wrapped up with Chloe that I didn't want to act on it. But the night before Jade had left Chloe's cousin's house, I had. Maybe it had been the fact that I hadn't had sex in months or the fact that I could hear Amber and Adam going at it like animals in the bedroom next to us, or maybe it had been the way Jade's tiny shorts showed too much. Before I could think about what I was doing, I'd rolled over and closed the space between us.

I shoved the pillow that had been serving as a barrier between us out of the way. I moaned as I pressed my body against Jade's. My dick throbbed as I shoved it against her ass. I needed release, and I was hoping that Jade would help me out with that. My fingers found the hem of her shirt and slid underneath to the warm skin of her stomach. I explored her, slowly making my way up to her breasts. I slid my fingers under the cup of her bra and ran my thumb across her nipple. She moaned, but I could tell that she wasn't awake yet.

I rolled her over onto her back and started kissing along her jaw and neck. She moaned again as I covered her mouth with mine. She still wasn't fully awake, but she kissed me back. I sighed in relief as I moved back down to her neck. I pinched her nipple between my fingers as I ran my tongue over her skin.

"Logan, what are you doing?" she finally whispered.

I ignored her question as I continued to explore her neck. God, she tasted like heaven.

"Logan! What are you doing?" she asked again.

"Shh...just kiss me, please," I whispered as I sought out her lips.

She hesitated for a second before kissing me back. Her lips parted, and I slipped my tongue inside to explore. Without realizing it, I'd climbed on top of her. I pressed my hips against hers, and we both moaned in unison.

Her chest was rising and falling rapidly. I smiled against her lips as she wrapped her arms around me. She shuddered when I pulled my mouth away from hers, and I nibbled on her ear. My thumb started stroking her breast again, and her breath hitched.

"Logan, stop." She moaned, her body still begging for my touch.

I ignored her as I continued to taste and explore every bare inch of her skin.

"Logan, stop. I mean it." She shoved against my chest.

I groaned as I rolled away. My dick was throbbing so much that it was actually painful. "What? What's wrong?"

"What do you think you're doing?" she asked angrily.

"Kissing you?"

"No, you were trying to molest me in my sleep. What the hell?"

"Don't try that. You were as into it as I was," I shot back.

"You didn't even ask. You just took! That's bullshit, Logan! I don't fuck guys who I'm not dating. I'm not a whore."

"I never said I thought you were!"

"You don't have to. Your actions are enough!"

"What the fuck do you want from me, Jade? A ring? Jesus. I just wanted to fuck. I don't want two kids and a picket fence."

Her mouth dropped open in shock. "You're nothing like I thought you were, Logan. You're a total and complete asshole hiding behind an angel's face!"

I watched as she stood and stomped out of the room. I groaned as I stood and walked to the bathroom. I was going to get off one way or another.

I had intended to get her alone the next morning, so I could apologize, but I'd never gotten the chance. She'd made sure of that by sticking to Eric like glue. The only time she had looked at me was when she was getting ready to climb onto their tour bus. She'd shot me a look that could slaughter kittens. That was the last time I'd seen her.

And now, it was obvious that she still hadn't forgiven me.

I looked up as another car approached. I whistled under my breath at the sight of the expensive Mercedes. It pulled up next to me, and Danny—Chloe's rich cousin from Maryland—stepped out.

He shot me a grin. "Logan, long time, buddy."

I walked over and gave him a quick hug, pretending not to feel the heat of Jade's gaze on my back.

I liked Danny a lot. He was rich as hell, but no one would ever know it by meeting him on the street. Everything about him—his clothes, his shaggy hair, the Converse on his feet—screamed typical twenty-year-old. I knew better though.

When his mother had died, she'd left him millions of dollars, real estate out the ass, and several large companies. The guy wouldn't have to work a day in his life if he didn't want to, but he was still going to college while his mother's lawyer and close personal friend watched over her estate. He'd told me once that he planned to finish college like a normal guy, and then he would dive right into managing her companies.

"Now that we're all here, let me explain everything," Amber called from behind me.

We all turned toward her, waiting on instructions. She glanced around nervously as she realized that everyone was giving her their undivided attention.

"Okay, so…yeah, Drake said Chloe wanted a low-key wedding, which is why we are the only ones here. He wants the ceremony to take place over there"—she pointed to a spot overlooking Cheat Lake—"with Eric as best man. Obviously, I'll be Chloe's maid of honor. The rest of you just have to stand around and look pretty. Drake texted me when they landed, so they should be here any minute. Any questions?"

We shook our heads. This was probably the easiest wedding in the history of the universe. I just hoped that it wouldn't turn out to be a joke in a few months. As much as I hated the thought of Chloe and

Drake being together, I didn't think I could handle seeing Chloe get devastated by him yet again. It would crush her.

I felt my stomach knot up when I heard a car approaching. I looked up to see Drake and Chloe pulling into the clearing. As soon as she stepped out of the car, the confused look on her face made it obvious that she had no idea what was going on. She looked beautiful in a white sundress. Her blonde hair had been straightened, and was hanging over her shoulders. I couldn't help but grin at the purple streaks running through it. They were so Chloe.

"What's going on?" Chloe asked as she approached us.

"I thought you would have figured it out by now." Drake grinned down at her.

"I have no clue what you guys are up to."

"You're an idiot, Chloe. You're about to get married," Amber said as she handed her a bouquet of flowers.

Chloe's mouth dropped open as she looked from Amber to Drake to where everyone else was standing. "No way."

"Way," Amber said matter-of-factly. "Come on, let's get started."

"Did you plan this by yourself?" Chloe asked Drake.

"Nope. Amber helped. I called and explained to her that you were freaking out about planning a wedding, so I wanted to have the most non-wedding possible. I told her about this spot, and she arranged for everyone to meet here. The only thing that makes this a wedding is the preacher, who is hiding behind Adam and the flowers."

Her eyes filled with happy tears, and I felt like I was getting a swift kick to the balls.

"I don't even know what to say."

"All you need to say is, I do. I think you can handle that." Drake took her hand and led her to where everyone else was standing.

Chloe smiled and hugged everyone, obviously shocked that we had all been in on the plan. When her eyes landed on me, they softened.

"I'm so happy for you, Chloe," I whispered. I kissed her cheek and hugged her. "You deserve to be happy."

"Thank you," she whispered back.

I felt like a dirty bastard when I saw the relief fill her eyes. She'd been worried about whether or not I was okay with this, and I'd lied right to her face. I wasn't okay, and I wasn't sure I would ever be okay.

I released her, and Adam quickly took my spot. After giving him a quick hug, she and Drake walked hand in hand toward where the preacher was standing. The rest of us lined up behind them as Amber and Eric stepped forward.

"Chloe and Drake, are you ready to begin?" the preacher asked.

"I am," Drake said.

Chloe nodded.

"Good. Let's begin." The preacher looked around at everyone. "This is where I would normally welcome you all and ask Chloe and Drake to repeat after me, but I was informed that this is going to be the most casual wedding ever planned."

There were several chuckles from our group.

"Anyway, I'll let Drake and Chloe say what they need to say. Drake, care to go first?" the preacher asked.

"Sure." Drake turned to Chloe. "Chloe, there's not much left to say since I've already said it all to you. Someone like you comes around once in a lifetime, and I'm lucky to have found you. From the moment I saw you when you sat down next to me in class, I knew you were mine. I've never wanted or cared about another person the way I do with you. Neither of us is perfect, but you come pretty damn close. No matter how long I live, I'll never be able to tell you that I love you enough times. Life will throw shit at us because it always does, but we'll make it through. There is nothing in this world that could tear me away from you. I love you."

She opened her mouth to speak, but he stopped her.

"Oh, and I think I was supposed to say, I do."

The preacher smiled. "Not yet. Chloe needs to make her speech first."

"My bad. Go ahead and tell everyone how much you like me, Chloe."

Chloe laughed. "I'll try." She took a deep breath. "You were an asshole when we met. I wasn't sure if I liked you or hated you. From the first time you looked at me, you threw my entire world into chaos. Once I really got to know you, I realized you weren't an asshole at all. You're the kindest person I've ever met. No matter how bad things got, you never gave up on us even though I did. I don't know what I ever did to deserve you, but I'm grateful for every day I've spent with you and for every day that I will spend with you. I will never give up on us. I will never hurt you. We're in this until the end. I love you, Drake Allen."

My heart stopped. I saw the pure love in both of their eyes. *Jesus.* My mind screamed at me to look away, but I couldn't. Instead, my eyes focused on Drake. *How the fuck did I miss it before?*

He'd admitted to being in love with her the night that my relationship with her had fallen apart, but I'd assumed that he didn't mean it after everything he had put her through. But now, I could see that he was looking at Chloe like she was everything to him. She was his whole world. Up until this moment, I'd thought that Chloe cared more about Drake than he cared about her. I knew that was a lie. I could see just how much he loved her. It was like she was air, and he was starving for oxygen.

I squeezed my eyes shut as I tried to process what was happening inside of me. She was his.

His.

He would take care of her. I didn't have to anymore. I was in physical pain as I realized that she really wasn't mine.

"Does anyone have a reason these two should not be joined in holy matrimony?" the preacher asked. When no one spoke up, he continued, "All right then. Will Amber and Eric please bring up the rings?"

I watched in shock as Eric gave a ring to Drake, and Amber handed Chloe one. Then, both of them walked back to where they were standing.

"Drake, do you take Chloe to be your lawfully wedded wife?"

"I do," he said proudly.

"Please place the ring on her finger."

He reached for Chloe's hand and slid the ring onto her finger. Tears formed in her eyes as she stared down at it.

"Chloe, do you take Drake to be your lawfully wedded husband?"

"I do," she whispered.

"Please place the ring on his finger."

I still couldn't move as I watched her place the ring on his finger. This was it. The end. The last six years no longer mattered. She wasn't mine, and she never had been.

"By the power vested in me by the state of West Virginia, I now pronounce you man and wife. You may kiss the bride."

I let her go.

The words were barely out of the preacher's mouth before Drake had Chloe in his arms, kissing her like he was starving. I heard everyone cheering and shouting around me, but I couldn't make my voice work. My mind was too busy with trying to process what had just happened. My life had been altered completely in the last ten minutes, and I wasn't sure where the hell to go now.

"I fucking love you, Chloe Allen," Drake said after he pulled away at last.

Allen. She wasn't my Chloe Richards anymore. She was his.

"I fucking love you, too, Drake Allen."

The preacher laughed. "I'd like to introduce Mr. and Mrs. Drake Allen."

Holding each other's hands tightly, Drake and Chloe turned to face everyone as man and wife for the first time. This was only the beginning of their new life, but it was the end of mine.

I started to leave as soon as Chloe and Drake's car disappeared down the narrow road. Everyone else was standing around, talking about how happy they were for Chloe and Drake, but I couldn't handle it right now. I couldn't fake my happiness and pretend that the whole fucking world wasn't crashing down around me.

I barely managed to get a quick good-bye out to everyone before heading for my car.

Amber chased after me. "Logan, wait! Logan!"

I ignored her as I opened the door and got in my car.

"Logan, talk to me. Please."

"My head is so fucked-up right now, Amber. Just let me go. I need to be alone." I started my car.

"No, the last thing you need right now is to be alone. We're all going to Gold's for a little while. Come with us."

I shook my head. "I can't. I'm going back to the house."

"Please, Logan, come with us, or all I'll do is worry about you. Come on, it'll be fun."

I snapped. Something in me just lost it, and poor Amber got the shit end of the deal. "Yeah, it'll be real fucking *fun* to sit around and talk about how happy we all are that Chloe and Drake found their happily ever after. It'll be real fucking *fun* to sit there and pretend like I'm happy while I'm drowning on the inside. *Fuck off, Amber!*" By the time I finished, I was shouting.

The others were close enough that they had heard every word I just screamed into Amber's face. No one spoke a word as they all stared at me in shock. Amber looked devastated, but I didn't apologize. I couldn't. I couldn't even speak anymore. I slammed my door shut and tore out of the clearing like my ass was on fire.

I didn't slow down until I pulled into my driveway. As soon as I cut the engine, I all but ran to the house. I unlocked the front door and went straight to my room. Once I made it there, I stopped in the middle of it and just stood there. My chest was heaving as I fought to control the emotions raging inside me. Hurt, anger, betrayal—they all made an appearance. Finally, rage won out.

I walked to my nightstand and picked up a picture of Chloe and me. It had been taken only a few months after we met. We both looked so young and innocent in it. With more force than I'd realized I was capable of, I threw it against the far wall. The glass shattered and fell to the floor. I didn't stop there though. I grabbed other photos of Chloe and me off the walls and flung them, too. They were pictures of moments in our lives that were important to me—the two of us in freshman English, at lunch, sitting together in a movie theater, curled up on Amber's couch, prom, graduation night when we spent the entire night out together, the day we moved into our dorms, the day she finally agreed to be mine. All of them were just reminders that everything I'd dreamed about was a lie.

My bedside lamp went next, and it left a hole in the drywall. *Goodbye, deposit.*

When I ran out of things to throw, I sank down to the floor of my bedroom and held my head in my hands. I pulled them away, and I was shocked when I noticed that they were wet. *Jesus Christ, I'm crying.* I was a grown fucking man, and I was crying over a relationship that had ended over a year ago. I wasn't sure how much more of a fuck-up I could possibly be.

I jumped when a hand touched my back. I looked up to see Jade standing behind me. Shame filled me as I looked around the room. I'd destroyed everything that I associated with Chloe, and now, I was crying.

"You shouldn't be here," I spit out.

"Logan—"

"Don't, Jade. I don't want your pity. Just go."

She walked around me and crouched down until we were eye-to-eye. "I'm not leaving you."

"I don't want you here!" I shouted at her. I didn't mean to be so cruel, but I couldn't handle seeing her look at me like that.

"I really don't give a fuck what you want, Logan. I'm not leaving," she shot back, not at all bothered by my rudeness.

"What do you want from me?" I asked, defeated.

"I don't want anything. I'm just…here. You can talk to me or pretend like I don't exist. It doesn't really matter to me."

"Why do you even care? I fucked up royally with you."

"You did, and I was pissed at you for a really long time, but I know you're not the person you were that night. You're a good soul, Logan. You're just hurting."

"You're wrong. I *am* that guy. I'm an asshole. I'm not the same guy you met when I was with Chloe. I'm bitter and angry and fucking self-destructive."

She shrugged. "I am, too, sometimes, especially when I think about my past. But you know what? I don't care. It's part of who I am. Sometimes, it makes me weak, but sometimes, the hate and anger I feel makes me stronger."

I didn't know what to say to that, so I didn't say anything at all. Neither did she. Instead, we sat together on the floor in silence. I couldn't bring myself to look at her again until the tears dried on my face. I vowed then and there that I would never cry again over Chloe. What had been done was done, and it was time that I *finally* moved on with my life. Chloe had obviously found happiness, and it was time that I did, too.

"You know what sucks the most?" I finally asked.

She looked over at me. "What?"

"I didn't realize until today that Drake really does love her. I always knew he cared, but I thought that he would eventually get bored and move on. I never realized just how much he loved her."

She gave me a sad smile. "He's been in love with her since they met. It took him a while to figure that out, but once he did, he was done. I've never seen him act the way he did when they were apart. It was horrible, Logan. Between the drugs and losing her, I was terrified that he was going to kill himself. Every night, I would pray that he'd be okay and still be with us in the morning. After he got clean, all he talked about was finding her. He was a man possessed. I've never seen him like that in my life. When she took him back, it was like he became a totally different person. He smiles and laughs all the time now. I know you're scared that he'll hurt her, but I want you to know that he never will. He cares way too much about her to screw up and lose her again."

"I really hope you're right. No matter how much it hurts me to know they're together, I just want her to be happy. That's all I've ever wanted…even if it means I'm broken."

Jade flung herself at me suddenly. Caught off guard, I fell back against the floor with her on top of me. She shocked me when her lips found mine, and she kissed me with such fierceness that I was paralyzed. Finally, my brain seemed to wake up, and I kissed her back. Her tongue slipped inside my mouth to caress mine. We were nothing more than a tangle of limbs as her hands found my hair, and I grabbed her hips to pull her body closer to mine. Out of my control, my dick swelled as her heat pressed against me.

I was jolted back to reality as a moan escaped her. I explored her mouth with mine one last time before pushing her away. She fell back onto the floor beside me, breathing heavily.

"I think it's my turn to ask, what the fuck are *you* doing?" I finally managed to pant out.

She stared at me. Her eyes were glazed over with lust and something else I couldn't identify.

"You don't deserve the pain you're feeling. As long as I've known you, you've always put others first. You've never asked anyone for anything, and I'm tired of seeing you be miserable. You deserve to be happy even if it's only for a few minutes."

I stared at her with my mouth hanging open. I was torn between pulling her body back on top of mine and laughing at her. While my head was still confused about what the fuck had just happened, my body had a crystal-clear picture of her and me together—naked and sweating while we took out our frustrations on each other.

"Stop looking at me like that, Logan, or I won't stop once I start again," she said after several minutes of silence.

I gave her a weak grin. "I thought you didn't want to be my rebound."

"Whether you realize it or not, I wouldn't be." She leaned in and pressed a gentle kiss against my lips. "You know, I hated Chloe for a while."

I raised an eyebrow. "Why?"

"Because she had you, but all she did was chase after Drake. It wasn't fair to the rest of us."

"Huh?"

She rolled her eyes. "Are you really going to make me break it down for you? I was *jealous* of her because she had you. That first night we all hung out together, I couldn't stop staring at you after you walked into the bar with her. I was hoping that you weren't her boyfriend because I'd never seen a man more beautiful than you." She paused to grin at me. "I was wrong, of course. You look even better now than you did then. Your hair looks better shaggy, like how you keep it now, but it was your eyes that drew me in. They're the prettiest blue I've ever seen, and they're so open. Anyone could see every emotion you feel if they look close enough into your eyes."

69

"You were interested in me?" I asked incredulously. "You are around Eric, Adam, and Drake twenty-four/seven. But you noticed me? The boring guy?"

"You're anything but boring. And those guys are like my brothers. I'd never look at them like that."

"I don't even know what to say here," I mumbled, trying to process the fact that someone like Jade had noticed me.

Sure, I'd noticed how beautiful Jade was, but I never thought we would have any kind of relationship. I'd been too stuck on Chloe to even entertain that kind of thought.

"I knew that your relationship with Chloe would eventually end, so I waited. I never thought things would go down the way they did though. I knew you would never even think about having a relationship with me, so I got close to you the only way I could. I became your friend. Then, things got awkward, and I wasn't sure how to fix it, so I stayed away. That night at Chloe's aunt's house, I was so confused because I knew you still loved her. I didn't want to be the girl you passed your time with while you waited for her. I wanted to be the girl you thought about all the time, the one you couldn't wait to see. So, I did what I do best. I ran from you."

"You had every right to get pissed and run from me. I was a total jackass to you," I told her honestly.

She shrugged. "I knew you weren't in a good place."

"Why are you telling me all of this now, Jade?"

"Because I want you to know that you're not alone. I know you've always been fixated on Chloe, but you have other options out there. I'm not asking for anything from you. I know you're not ready for that. Just know that when you are, I'm here, okay?"

I nodded. "Thank you for not pushing me. I've been in a really fucked-up place for a long time now. I need to get my head screwed on right and figure out where I want to go from here."

70

"I know you do. Take as long as you need." She paused for a second. "Do you remember me telling you about my sister?"

"Yeah," I said, wondering where this conversation was going.

"Once we finish this tour, I plan on finding her. We have all U.S. dates right now, and the tour will be six months long. If it does well, the label wants to send us overseas for another six months. The way our sales have been building, I think it's a good possibility that the tour will end up lasting for a year. We'll write new music on the road, but they'll let us take a few months off between the tour and when we start recording again. I want to take that time to find my sister and get to know her again. I want you to come with me."

"Me? Seriously? Why the hell would you want me to tag along?"

"Because I don't want to do it on my own, and I think you need some time away from everyone."

I shook my head. "I have school. I can't just up and leave it all for a few months."

"We'll be back right after the spring semester ends next year. The two of us can go and come back before school starts in the fall."

"Let me think about this, okay?" I asked.

It was a lot to take in. First, I had to process finding out that Jade had been harboring feelings for me all this time. Then, I had to think about her asking me to go with her to where she had grown up, where all of her bad memories were.

"You have a year to think about it." She smiled at me.

Unable to stop myself, I leaned over and kissed her again. Her lips parted easily, and I didn't hold back. The kiss was short but hot, and I tried to memorize the taste of her. When I pulled away, she rested her head on my chest and took my hand in hers.

"You're going to be okay, Logan. I know you will."

I stared down at her. I hoped she was right.

Jade spent the night with me, and we slept on the floor. When I woke up the next morning, my back screamed at me for being such an idiot and not moving us to my bed, but I couldn't bring myself to regret it. We spent an hour cleaning up the disaster that was my room. Afterward, I gave her some of Amber's clothes, so she could shower and change before she met up with the guys.

The band was leaving to go back to L.A later today. Drake and Chloe would be away on their honeymoon until right before the tour started, leaving the others to take care of any last-minute details for the tour.

I didn't want Jade to go. After my breakdown and heart-to-heart with her, I felt like I was losing something important as we walked out of my house.

She sent a quick text to the guys, letting them know that she would meet them at Drake's old house in a few minutes. I drove her to his house since Amber had dropped her off the night before and she didn't have a ride. The drive to his house was silent, but it wasn't awkward.

"I'll go with you," I told her when I pulled up to the house.

"Really?" she asked, surprised that I'd made my decision already.

"Yeah. I figure, why the hell not? I could use a vacation."

She smiled at me. "Thank you. It means more to me than you know."

"Yeah, yeah. Don't get all emotional on me. Guys hate shit like that."

She playfully stuck her tongue out at me. "My bad."

We both stared at each other, unsure of how to say good-bye.

"Thank you for last night," I finally said.

"What are you thanking me for?" she asked, confused.

"For being there when I needed someone and for showing me that things will get better."

"If you ever want to talk, just call me. I mean it. I'll listen."

"I know you will." I reached out and cupped her cheek. I pulled her closer and kissed her softly. "Be safe."

"I will."

She was gone after that. I watched as she walked to Drake's front door. Once she was safely inside, I turned the car around and drove back to my house.

I spent an hour staring at the television before Amber finally made it home. When she saw me sitting on the couch, she approached cautiously. I winced, realizing that she was probably afraid I would start yelling at her again.

"I'm sorry for yesterday, Amber. I shouldn't have yelled at you like that," I said as I shut off the T.V.

"It's okay. I knew you were upset, but I kept pushing you."

"It's not okay, not by a long shot. You didn't deserve to be yelled at like a dog."

"So, how are you today?" she asked.

"I'm...okay. Well, I'm not okay exactly, but I will be. I talked with Jade last night, and she made me realize a few things. It's just hard, you know?"

"I know. If there's anything I can do to help you, you'll tell me, won't you?"

I nodded. "I will, I promise. Everything just hit me at once yesterday, and I lost my cool. Seeing them get married made me realize that I wouldn't get a second chance with her. It hurt like a bitch, but I'm glad I'm finally seeing the truth."

She leaned over and hugged me gently. "I love you, Logan. You're like a brother to me. All I want is for you to be happy."

"And I think of you as an annoying little sister. I love you, too, kid. I promise, I'll be okay. Now that I'm seeing things from the right perspective, I can move on. I promise that the old me will come back."

"Good. I've missed him."

We chatted for a few more minutes before I told her that I wanted to go to my room for a while. She seemed to understand that the one thing I needed more than anything right now was alone time. She left me alone once I was in my room.

I dropped down onto my bed and stared out the window. The last twenty-four hours had been eye-opening for me. The world didn't look the same today as it had yesterday. I knew I wouldn't be okay today or even tomorrow, but soon, I would go back to how I used to be. I vowed that I would stop using women the way I had before. It wasn't right, and I knew that my guilt from using them was part of my problem. I had to let all of that guilt and regret go, so I could move on.

"When you come back, I'll be a new man, Jade. Maybe then, I'll be ready for something more."

It took me a long time to feel like myself again after that day, but I did it. I'd suffered for months. One minute, I would feel almost human. Then, the depression would take hold, and I'd start to spiral out of control again. I forced myself to keep moving forward, and I tried not to think about the darkness that seemed to take over sometimes. When I was at my worst, I would think about Jade and what she'd said to me the night of Chloe's wedding. I had to keep going, and I had to move on if I wanted any kind of future with her.

By the time Jade made it back to me, I was a different man. I still loved Chloe—I probably always would—but now, it wasn't an all-consuming fire. It was more like a small flame. She was happy with Drake, and for the first time in a long time, I was starting to find happiness, too.

Part 2   JADE

Thump. Thump.

This is for you, Dad—for being a controlling, abusive, arrogant fuckhole who did nothing but screw me up.

Thump. Thump. Thump. Thump.

This is for you, Mom—for sitting around and watching as he tried to break me. You should have been on my side instead of hating me for driving a wedge between the two of you.

Thump. Thump.

This is for you, Bethaney—for being the one who was loved while I went through hell. Even if it wasn't your fault, I can't help but feel anger toward you sometimes.

Thump. Thump. Thump.

This is for you, Chloe—for breaking Logan so bad that I don't know if I'll ever have a chance with him.

Thump. Thump. Thump. Thump.

This is for you, Mikey—for all the times you tried to control me. I can't be controlled or contained. My stepdad tried for years, and he never managed it.

Thump. Thump. Thump.

This is for you, world—for fucking me over every time I turn around.

Thump. Thump.

Thump.

Thump. Thump. Thump.

Thump.

Thump. Thump. Thump. Thump. Thump. Thump.

My drumsticks hit the drums one last time, and the crowd roared as the song ended.

Fuck you, world.

9

Sweat coated my body as we ended the last concert of the tour. I was sticky and gross, but I didn't give a damn. The adrenaline pumping through my veins made me feel invincible. As I stood to walk offstage, I glanced back at my drum kit longingly. She'd been my best friend for the past year, and I wasn't sure how I felt now that I wouldn't be with her every night. *Good God, I need to get laid before I start whispering sweet nothings to my foot pedal.*

Drake finished up with telling the crowd how fucking awesome they were just as I reached the edge of the stage. I could hear the crowd, most of them female, screaming and begging for us to come back onstage—or more like, begging Drake to come back. I didn't know how Chloe did it. Those bitches *knew* he was married, but they didn't seem to care. Night after night, show after show, they would continue to throw themselves at him. He'd gently push them away as they tried to climb on top of him. It was gross, and it made me want to vomit.

Chloe never said anything in front of the guys or me, but I knew it caused tension between Chloe and Drake. It would cause tension in any relationship, but she had known what she was getting into when she married him. She'd seen it happen all the time when they first met, but now, it was amplified tenfold. I knew that both of them were relieved now that the tour was officially over.

We'd played for almost nine months straight. I was exhausted, and I knew the guys were too. I couldn't wait until we were big enough to have a say in our tour dates. For now though, the label was concentrating on making us as big as possible, and so far, it seemed to be working. Just as I'd suspected, the U.S. tour had been a huge success, so the label had lined up a U.K. tour as well. Thankfully, they'd decided to keep it to three months instead of six, like the U.S. tour. I was exhausted. Now that the U.K. tour was over, all I wanted to do was get back to L.A. and sleep for ten years.

The guys followed me offstage. Without missing a beat, Drake walked straight over to Chloe and picked her up. I couldn't help but grin at the way she squealed. He brought his mouth down onto hers, and the rest of the world was lost to them. I felt a little twinge of jealousy as I watched them. Out of all of us, I always thought it would be Eric who settled down first. He was the...calmest one of our group. Adam and Drake were the man-whores, and I was the one who didn't have any emotions whatsoever, so Eric had been the obvious choice. Instead, Drake had traded in his man-whore card for a certified and sealed Chloe card.

I was happy for them most of the time. I really was. Drake deserved some happiness, and Chloe was one of the nicest girls I'd ever met. I tried to tell that to the jealousy running through my veins, but it still reared its ugly head. I couldn't help it. Sometimes, I hated that they were so happy while I was alone and miserable. Maybe if they hadn't fucked Logan over so hard, I'd be with him now. Maybe I would have been in his arms at this very moment. So many maybes.

I growled in aggravation as I walked past them and down the hall to my dressing room. I had it bad for Logan. I knew it, and after our talk before I'd left for the tour, he knew it, too. I just wasn't sure what would happen once I saw him again. Truthfully, I was kind of scared to see him again. It had been over nine months since I saw him last. He'd been a wreck then, and I wasn't sure what I would come back to. We'd texted and talked a few times, but I could never gauge his mood.

As soon as I closed the door to my dressing room, I sagged in relief. I loved this life, but it was always so fucking loud. The only time we would have any peace was when we were on the bus, traveling from show to show. Even then, it would never be completely quiet. We'd been working on our next album as we toured, trying to figure out which of our old songs we wanted to use while working on new ones as well. I didn't know how many times I'd thrown my pillow at Eric and Adam because they had been playing their fucking guitars at four in the morning while I had been trying to sleep.

Peeling off my clothes, I walked to the back of the room. I fucking smelled, and the shower in the back of the room was calling—no, screaming my name. I turned on the water and waited until it was scalding to jump in. I moaned in relief when the spray hit my back. I took my time with scrubbing every inch of my skin before shutting off the water. I wrapped a towel around myself and stepped out into the chilly room. Goose bumps rose on my skin, and I shivered as I walked over to where I'd left my clean clothes earlier.

I dropped my towel, and I pulled on my jeans and a loose-fitting Escape the Fate T-shirt. I'd had it for years, and it was worn in places, but I didn't give a damn. It was comfortable, and after wearing a miniskirt and a practically see-through, skin-tight shirt all night, my body was begging for comfort. I was slipping my feet into my favorite pair of Converse when my dressing room door opened. I looked up to see Chloe poking her head in.

"Hey, the guys are ready to leave. They wanted to know how much longer you might be," she said.

I smiled as I finished tying my shoes. "I'm ready. I had to shower. I could barely stand to smell myself."

She laughed. "I wish Adam would take a fucking shower. He chased me down the hall earlier when I told him he smelled like ass."

I shook my head as I opened the door the rest of the way and followed her out. One thing was for sure—Chloe fit in perfectly with the band. Adam tried to give her a hard time daily, but she never let him get to her. Instead, she would come back with a smart-ass remark that would leave his mouth hanging open in shock. Eric thought the world of her, and so did I. She just…fit. I couldn't even bring myself to be mad at her for hurting Logan—well, most of the time. Sometimes, especially when I was PMSing, I would get a little pissy with her. The guys, like the good little boys they were, had quickly learned what times of the month to avoid Chloe and me. All it had taken was one freak-out from Chloe when Adam had eaten all of her chocolate, and they had all gone running to their bunks.

The guys were a little ways down the hall, and Chloe and I hurried to catch up with them. Drake caught sight of us and stopped to wait. As soon as Chloe was within grabbing distance, he tugged her to his side and kissed her forehead. His hair was wet, and I noticed Eric's hair was, too, so at least those two had had the common sense to shower.

I watched as Chloe leaned into Drake and kissed his chin. I could see why the girls went wild for him. His dark eyes had a way of pulling you in—that was, if you could see them. Most of the time, his shaggy black hair would cover them. He had piercings in his eyebrow and his lip as well as a few tattoos poking out of his shirtsleeves on both of his arms. He was built, and if I didn't think of him as my own blood, I might be attracted to him.

Eric and Adam were just as attractive. Adam would use his looks to his full advantage, trying to pick up every chick from L.A. to London. His hair was dyed an electric blue and styled in a Mohawk that stood several inches high. He'd worn it like that for years. His eyebrows were both pierced twice, and he had a set of snakebites. He also had several tattoos on his arms, chest, and back. I knew them all by heart since I'd seen him shirtless enough times. The boy hated wearing clothes.

Where Adam went for shock value, Eric was the opposite with his looks. His hair was styled the same as Drake's, but it was a light brown. He didn't have any piercings at all. The only rocker thing about him were the tattoos on his arms, and there weren't many there.

He would pick up a groupie from time to time, but it was nothing compared to Adam. Eric had always been the quiet one, the thoughtful one, but I'd seen glimpses of another side of him. I would try not to dwell on it too much, but I knew Eric had a history.

"I'm ready to get the fuck out of here and on a plane home!" Adam shouted as we approached the doors that led outside.

"Me, too. I love you assholes, but I'll be glad to get rid of you. There's only so many months I can spend locked on a fucking bus with guys," I said.

"Aw, I thought you liked to cuddle with me, Jade," Adam joked.

"And get an STD on contact? No, thanks."

Eric, Chloe, and Drake howled with laughter.

"Dude, she just handed your ass to you," Drake said as he opened the exit doors.

I squinted my eyes once I made it through the doors. People were lined up along the barricade from the doors to where our bus was parked. Most of them had cameras, and every single one of the flashes hurt my eyes. I blinked a few times, hoping to get rid of the spots dancing in front of me. When they cleared a bit, I smiled and started walking toward the bus. Most of the fans were interested in Drake and the guys, but a few called my name. I signed a few things and posed for pictures as we slowly made our way to the bus.

Once we were free from the grabbing hands, I threw the bus door open and hurried inside. Drake, Chloe, and Eric followed, but Adam wasn't with them. We looked back to see him kissing some chick like he was about to lift her skirt and take her right there in front of everyone. Chloe rolled her eyes.

Eric barked at him, "Adam! Let's go!"

He released the girl and frowned at Eric, but he finally started walking toward the bus. Once he was inside, our driver, Andrew, pulled out of the lot.

"You guys ruin all the fun," Adam joked as he dropped down onto the couch.

"Do you want to fuck a groupie or sleep in your own bed?" I asked. He opened his mouth to reply, but I shook my head. "Don't answer that."

He laughed. "Jealous, Jade? Come here, and I'll make it all better."

I rolled my eyes as I sat down on the other side of the couch. Adam was one big, perverted pickup line, but I knew he never meant what he said to me. I'd known him for years, and he never once tried to sleep with me. I counted my lucky stars daily. The guy didn't know how to keep it in his pants.

"Please go shower before we get to the airport. I don't think my stomach can handle your ass-smell through a twelve-hour flight," Drake said. He sat down on one of the chairs and pulled Chloe onto his lap.

"Fine," Adam grumbled. He stood and started walking to the back of the bus.

Once he disappeared into the tiny bus bathroom, I sighed in relief. Adam was a lot to handle. I leaned back into the plush black couch and relaxed. I looked around the bus and smiled. We'd come a hell of a long way since our first tour bus. The bus Drake had rented for us wasn't bad, but it just wasn't in the same league as this one. This one was twice the size of our original one. A large black couch took up a good portion of the front of the bus with two matching chairs sitting across from it. While our bunks were no queen-sized beds, they sure had a lot more room than the ones we'd been in before. I could actually roll over without face-planting into the wall or falling out of the bed.

Adam came out of the bathroom just as we pulled up to the airport. After climbing out of the bus and grabbing our bags, we bypassed security and walked straight to the label's private jet. It was almost the same as the one the label had originally sent to West Virginia before we even signed with them. Five seats were on each side, and in the back, two couches were situated directly in front of two flat-screen televisions mounted on the wall.

The first time we'd stepped onto a plane like this, the entire band had been amazed at the extravagance of it. By this point, we were used to it. Things had changed so much since then. I'd barely had enough money to pay bills before we left West Virginia. Now, I had my own place in L.A. where the rent was more than three times the amount of the old place I'd shared with Eric. Money wasn't a problem anymore. That was probably my favorite thing about signing with the label. After spending years of just barely making it, it was nice to buy what I wanted.

I settled into one of the seats and hooked my seat belt. The rest of the band and Chloe did the same as we waited for takeoff. Once we were in the air, I took off my seat belt and reclined my seat until I was almost lying down. I took the blanket Eric handed over and threw it on me. Within minutes, I was asleep. Lucky for me, Logan was waiting for me behind my closed eyes.

I awoke several hours later to Eric nudging me. I opened my eyes and stared up at him.

He dropped down into the seat next to me. "We'll be landing soon."

"Thank God. All I want to do is go home and sleep for a week."

"Me, too. This tour kicked my ass," Eric said.

I looked out the window to see that it was still dark. Even though we'd left at just after midnight in London and traveled a little over ten hours, it was still dark here. Time changes always fucked with me when I was flying. I felt like it should be early morning.

"So, what do you plan to do while we have some time off?" Eric asked.

I hesitated. Eric of all people knew how bad my home life had been. He'd picked me up not long after I ran away, and he'd seen how fucked-up I was. I knew he wouldn't approve of me going back for the ultimate family reunion.

"I'm going home," I said quietly.

"What? Back to West Virginia? How come?"

I shook my head. "I'm going *home*."

"Oh." He was quiet for a minute, obviously trying to figure out why I would want to do something stupid like that. "Why?"

"Bethaney."

He nodded. "She's what? Eighteen now?"

"Yeah. I wanted to wait until they couldn't stop me from seeing her. I just hope that she *wants* to see me after all this time. She probably thinks I abandoned her."

"She saw what he did to you, right?"

I nodded.

"Then, I'm sure she understands why you left when you did. A person can only take so much, Jade."

"I know. I just hope she sees it that way. I'm nervous to see her again. She won't be the little girl I left behind."

"You're still her big sister. I'm sure she'll be excited to see you."

"I hope so. I can't wait to hug her again. I've missed her so much."

"I know you have. You know, I don't have any plans for this summer besides sleeping. Do you mind if I tag along with you? I don't want you to go by yourself, especially since I'm sure you'll run into your stepdad."

I bit my lip. "That's okay. Someone already offered to go with me."

He raised an eyebrow. "Who?"

He knew that the only friends I had were the guys and Chloe, so I understood his surprised look.

"Uh...Logan."

His eyes widened before he glanced over to where Chloe and Drake were sitting. "Chloe's Logan?"

"He's not *hers*, Eric."

"No, that's not what I meant. I just...shit, sorry. You just surprised me. I didn't even know you two were friends."

I gave him a meaningful look. "We all have our secrets, Eric. You should know that better than anyone."

He looked away, and I knew he wouldn't push the subject anymore. If he did, it meant that I would ask him questions he wouldn't want to answer.

The seat belt light came on, and we buckled up as the plane slowly descended into the lights of L.A. It was good to finally be done with the tour and back in America.

"You'll call me if you need anything, right?" Eric finally asked.

I nodded. "You know I will. You're the closest thing to family I have, Eric."

"Good. I don't want to worry about you."

"I'll be fine. I have every intention of confronting my stepdad while I'm there. David is nothing more than a bully, and it's time someone put him in his place. I'm going to tell my mom what I think of her, too, but my main focus will be spending time with Bethaney."

Eric took my hand in his and squeezed. "Give 'em hell, kid."

I grinned. "Oh, you can bet your ass I will."

I spent two days sleeping and recovering before packing some of my clothes and flying back to West Virginia. Besides Eric, no one knew what my plans were, and I wanted to keep it that way. Mentally, I knew that I would be fucked-up by the time I returned to L.A. I just wasn't sure if it would be Logan's fault or my stepdad's.

I'd called Logan the day before I left to let him know that I would be flying in and to make sure that he still wanted to go with me. I had been relieved when he said he was still up for the trip. I almost hadn't asked, afraid that he'd changed his mind. I'd called and texted him once or twice while the band was on tour, but that had been it. I had no idea what to expect when he picked me up from the airport. I had intended to rent a car and drive to his place, but he'd insisted that it wasn't a big deal to pick me up. I knew for a fact that he had been lying since I would be landing in Pittsburgh, and it was over an hour drive there from Morgantown. It made me smile to realize that he cared enough to come get me.

I spotted his car as soon as I walked out of the airport. My breath caught in my throat as I stared at him. He was gorgeous. He'd said before that he couldn't compete with my bandmates, but he obviously didn't look in the mirror that often. He'd trimmed his hair, but it was still shaggier than I was used to seeing on him. His piercing blue eyes were crystal clear, and I couldn't help but notice both of his dimples. He was grinning from ear to ear as he took my bags from me. After shoving them into the trunk of his car, he pulled me into a hug.

"Well, hi to you, too," I joked.

"It's good to see you. Did you have a good flight?" he asked as he released me.

I instantly missed his touch.

"Yeah, I slept through most of it," I said as we got into his car.

We were both quiet until the airport was nothing more than a memory in the rearview mirror.

"So, how have you been?" I finally asked.

He smiled as he glanced at me. "I'm good—not great, but good. I'm a lot better than I was the last time you saw me."

"I'm glad to hear it. I was worried about you."

"I was worried about me for a while, too, but I focused on my classes and my job to pass the time. It took me a few months, but I finally figured out what a fucking sap I had been. I know how stupid I was to hang on to her."

"You weren't stupid, Logan. Never think that."

He shrugged, clearly finished with our discussion. "So, how was the tour?"

"It was great. I loved every minute of it. The fans were insane, and I got to see a lot of places I never thought I'd see."

"That's awesome. I bet you're sad that it's over."

I shook my head. I was right where I wanted to be. "I can only live on a bus with Adam for so long before I lose my ever-loving mind. We barely got a chance to rest, so I'm beat. I'm looking forward to just relaxing for a while."

"How long do you guys have off?"

"Well, technically, two months, and then we're supposed to finish writing the rest of the album after that. The label doesn't need to know that it's already done, so we'll get a few extra weeks off."

"Sneaky," he joked.

"You say sneaky, and I say smart. I'm just looking forward to getting away for a while."

We chatted most of the way to his house, but neither of us talked about anything too deep. It was refreshing to just hang out and talk with him. We'd never done this before. He had always been so torn up over Chloe that it was impossible to talk about the little things in life. I loved the way his eyes would light up when he laughed at something I'd said.

When we pulled up to his house, he grabbed my overnight bag and carried it inside to Chloe's old room. I was staying with him and Amber tonight. Logan and I planned to leave early in the morning for Tennessee. The trip back to my hometown of Crossville would take a little over seven hours, so we wanted to start as early as possible.

Nervousness filled my stomach when I realized that I would be going *home* tomorrow. It was the one place I considered my own personal hell. It'd been just over six years since I ran away, but it felt like a lifetime ago. The things I'd experienced since leaving my old life behind had changed me. I wasn't the scared seventeen-year-old who had run away from her problems. The music my stepdad always bitched about hadn't destroyed my soul. Instead, it had changed my life.

When I walked back into that house, I would do it as a successful woman—a *signed* drummer with an entire company behind her. As immature as it sounded, I couldn't wait to rub my accomplishments in my mom's and stepdad's faces. I wanted them to see that I was more than an accident. I was more than the stepdaughter who was always in the way. I was no longer the living and breathing reminder of my mother's mistakes. I was me, and it felt damn good to know where I stood in life.

"You hungry?" Logan asked.

I dropped my bag onto the bed. "Starving. Airplane peanuts aren't what I consider dinner."

He grinned. "Come on, we'll go get something to eat. Anyplace specific you want to go?"

"What? You're not going to cook dinner for me?" I joked.

"Nah, I like you too much to make you suffer through that." He took my hand in his and forced me to follow him back to the front door.

I couldn't help but look down at our joined hands. No one had ever touched me like this—with the exception of Eric, and his touches were rare. Even when I was with Mikey, he wasn't the type to hold hands. It might not mean anything to Logan, but it did to me.

"Where's Amber?" I asked as we walked outside to his car.

I was surprised to see that it was almost completely dark outside now. It was barely six o'clock back in L.A., and the time change was screwing with me.

"Out as usual. She's never home anymore."

So, that means that we'll have the house to ourselves tonight. "I see."

"She drives me nuts. She tried bringing guys back to the house when Chloe first moved out. I got tired of hearing her screwing them, so I told her she couldn't do that anymore. Now, she goes home with *them*, but that doesn't really make me feel any better." He looked pissed.

I frowned as we got into the car. "She's a big girl, Logan. I know she's your friend, but you can't worry about everyone all the time."

"I know that. I'm just worried because she's not the same as she used to be. When we started college, she turned into a completely different person. She had gone through a nasty breakup right before we came here, but I don't see how that could still be bothering her. It wasn't like she was planning on marrying the jackass. It's like she stepped onto campus and signed up for *Girls Gone Wild.*"

"People change as they get older, Logan. She isn't the eighteen-year-old you came here with. Just let her figure out her problems on her own."

"I know, I know. You're right. The thing that bugs me most is that"—he cursed softly under his breath—"for a while, I was one of the guys she took home."

I froze in my seat. "You slept with Chloe *and* Amber?"

Could I pick anyone more fucked-up than Logan?

His eyes widened. "What? No! Oh shit! *No!* That's just…wrong. I meant, I was like those guys for a while. I would go to the bars and pick up girls just to fuck them."

I hadn't expected that from him. I'd just assumed that Logan wouldn't touch another woman while he was pining away over Chloe. After spending nine months in an enclosed space with man-whore Adam, I didn't like this information one bit. I didn't want someone who spent all his time fucking other girls.

"How long has this been going on? Have you done it recently?" I finally asked as we pulled into the parking lot at Denny's. If I hadn't been so focused on what he was about to say, I would have smiled at his choice of restaurant. I loved this place.

"I haven't done that in a long time. I stopped when you left town."

My head whipped up to look at him. "What? Why?"

He had the decency to look embarrassed by this whole conversation. "I don't know. It didn't feel right. I got off on degrading those girls more than anything, and then after everything happened with you, I realized what a dirty bastard I was. So, I quit going out. I went to school and work. That was it. It helped a lot because I didn't have to worry about feeling guilty."

I wasn't sure what to say, so I stayed silent as we stepped out of the car and walked across the lot to the restaurant. He held the door open for me, and we stepped inside. Even though it was after nine, the place was packed. It always was. In a college town, places that stayed open all night were usually swamped by this time.

We had to wait a few minutes for them to clear a table for us. Once we were sitting down, I opened my menu and stared at it blankly. I wasn't seeing any of the words or pictures that normally made my mouth water. Instead, all I could see was Logan going home with girl after girl. It shouldn't bother me like this. I had no claim on him. I wasn't even sure if he really considered me a friend.

"I fucked up with you, didn't I?" he finally asked.

I looked up to see him staring at me. "What do you mean?"

"You've barely looked at me, and you haven't said a word since I told you that stuff in the car."

"Logan—"

"No, it's okay. I get it. I knew what I was doing wasn't right, but I didn't care. I deserve whatever it is you think of me," he said as he looked away.

He looked utterly defeated. His features were darkened with a frown, and I could see storm clouds raging behind his eyes. Without thinking, I reached across the table and took his hand. His eyes widened as he glanced up at me.

"What you did was wrong. I won't lie and say it wasn't. But the fact that you *know* you messed up says that you regret it. We've all messed up in our lives, and we'll all mess up again—several times. What matters is that you're trying to do what's right. I'm not angry with you, honest. It just kind of surprised me. I have this picture of how you used to be in my head, and that's how I see you. When you tell me stuff like this, I don't know what to think."

He looked down at our joined hands and then back up at me. "Thank you."

I stared at him, confused. "For what?"

"For not giving up on me and not thinking the worst when it comes to me. I don't know what I did to gain your loyalty, but it means more to me than you know."

He looked like he wanted to say something else to me, but our waitress decided to show up at that exact moment.

"What can I get y'all tonight?" she asked without looking up from her notepad.

Once she took our orders and menus, she glanced up at us for the first time. When her eyes landed on me, I saw recognition in them.

"Holy shit! You're Jade from Breaking the Hunger!" she said in an excited whisper.

I glanced around to make sure no one else was paying attention. The last thing I wanted tonight was for a room full of people to realize who I was. No, I wasn't as big as Drake or even Eric and Adam, but people knew who I was, too.

I gave her a pleading smile. "Yeah, that's me. We came here for a *quiet* evening together."

She smiled knowingly. "Gotcha. I won't say a word. Can you sign something for me though?"

"Sure."

I waited as she tore off a piece of paper from her order pad.

She handed it to me. "Can you make it out to Jennifer?"

I wrote her name on the paper and then signed my name at the bottom. I couldn't help but smile at the look on her face. It was like Christmas had come early for her.

"Thank you! I've been following your band forever! I'm so excited that you guys are getting so big now! Don't worry. I won't let anyone know who you are."

I breathed a sigh of relief as she stuffed the paper into her pocket. "Thank you."

"I'll bring your food back shortly," she said before she turned and hurried to the kitchen.

I glanced up to see Logan smiling from ear to ear. "What?"

"You. It's so weird to see someone react to you like that. I keep forgetting you're some famous drummer now."

"I'm not famous!"

"Sure you're not," he joked. "Don't worry. I'm just teasing you, but I do think it's cool."

"Well, thanks, I guess," I mumbled.

"You're embarrassed."

My cheeks flamed. "Am not."

"Yes, you are. It's cute. You're always so hard. It's a nice change."

I raised an eyebrow as I chuckled. "Sorry, Logan. I don't have the right parts for that."

It took him a minute to figure out my sarcastic remark to what he'd said. Once he did, he laughed. "Smart-ass."

The waitress appeared a few minutes later with our food. With the exception of her checking on us every two-point-five seconds, dinner was peaceful. When she brought our bill to the table, Logan snatched it up before I had a chance.

"Hey! I was going to pay."

He shook his head. "Nope. My treat."

I grinned as he walked to the register to pay. Sitting here with him tonight and the fact that he was paying made me feel like this was a date. It was stupid because it obviously wasn't. He was just being nice.

The drive home was silent. By the time he pulled into his driveway, my eyelids were so heavy that I could barely keep my eyes open. I cursed at my ever-changing time zones as we walked into the house. I didn't want to go to sleep yet, but my body was begging me for relief. I'd planned to get the travel grime off of me before I went to bed, but I knew I'd never make it through a shower. Instead, I told Logan good night and walked to Chloe's room. Without a second thought, I collapsed onto the bed and passed out.

I woke up to sunlight filtering through the window. I rolled over so that I could check the time on my phone. Seeing that it was already after eight, I jumped out of bed. Our plan had been to leave the house at seven. I had no idea why Logan hadn't woken me up yet. I grabbed clean clothes and hurried to the bathroom to shower. After taking the fastest shower on earth and drying my hair, I threw my dirty clothes in my bag and carried it to the front door.

I glanced into the living room to see Amber and Logan sitting on the couch, watching TV.

He glanced up at me and smiled. "Morning."

"Why didn't you wake me up? I thought we were going to leave early."

He shrugged. "I started to wake you up, but you looked so peaceful, so I let you sleep in a bit. I know you're tired from traveling so much."

His thoughtfulness touched me, and I grinned back at him. "Thanks. I'm up now, so if you're ready to go…"

He nodded as he rose from the couch. "Let me grab my bags and throw them in the car."

He walked past me, leaving Amber and me alone. I glanced over to see her watching me. I looked away and stared at the TV. Amber seemed nice enough, but we'd never really talked before.

"I have to say, I'm surprised," she finally said.

I glanced at her. "Huh?"

"That Logan is going with you. He's even excited to take a spur-of-the-moment vacation to meet your family. I didn't realize you two were so close." She raised an eyebrow as she waited for my response.

"Oh…well, I wanted to get away for a while, and I didn't want to go alone, so I asked him to come with me."

"To meet your parents."

He obviously hadn't told her what my plans were or the circumstances surrounding my *parents* and me.

"It's not like that."

She grinned. "Jade, I'm not his mother. I don't care what's going on between you two. Just do me a favor, okay? Don't break him. He's had enough of that."

My eyes widened. "I wouldn't do that to him."

"Good. As long as he's happy, I'm happy."

Logan walked back into the room and glanced between the two of us. "I'm ready if you are."

I nodded and walked past him. I could hear him and Amber saying their temporary good-byes before the door closed behind me. I tried not to think about what Amber had said. *Don't break him.* I had no intentions of doing that. In fact, my plans were the complete opposite. I wanted to help him heal, not drag him further down. He seemed to be doing just fine on his own, but I'd only been with him for a day. Just because he seemed okay didn't mean that he was.

I walked over to Logan's car and leaned against the passenger-side door. I'd offered to rent a car for the trip, so we wouldn't put extra miles on his car, but he'd refused. It didn't matter to me as long as he was okay with it, so I didn't argue with him.

A car pulled up to the curb in front of the house. My mouth dropped open in shock when I saw Chloe and Drake getting out. The shock was evident on their faces as we stared at each other.

"Jade? What are you doing here?" Drake asked as they walked over to where I was standing.

Fuck! I'd told everyone that I was going to hang around L.A. for a while and that I didn't want anyone to bug me.

Drake and Chloe obviously knew that was a lie now.

"I, uh…"

"Chloe? Drake? What are you guys doing here?" Amber called as she walked outside with Logan.

Chloe ran over to her and Logan and hugged them tightly. My stomach dropped when I saw how tightly Logan was holding her back.

"We came to surprise you guys, but it looks like we're the ones who got the surprise," Chloe said as she glanced over at me. "We didn't know Jade would be here."

"I'm so glad you're here," Amber squealed.

"Me, too. I've missed you both so much, so Drake agreed to come back to West Virginia while he had some time off. We can spend the summer together!"

My stomach dropped until it was no longer part of my body. Chloe was back, and she wanted Amber and Logan to hang out with her this summer. There was no way that he'd choose me over her. It looked like I'd be making my way to Tennessee on my own. The thought alone made me want to cry. I hadn't wanted to go by myself, and I'd stupidly relied on Logan to keep me company.

"Oh," Logan said, shock clearly covering his face. He glanced at me. "We were just about to head out."

"Where to? We can all go," Chloe said.

I noticed Drake watching me. He knew something was up.

Fuck. My. Life.

Before Logan could spill where we were going, I cut into the conversation, "Actually, I was just leaving. I'm going to take a road trip." I pretended to glance at my phone. "I'd better head out. I'm already starting late."

I stupidly realized that I didn't have a car as soon as the words were out of my mouth. *Perfect, just fucking perfect.* I just kept digging my hole deeper and deeper.

Logan walked down the sidewalk to where I was standing. "Jade…"

"No, it's okay. I get it," I whispered before raising my voice so that everyone could hear me. "Would you mind taking me to the car rental place?"

He kept looking back and forth between Chloe and me. Finally, his eyes hardened as he made his decision, and he turned his attention to me.

Just say it, and get it over with, Logan. Come on, tell me that you'll take me to the rental place and be rid of me.

Then, he looked back to Chloe. "Sorry, Chloe, but I won't be around for the summer. I'm going with Jade."

I looked up at him in surprise. *Did he really just choose me over her?*

I glanced over at Drake to see him frowning as he watched Logan carefully. His eyes flicked over to me, and I saw the light bulb come on. A small smile lifted the corner of his mouth.

"Aw…are you sure?" Chloe asked.

I could tell that she was upset because I was taking Logan from her, but I couldn't bring myself to feel bad. She'd had *years* with him. All I wanted was a few weeks. Besides, she had Drake to keep her company. She didn't need Logan for that anymore.

"Sorry, Chloe, but I promised Jade. Maybe I'll be back in time to hang out some." He shrugged his shoulders like he didn't really care if they spent time together or not.

I knew it was an act, but I still felt like doing a victory dance around his car.

"But—"

Drake cut her off, "Let them go, Chloe. Jade said they needed to head out."

She frowned but nodded. "I'm sorry. I didn't mean to sound rude. I'm just surprised." She walked over and wrapped her arms around Logan.

I looked away, suddenly uncomfortable. I wasn't sure if or when I'd ever be comfortable with them touching.

She released Logan and turned to hug me. "Take care of him, Jade. Please," she whispered in my ear.

"I will." I hugged her back before stepping away.

Drake's knowing gaze drilled into me as I climbed into the car.

We waved as Logan backed out of the driveway and started down the street. I still couldn't believe that he'd chosen me over her. I couldn't remember him ever telling her no or turning her down.

My phone beeped, and I looked down to see a text from Drake.

Drake: Didn't expect that one.

Me: I have no idea what you're talking about.

Drake: Have fun. ;)

Me: Asshole.

Drake: Love you, too. :P

I rolled my eyes and shoved my phone into my pocket.

"You could have stayed," I mumbled once the house disappeared from sight.

"I could have, but I didn't want to. What I *do* want is to spend the summer getting to know you better." He didn't look at me when he spoke, obviously unsure of how I'd respond to his words.

I leaned across the console and kissed his cheek. "I want to get to know you better, too."

I had no idea how long we would be in Tennessee. If things went my way, I'd probably spend most of my time off with my sister. Otherwise, we'd probably be back here in a week. Regardless of how long the *vacation* was, I wanted to spend it with him.

Let the fun begin, I thought as we hit the interstate.

11

I'd spent so much time traveling over the past year that being in a car didn't even faze me. When we'd toured the summer before last, I'd been climbing the walls of the bus to get out. At least, I had been in my head. I never let the guys know when something was bothering me. Being the only chick in the band, I always felt like I had to make sure that I fit in. That was stupid because I'd been with the guys for years, but a part of me—a teeny-tiny part—was afraid that they'd decide they were better off with all guys, and then they'd leave me behind.

Now, traveling was my norm. Where I should have felt confined by the small interior of Logan's car, I felt only comfort and security instead. Despite just waking up and trying my hardest to keep my eyes open, I slipped into a peaceful oblivion less than an hour after we'd left the house.

I awoke when the car door slammed. I opened my eyes to see Logan pumping gas. I frowned when I realized that he'd paid for the gas. From the very beginning, I'd told him that I would pay for *everything* on this trip, and I'd meant it. I didn't want him to waste his hard-earned money on stuff for me even if it was only gas.

Logan finished filling the car and climbed back in. He smiled when he noticed that I was awake. Before he could say anything, I grabbed the gas receipt out of his hand.

"Hey!"

"I told you I didn't want you to pay for anything on this trip. It's because of me that we're doing this, and I won't let you waste your money on me," I said as I shoved the receipt into my pocket.

He rolled his eyes. "It's just gas, Jade."

"I don't care. I'll pay you back when I can get to an ATM."

While I knew Logan wouldn't be hanging out at the local homeless shelter anytime soon, I also knew that he was barely making enough to cover bills and food. I'd been in the same situation before I moved to L.A. I didn't want him to waste a dime on me.

"Where are we?" I finally asked.

He pulled out of the gas station's parking lot. "Just south of Princeton, West Virginia. We'll be in Virginia soon."

"Dang, how long did I sleep?"

"Only a couple of hours. You can go back to sleep if you want. I know you're tired."

I shook my head. "I'm fine now. I feel wide awake."

"Okay. Mind if I turn on some music?" he asked.

"Sure."

He reached over and turned on the radio. We heard static for a split second before he pushed the CD button. I winced when I heard the beginning of a country song. I'd forgotten that he liked country music.

"Bleh," I muttered as the song filled the car.

He laughed. "What? You don't like 'Country Boy'?"

"You know I hate country. My ears are already bleeding," I joked.

"Oh, come on. It's better than that screaming shit Amber, Chloe, and you seem to like."

I rolled my eyes. "It's not screaming shit. It's rock. So, I take it you don't like my band's music?"

He shook his head. "I like your songs. Drake doesn't scream like an idiot when he sings them."

I frowned. Logan would hate the new album we were working on. There was more than one song that had Drake *screaming*. We'd tried a few of them on the bus to make sure that Drake could get the vocals right, and he had. I was excited to start working on them. The guitars were faster, but the drums carried those songs. To perfect the songs we'd created, I'd be playing harder than I ever had.

"What's wrong? If the music is that bad, I'll turn it off."

"It's not that. I'm just realizing how different we are. I live and breathe the music you hate."

"I don't hate all of it. Pick a few of your favorite songs, and play them on your phone. I'll tell you what I think."

I nodded as I tried to think of a few songs that had stuck with me. I knew my favorite—The Amity Affliction's "Open Letter"—wouldn't go over well with him, so I decided not to play it. Once I figured out what I wanted him to hear, I pulled up one of the songs on my phone.

"Okay, listen to this one," I said as I pushed play.

We were both silent as we listened to Chevelle's "The Red." This song meant more to me than he realized. It was an older song, one that I'd heard when I was still living at home. The bullying, the anger—it all played out in this song, like it was the anthem to my life then. I hoped that he could understand why I'd played this song.

When it ended, I didn't say a word. Instead, I clicked play on Stone Sour's "Tired." It was a newer song, but I'd fallen under its spell after the first time I heard it on the radio. Again, I let the lyrics speak for me. I wanted them to tell Logan everything that I couldn't. I wasn't good with my feelings. I never had been, but with him, I wanted to be. I wanted him to be the one who kept me safe.

When the final verse ended, Logan was gripping the steering wheel so tightly that his knuckles were white.

"Logan?" I questioned.

He shook his head as he pulled the car off the interstate, ignoring the signs that said to pull off in an emergency only.

"Logan, what are you doing?" I asked as the car came to a stop.

He leaned across the console and grabbed my face with both hands. He stared straight into my eyes. "Is that what you want?"

"What?"

"You want me close? You want me to make you feel safe?"

I tried to look away, but his hands kept me from moving.

"I'm not...I don't..." he growled. "Damn it, this isn't coming out right at all!"

I expected him to pull away, but instead, he pulled my face to his, and he kissed me. It wasn't safe or sweet. It was hungry and angry. He never gave me a chance to stop him before his tongue plunged into my mouth. A small moan escaped me as he explored. Fire shot through my veins as I kissed him back. This was all I'd wanted. Being with him like this made me feel alive. Feeling his hands on me made me feel safe.

He finally pulled away from me and grinned. His grin turned into a full-blown laugh as we caught the lyrics of another song playing. "I guess the song is right. It *does* feel good when I lose control."

I glanced down and pushed pause, cutting off "Temper Temper" mid-song. "What was that kiss for?"

He tilted my chin up, so I was looking at him again. "Because I suck with words, and I've wanted to kiss you since you walked out of the airport yesterday."

"Really?" I asked, my heart thumping wildly in my chest. Maybe this wasn't all one-sided. Maybe, just maybe, I had a chance with him.

I shouldn't want that though. After all, I'd done fine on my own for the past few years. What was it about Logan that made me want to go and fuck up my perfectly put-together new life?

"Really. And now that I've started kissing you, I don't want to stop. Look, I'm not good with words or relationships. I thought I was, but I'm not. I'm not saying that I want us to suddenly jump into something serious, but I've waited almost a year for you to come back to me. The things from before still get to me from time to time, but I want to try to take this somewhere with you. Is that what you want? Or am I making a fool of myself?"

I stared at him in shock. He wanted an *us?* "I don't know what to say. No, that's a lie. I totally know what to say. I've wanted to be with you from the moment I saw you."

"Is that a yes then?" he asked as he grinned.

I nodded. "It's a yes. I have baggage, lots of it, and you do, too. The good thing is that we both know what happened to the other. We'll figure things out together. How does that sound?"

"Sounds like a plan." He leaned over and kissed me softly. "I'm going to kiss you a lot. I hope that's okay."

I wrapped my arms around his neck and pulled him closer. "It's more than okay."

We kissed on the side of the interstate until both of us were gasping for breath. When we finally separated, he pulled the car back onto the interstate.

For the next few hours, he held my hand without a word.

The ride home was so different from the one I'd taken with Eric when I was running away. While I was nervous about seeing everyone again, I wasn't terrified like I had been when I left. I wasn't sure if it was because of Logan or because I was in control of the situation this time. Regardless of the reason, I no longer feared the future.

Back then, Eric had picked me up on I-40 just outside of Knoxville. I'd been stupidly trying to hitchhike my way to New York City at the time. I'd been desperate enough to get in the car with him when he said he'd take me to northern West Virginia even though I didn't know him. Back then, I had been terrified of what life would throw at me. I had been afraid that my stepdad would try to find me and force me to come back home.

Even then, Eric's presence had calmed me. We'd talked casually as he drove me closer and closer to his home. He'd told me he was visiting his real dad in Tennessee, but he lived with his adoptive parents. He'd never mentioned his mom, and I hadn't pried. I'd told him about my stepdad, my mom, and Mikey. When I'd told him I could play drums, he'd said he played guitar. Once we'd started talking about music, we'd never shut up. By the time we'd arrived at his house, I'd agreed to hang out for a few days and jam with him as long as his parents were okay with it.

By the end of that first week, his parents had offered to let me stay with them until I got back on my feet. They had been so kind to me, and I'd kept waiting for them to change and start screaming at me. They never had. Instead, I'd stayed with them until Eric and I were able to get a place of our own. For the past six years, Eric had been my best friend, and he still was. He knew more about me than anyone, even Logan, and Logan knew a hell of a lot.

It'd been hard to hide things from Eric when I would wake up screaming and crying in the middle of the night. The day I'd told him how my stepdad had blackened one of my eyes because I got a D on a report for school, I'd thought he was going to drive back to Tennessee and kick his ass.

I hadn't been the only one who had nightmares though. Eric had had his fair share, and he'd finally come clean to me about what happened to him and the things he witnessed. I couldn't even process it. Eric was always so calm and put together on the outside, but on the inside, he was broken beyond repair.

"So, want to give me a little Jade history before we get there?" Logan asked.

We'd just stopped at a small diner for lunch and were now back on the interstate. We had less than an hour before we arrived in Crossville.

I tapped my finger against my chin as we merged back onto the interstate. "Let's see. My stepdad's name is David, and my mom's name is Elizabeth. I look nothing like my mom. My little sister's name is Bethaney, and I look nothing like her either. I grew up in a middle-class family. David was a pharmacist while Mom stayed home with us. Crossville is a small town, so there isn't a lot to do there. We have a bowling alley, a movie theater, a Sonic, and a Walmart. I didn't really have any friends, except for Mikey and his friends. My sister, on the other hand, was a social butterfly."

Logan nodded. "Where are we going when we get there?"

"Well, I thought we could rent a hotel room and get settled in tonight. Then, we can go confront my parents and try to steal Bethaney away tomorrow. For all I know, she doesn't even live at home anymore. She's nineteen now. Once I meet up with her, I'll know how long we'll stay in town. If she hates me, we'll leave. If she wants to spend time with me, maybe we can look for someplace to stay for a month or two."

"Are you sure you're okay with seeing your stepdad again? You know you don't have to. There's got to be another way to get in touch with Bethaney. Maybe go to one of her friend's houses and have them call her?"

I shook my head. "Nope. I'm going to confront the bastard. He made me feel like I was worthless, and I can't wait to tell him just how much I've accomplished since I ran away. I want him to know that he didn't win. I'm not afraid of him anymore."

"Fair enough."

We were both quiet as we sped toward my past. I couldn't help but wonder what Bethaney looked like now. When I'd left, she was nothing more than a mouthy preteen. I couldn't imagine her all grown-up. To me, she would always be my baby sister.

"Do you plan to look up Mikey while we're here?" Logan asked.

His tone had indicated that he didn't care, but I knew better. He was back to gripping the steering wheel like he wanted to break it. I couldn't hide my smile. He was jealous—because of me.

"Nah. I'm over him, and I have been for a long time. I'm sure he feels the same. There's no point in finding him. All he would do is yell at me for leaving and then send me on my way."

Logan seemed satisfied with my answer. "Okay then."

We started passing signs leading us to the exit for Crossville. My palms turned sweaty when I realized I was really going home. No, I was practically home now. Nerves fluttered in my stomach as I tried to keep my breathing normal.

"You okay?" Logan asked as he took the exit.

"I'm fine," I said in a small voice. I wasn't fooling either of us though.

"Jade, we can turn around right now and go home. No one will ever have to know that we came here. Or we could even take a road trip like we told everyone. It doesn't matter to me. You're in control here."

You're in control. I sat up straighter and forced the butterflies in my stomach to take a flying leap. *I. Am. In. Control. I can do this.*

"Nope. We've come this far. I'm seeing this through to the end, no matter what."

"Which way?" Logan asked when we stopped at the end of the exit ramp.

"Right. There's a motel a few miles down the road. We can stay there until we know what we're doing."

Neither of us spoke as Logan drove toward the motel. Once we arrived, I checked us into a room with double beds. Logan and I each carried our overnight bags up to the room. There was no point in carrying all of our things up if we were only staying here for a day or two. If I remembered right, there was another place that rented rooms by the month. We could move there if things worked out since we'd be in town for more than a few days.

"Which bed do you want?" I asked once we were inside the room.

It wasn't anything fancy, but it would do. I actually preferred staying in places like this rather than the five-star rooms the label had put us in. It was also nice not to be swamped by security. I wasn't Breaking the Hunger's Jade here. I was just plain old Jade, and I loved it. I didn't have to pretend for anyone, especially not Logan.

"Doesn't matter to me," Logan said as he dropped his bag onto the floor in front of the dresser.

I shrugged as I dropped my bag in front of the bed closest to the window. "I'll take the window then."

He grinned as he lay down on the other bed. "What do you want to do for dinner tonight?"

I couldn't help but smirk at how domesticated he sounded. We were talking like we were an old married couple.

"Let's order room service. I'm too tired to go out tonight." I grabbed a menu off the hotel nightstand.

The prices inside were ungodly, but it was better than taking a chance of being seen in town before I was ready to let anyone know that I was here. I wanted the element of surprise on my side. If David knew I was back, it would give him time to prepare. I wasn't going to let that happen.

Once room service arrived, Logan and I sat together on my bed, eating our food and watching TV. Everything was fine until the food was gone. It was like a switch flipped, and we'd gone from two friends hanging out to two people who were very attracted to each other and sitting on a bed together. I couldn't look away from him, and he couldn't seem to bring himself to tear his gaze away from me.

The temperature in the room went from cool to scorching hot in about two seconds flat. I waited, anticipation running through my veins like a drug, until he finally made his move. I closed my eyes a split second before his lips found mine. The oxygen was sucked from the room as I lost myself in his kisses. They were nothing like the one in the car. These were sweet, gentle even. My fingers found his hair and tugged on it until we fell back onto the bed.

I felt his hard body everywhere. My body hummed with need as I tried to press closer to him. Our kisses became fast and furious as primal instinct took over and controlled us both. He bit down on my bottom lip, and I moaned into his mouth. God, all I wanted was to feel his skin against mine.

I started tugging on his shirt, trying to pull it up and over his head. He pulled away, gasping, and gently moved my hand away from his shirt. I questioningly looked up into his blue eyes. They had darkened to a blue so deep that they matched the sea. The only thing I could see in them was lust. So, why had he stopped me?

"Too fast," he whispered before kissing my nose.

"Too fast?" I questioned.

He nodded. "I'm not going to screw this up before we even get started, regardless of what my body is demanding."

I could feel his body's *demand* as it dug into my thigh.

"We're not going to screw it up, Logan. Take what you want from me. I don't care."

He groaned. "Don't say shit like that, Jade. It makes it ten times harder for me to get off this bed."

I was about to tell him that there was no way in hell I would let him move when he pushed away from me.

"I'm going to go take a shower."

I watched in silence as he dug clothes out of his bag and walked to the bathroom. As soon as he closed the door behind him, I let out a loud sigh. If he didn't want to give me what I wanted, I'd have to change his mind. I could be very convincing when I wanted to be. Poor Logan had no idea what I had in store for him.

12

I was up early the next morning. Between my evening make-out session with Logan and the thought of seeing my family again, sleep had evaded me. After tossing and turning for several hours, I finally gave up and crawled out of bed. Logan was still asleep as I walked silently to the bathroom. I closed the door behind me, so he couldn't hear me moving around. I didn't want to wake him up.

After relieving my screaming bladder, I washed my hands and then brushed my teeth. Once I was satisfied that I wouldn't kill anyone with my morning breath, I wiped my mouth and stared at my reflection in the mirror. The girl in the mirror stared at me defiantly. She looked confident. She looked like she could take on the world. Well, once her hair was tamed and her makeup was applied, she could.

I closed my eyes and tightly gripped the sink. I vowed that it would be the only sign of weakness I showed today. I wouldn't let any of them know how scared I was of what today might bring.

I started on my hair first. I'd let it air day last night as I slept, and it was a disaster. I washed it again quickly and then blow-dried it straight. Next, I applied mascara and eyeliner to my eyes, both black to make them look darker. I never bothered with eye shadow unless I was performing. Once I finished, I applied my foundation and checked myself over carefully. With my dark makeup and my hair flowing around me in black and red strands, I looked like someone no one would want to fuck with. Sure, I was barely over five foot two, but that didn't seem to matter when my body was living off of hate and anger. Those two emotions could turn anyone into the heartless bitch staring back at me.

Only, I wasn't a heartless bitch, not anymore. When I'd left Crossville six years ago, I had definitely been one. But spending time with my band and Logan had softened me. While I was no longer heartless, I also wasn't someone to be fucked with. Being one of the few women in the rock industry, I couldn't afford to ever let my guard down.

I crept back into the room to see Logan in the same position he'd been in earlier. Careful not to wake him, I unzipped my bag slowly and pulled out an outfit for the day that consisted of a T-shirt, jeans, and my Converse with the lime green shoestrings. I loved those fuckers. They were by far my favorite pair. I grinned as I shimmied out of my sleep shorts and tank top before slipping on my Breaking the Hunger T-shirt. I totally planned to rub the band's success in my stepdad's face as much as possible.

"That's a view I definitely don't mind waking up to," Logan mumbled from his bed.

I froze for a split second before straightening my back and turning to face him. I suddenly felt shy. Without the lust from last night running through my veins, I didn't feel quite as brave as I realized just how much of my body Logan could see. I was standing in the middle of our room with nothing more than a T-shirt and a black thong. No one had seen me like this since Mikey.

"Morning," I mumbled as I grabbed my jeans and pulled them on quickly.

Logan laughed as he sat up in bed. He looked adorable with his shaggy hair sticking up all around his head. "I never took you for the shy type."

"I'm not shy," I said quickly.

"Then, why did you jump in your pants faster than I could blink?" When I didn't answer, he smirked. "That's what I thought."

"Get dressed, so we can get out of here." I sat down on my bed and started to pull on my socks and shoes.

I heard him moving around behind me. I collapsed back on the bed as soon as I heard the bathroom door shut. Only a few minutes later, Logan stepped back out, fully dressed and hair tamed.

"I was going to change in here, but I wasn't sure if you wanted a strip show, too," he teased.

I rolled my eyes. "Whatever." *Yes, please. I'd give anything to see you strip down to nothing.*

We stopped at a local diner for breakfast before heading to my parents' house.

I kept my mind blank as we crossed town. Now was not the time to lose my nerve, and I would if I *really* thought about what I was doing. When I told Logan to turn onto my old street, I sat up straight in my seat. My body was rigid as the house came into view.

"Here," I said as I pointed at my old house.

Logan pulled into the driveway. I stared out the windshield at the house. It hadn't changed much since I left. Now, I could see where the roofing tiles were darkening with age, and the blue siding was starting to fade. I couldn't help but find that strange. David had been all about making sure things looked perfect. At least, he would make sure things looked perfect on the outside. He had always worried about what our neighbors thought. If only he'd worried about the people, especially me, living inside of his home as much as he did his reputation, my life would have been so different.

"You ready for this?" Logan asked from beside me.

I nodded. "Yeah. Might as well get it over with." I opened my door and started to climb out.

He grabbed my arm to stop me. "I'm coming with you. I won't let you do this on your own."

My heart softened. "You don't have to."

"I know I don't. I want to." He released me and opened his own door.

He followed behind me as we walked up the sidewalk to where the front door was. I took a deep breath before ringing the doorbell. When no one came to the door, I rang it again. Still, there was no answer. I frowned as I rang it one more time. *Nothing.*

"Fuck," I muttered.

Mom was always home. *Always.* The only time she would leave was when she went to the grocery store or when she went somewhere with David. Most of the time, they would only go out together at night, usually for a private dinner or a party.

"No one's home," Logan said, pointing out the obvious.

I sighed in defeat and started walking back to the car. *Now what?* All my plans had been centered around someone being home. We'd have to go back to the hotel and wait for a few hours now. I hated waiting.

"Where to next, boss?" Logan joked as we climbed back into the car.

"Our room, I guess."

"Are you sure? Isn't there someplace else we could try?"

I shook my head. "I have no clue where they could be. David was almost never home, but Mom was home all the time. Obviously, things have changed."

"What about your sister?" he asked.

"What about her?"

"Do you have any idea where she might be?"

I shook my head. "She could be anywhere."

"You said she had a bunch of friends, right? Maybe she's with one of them."

I thought for a few minutes. "She had one friend that she was super close to—Lily. She lives on the other side of town. Well, she used to. I don't know if she would still be at her parents' house or not."

"Well, it's summer break, so she might be. It can't hurt to stop and ask."

I shrugged. "Sure. Why not?"

It was better than going back to our room and waiting. I gave him directions as he drove through town. It was a little surreal how everything looked exactly the same as it had when I left. For some stupid reason, I'd expected it to be completely different, but it was still sleepy little Crossville.

It took us a few minutes to find Lily's house. I'd only been there once or twice to pick up Bethaney when Mom couldn't, and that had been years ago. Finally, I recognized the mailbox. That was how I'd remembered it before. Instead of having a normal box, they'd had one custom made to look like a bird. No joke. The thing looked ridiculous.

Two cars were parked in the driveway, so we were forced to park on the street. I walked across their perfectly manicured lawn and up to the front door. I knocked softly since I saw no doorbell.

A few minutes later, a middle-aged woman opened the door and gave me a questioning look. "Can I help you?"

"Uh…yeah. This is going to sound strange, but I'm looking for my little sister, Bethaney. She and Lily used to be friends a long time ago, so I thought I'd check here."

The woman's eyes glanced behind me to where Logan was standing, and then she looked back to me. As she stared at me, recognition dawned.

Her mouth dropped open for a split second before her eyes turned cold. "Jade?"

I nodded.

"You have some nerve coming back to this town after all this time." Her voice was cold but calm.

I raised an eyebrow in surprise. "Look, I'm not here to explain myself to you. I'm just looking for my sister. Do you know where she is?"

She stared at me for a minute. I expected her to threaten me with the police if I didn't leave.

Instead, she called out to someone behind her, "Bethaney, can you come here, please?"

A few seconds later, I saw a young girl come into view.

She barely glanced at me before turning her attention to the woman. "What do you need, Marie?"

"Someone is here to see you."

My sister's eyes shifted to me. Once she got a good look at me, she stumbled back with her mouth hanging open. She opened and closed it a few times, but no words came out. I knew how she felt. All I could do was stare at my baby sister, but she wasn't a baby anymore.

She'd always been tiny like me, but she'd obviously hit a growth spurt sometime in the last six years. She was taller now, probably close to five foot seven. Her hair was the same light blonde it had always been, but it was cut short now. When I'd left, it had hung halfway down her back. Now, it barely brushed her shoulders. Her build was slim, like our mom's and mine. Her eyes were the same chocolate brown as mine. It was something else we'd both inherited from our mother.

"Beth?" I finally managed to get out.

My voice seemed to snap her out of it.

Her mouth finally closed, and she took a step closer. "What are you doing here, Jade?" she asked quietly.

"I came back to find you. I've missed you." I glanced at Marie, who was still glaring at me, before looking back to Bethaney. "Can we talk? Alone."

Bethaney nodded as she walked past Marie and closed the front door behind her. She walked over to a porch swing and sat down without taking her eyes off of me.

I sat down in a chair that was across from her. I wanted to grab her and hold her tight, but I wasn't sure if she'd be okay with that. The way Marie had greeted me made me think that maybe I wasn't wanted, even by my sister.

"You look different," I finally said.

"You do, too. Well, kinda. You still look like hard-ass Jade, but you're more grown-up."

"You're all grown-up, too. I can't believe it. I've missed you so much, Beth. I wanted to come back so many times, but I was afraid that David and our mom wouldn't let me see you. I planned to come back as soon as you turned eighteen, but then we signed with the label and went on tour. This is the first chance I've had. I'm so sorry that it took me this long," I said in a rush.

She snorted, and her eyes burned with anger. Besides shock, it was the first emotion she'd shown since she saw me. "Yeah, I'm sure it was hard to find time for me while you were off playing rock star. Do you know how horrible it was for me to have one of my friends tell me they saw you on TV? My own sister, and I didn't even know. I spent so many years worried about you, praying that you weren't dead! All that time, you were off playing your fucking drums and having the time of your life while I was here, all alone!"

Logan cleared his throat, and I glanced over at him.

"I'm going for a walk. Call me when you're ready," he said.

I nodded, and then he turned and walked back across the yard. Once he was out of sight, I turned back to my sister. She was staring at the spot where Logan had been standing earlier.

"Who's he? I know he's not from your band. I've watched your videos online, and he was never in them."

"He's my...he's Logan," I answered lamely.

"I thought for sure you'd be with that Drake guy. Lead singers were always your thing."

I shook my head in disgust. "Drake? Not a chance. He's family."

She sneered. "Family means nothing to you."

I frowned. "I wanted to call a million times, Beth, but I knew they'd never let me talk to you. What I did to you is the only thing I've ever regretted. I've hated myself for leaving you behind when I left."

"You mean, when you ran away!"

"I had to! You have no idea what he was like toward me! It was horrible."

"You're right. I had no idea what you went through until after you left. Then, I got to live it."

I stopped breathing. *No. He wouldn't.* Bethaney had been David's pride and joy. "What are you talking about?"

"When his favorite punching bag left, he found a new one. You left me alone with him. What did you think would happen?"

"No," I whispered. "He wouldn't do that to you. You were his."

She laughed, but it was humorless. "It didn't matter to him. Dad had anger issues, and he had no outlet after you left. He left me alone for a few months, but then I became the new Jade."

"I'm so sorry, Beth. I *never* would have left if I knew he'd start hurting you."

"Too little, too late, Jade. It doesn't matter now anyway. What's done is done, and there isn't a damn thing either of us can do about it. Besides, I moved in with Lily a year after you ran off."

I raised an eyebrow. "He let you?"

She looked sad for the first time. "He wasn't in any shape to take care of me."

"Huh? Why not?"

She stared up at me, sadness filling her brown eyes. "He was too busy mourning Mom. She's dead, Jade. She had a heart attack. She's been gone for five fucking years, and you didn't even know!"

My heart stopped. My lungs refused to suck in air. I stared at my sister as I tried to process what she had told me. *Mom is dead.* A cry erupted from my chest. My lungs were working again, but all I could manage to do was scream. This couldn't be happening. *No!* My mother couldn't be dead. She couldn't have been dead for *five years* without me knowing.

I heard footsteps running to me, and then Logan was there. He picked me up and pulled me into his arms.

"What did you do to her?" he shouted at Bethaney.

"I told her the truth. Our mother is dead, and she had no fucking clue."

I felt Logan's arms tense around me.

He cursed under his breath as he pulled me tighter against him. "Jade, calm down. Come on, it's going to be okay. Calm down."

I couldn't calm down, not entirely. My body shuddered as I continued to cry in his arms. Up until this moment, I'd thought I hated my mom. She'd idly sat by while David punished me over and over again, both mentally and physically. She'd never said a word, never tried to stop him.

But damn it, she was my *mother.* How could I not feel pain over losing her?

"How did I not know? Why didn't someone contact me?" I finally managed to get out.

"You disappeared, Jade. We looked for you for a long time after you left, but we came up with nothing. It was like you had vanished into thin air. How were we supposed to tell you what had happened when we couldn't even find you?"

"I want to see her," I said once my tears slowed.

Logan looked like he was about to argue, but I shook my head.

"*I want to see her!*"

All three of us winced at the shrillness in my voice.

Logan kissed my forehead before looking over at Bethaney. "Where is she buried?"

"The cemetery a few miles from here." She hesitated for a second. "I'll show you where. I don't think Jade could tell you where the front door is at this point."

He nodded as he stood up, still cradling me in his arms. He carried me to his car and sat me gently inside. Bethaney had disappeared inside the house, but she came back out and walked to the car. Once she and Logan were inside the car with me, she started giving him directions. Besides that, no one spoke.

Logan kept my hand in his as he drove. I felt comforted by the touch. *Logan was strong. He was good. He would take care of me.*

13

Why is the sun still shining so brightly? That was my first thought when we pulled through the cemetery gates. I felt like I'd lost a piece of myself, and it didn't seem right that the sun kept shining.

"Park over there," Bethaney said from the backseat.

Logan steered the car off the road and put it in park. After he turned the key to shut it off, we all sat motionless. The silence seemed to push against me. It was too much. The car suddenly felt too small. I shoved the door open and all but fell out. My knees hit the gravel, and I barely noticed when I heard my jeans rip on the jagged edges of the rocks.

Logan was out of the car and by my side in an instant. He crouched down beside me without saying anything and lifted me until I was standing. I turned my attention to Bethaney as she climbed out of the car.

"Where?"

She pointed toward a few graves in the back. "There."

I walked to where she'd pointed. I was surprised when my steps didn't falter. Instead, I kept a solid pace until I reached my mother's headstone. I stared down at it. Up until this moment, I'd hoped that Bethaney was simply playing a horrible joke on me. The words on the stone let me know just how serious she was.

Elizabeth Dawn Walters

Beloved Mother and Wife

1970-2008

I wiped my eyes as I stared down at the words engraved in the stone. She was really gone. For some reason, I didn't feel the overwhelming sadness I had felt when Bethaney told me. I was still hurting and definitely still in shock, but it wasn't all-consuming. Maybe I'd lost it before because it was such a surprise. Regardless of the reason, all I felt while staring at my mother's final resting place was a hollow ache in the pit of my stomach. This was the end of the road between the two of us. There would be no reunion, no peace.

I shook my head. *This isn't right. She should have to answer to me for what she did.*

"You got lucky," I said between clenched teeth. I was suddenly angry with my mother for leaving before I had a chance to say what I wanted to her. "Death was an escape from what you did. I hope you died regretting what you let him do to Bethaney and me."

I heard Bethaney's sharp intake of breath. *"Jade!"*

I ignored her. I didn't care if she was upset with me. "You just stood there and watched him hit me! And I'm sure that you did the same with Bethaney! What kind of mother does that?"

Logan wrapped his arms around my shoulders, but he said nothing. I leaned into him, letting him give me strength.

"I came here to confront you. I came here to show you and David that I made it. I escaped my childhood, and I became the woman I always wanted to be. I am successful. I am determined. I am *strong.* You were the weak one, the one who wouldn't even stand up for her own children. And you know what? You and David didn't win! You didn't strip me of myself. Instead, you were the reason I pushed myself so hard. I wanted to show you that I am better than what I left behind. So, here I am, Mom. I. Beat. You." I took a deep breath to control the rage building inside me. "You are my past. I am my future. The band is my future. Logan is my future. I will *never* look back."

I pulled away from Logan and walked back to the car. I didn't bother to look behind me. I'd said what I came all this way to say. As I climbed back into the car, I realized it hadn't brought me the peace I thought it would. Instead, I still felt hollow inside. I wished David were in front of me right now. I wanted to kick and hit him until the emptiness inside of me disappeared. I wanted him to know what it was like to suffer.

The driver's side door opened, and Logan sat down next to me. "Are you okay?"

"Fine," I muttered.

Bethaney climbed into the backseat. "Are you happy now?" she asked angrily.

"No, I'm not. I won't be happy until I find David."

"You're nuts, Jade! I can't believe you said those things to our *dead* mother. What the fuck is wrong with you?"

"You want a list?"

She frowned at me. "You're not the same Jade that you used to be. You're angry, and you're bitter. What happened to you?"

"Trust me, I was worse than this before I left. I just hid it better."

We glared at each other as Logan started the car. He pulled back onto the blacktop.

When we finally reached the main road, he glanced back in the rearview mirror at Bethaney. "Do you want me to drop you off at your friend's house?"

"Yeah," she muttered.

I turned to look at her again, but she refused to return my gaze. Instead, she stared out the window. I swallowed the lump in my throat as I watched her. Nothing was going like I'd planned. Once we dropped Bethaney off at Lily's, I knew Bethaney would never speak to me again.

"Bethaney—"

"Don't. You don't get to sound remorseful after that shit."

"I'm so sorry. Please don't hate me…I didn't come all this way just to walk away from you again. You're all I have left. I don't want to lose you, too."

"What do you want me to say? The things you said back there were wrong. Mom is *dead,* Jade. How could you say those things to her?"

"It was the truth, Beth. We both know it. They screwed us up so badly. The way we grew up…it wasn't right. Just because she's gone doesn't make what she did right."

"I know that," she said quietly.

"Look, we're both upset right now. Why don't we take a breather and try this reunion thing again? I swear, I'll do better tomorrow."

Her lips quirked up into a grin, but she hid it quickly. "I'm really mad at you."

"I know, and I want to make it right. Please let me try. Give me another chance before you decide to hate me."

Logan pulled up in front of Lily's house, and Bethaney reached for the door.

As she swung it open, she turned back to me. "Pick me up tomorrow at noon."

I smiled for the first time in what felt like years. "I will."

She stepped out of the car and slammed the door behind her, letting me know that she was still pissed. I watched her walk up to the house until she disappeared inside. Logan pulled away from the curb and headed back toward our hotel.

"That was fun," he said as he glanced over at me.

I gave him a sheepish grin. Logan had just seen the worst of me. He'd seen the monster that was always lurking just below the surface.

"I'm sorry. I lost it back there. I meant the things I said though. My mother was a coward for not standing up for my sister and me."

He frowned. "Hey, you don't have to explain anything to me. I watched Chloe's mother abuse her for years. I know what she went through. You both suffered so much, and no one did a thing to stop it. You have every right to feel angry. You're the victim, Jade, not your mom and certainly not David."

Even hearing his name sent waves of anger coursing through my body. "I want to go back to his house."

"Jade—"

"No, I want to see him. I'm already fired up, so now is a good time to have it out with him."

"I think you've been through enough today. You have all summer to confront him. Let's just go back to the hotel and chill, okay?"

I shook my head. "Take me to the house, or I'll get there myself."

He sighed. "If you're sure…"

"I am."

"What if he's not there?" Logan asked.

"Then, I'll wait until he comes home."

"What are you going to do when you see him?"

"I'm going to tell him what a no good piece of shit he is for hurting Beth after I left. I can handle the fact that he hit me. What I can't handle is knowing that she suffered at his hands. She's his daughter, for God's sake!"

"Don't do anything stupid, okay? I don't have enough money to bail you out."

I laughed. "I'll try my hardest."

He frowned. "I'm serious. Don't do something you'll regret."

I ignored him as we pulled into David's driveway again. This time, a car was parked out front. I smiled as I opened my door.

"Stay out here. I want to do this on my own," I said.

"I don't think you should be alone with him."

"Please, Logan, let me do this on my own. If I'm not out in fifteen, you can come inside."

He hesitated before finally nodding. "Fifteen minutes, and then I'm coming in after you."

I leaned over the console and kissed him. I felt his lips turn up into a smile as he cupped my face and pulled me closer.

"If you kiss me again, I'll drop it to ten minutes. Hurry up," he teased after we had pulled away from each other.

I gave him a grin before I stepped out of the car. As soon as I started walking toward the house, my smile faded, and I felt the anger from earlier return. I stopped and stared at the front door. The man behind this door was my physical embodiment of evil, of hopelessness. He was my own personal hell.

Before I could change my mind, I pounded my fist against the door several times. I stepped back and waited. Finally, the door opened, and there he stood in all of his asshole glory.

I felt like a bucket of cold water had been dumped on me as I looked at the man who had taken everything from me. He'd taken my childhood, my mother's love, my pride, my dignity, my self-worth…everything. The only things he'd ever given me were anger and hatred. He'd twisted me until those emotions were all I could focus on. When I'd left this house so many years ago, I'd been filled with so much hate. I'd hated myself and my life so much that I ran away from it all. If it hadn't been for Eric, Adam, and Drake, I would have been consumed by it. This man would have destroyed me.

He looks so much older, I thought as we stared at each other, *and so much weaker.*

"Jade," he said after a moment of hesitation.

"David." My voice held barely controlled rage. I wasn't calm or collected like I'd wanted to be. No, seeing him brought out the monster inside of me, and she was begging to be let loose.

"What do you want?" His voice held absolutely no emotion at all. He used the same tone that he would use to speak to a stranger.

"Aren't you going to invite me in?" I asked sarcastically.

He stepped out of the way and gestured for me to enter. I walked past him, careful to never turn my back to him. I didn't trust him. He closed the door behind me. I waited until he turned to face me to do what I'd wanted to do for years. I drew back and punched him as hard as I could. He stumbled back as blood started to trickle from his nose. It looked like years of pounding the shit out of my drums had come with another perk. I could hit as hard as some men.

Instead of feeling better after hitting him, I only felt angrier. Before I could even think about what I was doing, I hit him again. He hadn't even tried to block me. Years of pent-up anger and frustration were unleashed on him as I hit, clawed, and kicked every inch of his body that I could reach. Finally, I brought my knee up and hit him in the groin. He dropped to his knees and cupped himself as he moaned in agony. I felt a sick sense of satisfaction as I watched him suffer.

I stared at him, taking in all the damage I'd inflicted upon him. Blood was running from his nose and his lips. His left eye was already starting to bruise. I couldn't help but feel pride over that. I'd hit him *that* fucking hard.

"How does that feel?" I finally asked.

"Keep going, Jade. Don't stop until you feel better," he said as he looked up at me. Again, there was no emotion in his voice at all.

He was acting like I hadn't just kicked the living shit out of him. I knew he had to be hurting, but his voice had given no indication that he was.

"What the fuck is wrong with you?" I shouted.

He wasn't supposed to just lie there and take it. He was supposed to fight back. He was supposed to tell me how worthless I was. He was supposed to give me fuel so that I could light him on fire. I wanted him to tell me how pathetic I was, so I could shove the last six years of my life in his face.

"Why aren't you fighting back, you fucking asshole?" I asked when he hadn't answered my first question.

He looked up at me, and I gasped in shock when I saw tears filling his eyes.

"I have nothing left to fight for."

I dropped down to my knees, so we were eye level. Tears leaked from his eyes and ran down his cheeks as he met my gaze. This wasn't the man who had abused me for years. No, the man in front of me was broken. Even his body was slowly wasting away. His hair was now completely gray, and his skin was hanging off of his frail frame. But his eyes did me in. There was nothing in them besides pain. The anger I'd grown up with was nowhere to be found. I felt my own anger drain from my body. There was nothing here to be angry at. There was nothing here, period. This man, whoever he was now, was an empty shell. Nothing I'd wanted to do to him would give me satisfaction. The fucker had taken my revenge from me.

"What happened to you?" I whispered.

"Your mother," he said, sorrow thickening his voice.

"My mother?"

"She was everything to me, and she's gone now. Bethaney is gone, too. I have nothing left."

"How could you do the things you did to me?" I asked, refusing to think about what he'd just said.

"You were a reminder that your mother didn't love me—at least, not the way I loved her. I tried to give her everything, yet she still strayed."

"It wasn't my fault that she cheated! I can't believe the things you put me through just because you were angry with my mother!"

"It didn't matter. You were there every single day, living in my house. You were a constant reminder of what she'd done. I couldn't take it."

"Why did you hurt Beth when I left?" I asked.

The fight in me was gone. The man I'd wanted to hurt no longer existed.

"I don't know."

"You can't be serious. *You don't know?*" I stood and backed away from him. "I hope that my mother's memory haunts you until the day you die, David. I want you to suffer day after day just like I did." I stepped around him and walked to the door.

When I opened it, he called out, "Jade?"

"What?" I spit out.

"I...I saw you on TV with that band. Your mother would have been proud of you. She always loved you. She was just too afraid of me to tell you."

I turned to face him one last time. "It's too bad that I couldn't be proud of her. All those years, David, you tried your hardest to destroy me. I want you to know you didn't. When I left here, I found a new family, a family who loves me. I found my place in life right where I always wanted it to be—behind the drums you hated so much. I found someone I care about, and he doesn't think I'm worthless or in the way. I found a best friend who has taken care of me when I've needed him the most. I found myself, and after today, I will *never* look back. The minute I walk out this door, you are dead to me. You will rot away in this house by yourself, knowing that no one in this entire fucking world gives a damn about you. And while you're here, do you know where I'll be? I'll be out there—living, laughing, loving. I fucking found myself, and you'll never take that away from me. Good-bye, David."

I left him on his knees. I wanted that to be my last memory of David – bleeding, defeated, and broken. I walked back to the car and climbed in without once looking back.

Logan looked worried as he stared at me. "So?"

"It's done. Let's go."

"What's done? Jade, what did you do?"

I knew he was worried that I'd done something stupid.

"I punched him and kicked him in the balls. Then, I told him I hoped my mother's memory haunted him for the rest of his life. That's it. After that, I just walked out," I said calmly.

"That's it?" he asked, surprised.

"That's it. What did you think I was going to do?"

He shrugged. Then, he started the car and backed out of the driveway. "I had no clue. I never know what's going on in that head of yours."

"Neither do I, Logan. Neither do I."

Logan stopped at a pizza place and grabbed us dinner before heading back to the hotel. I hadn't even realized how late it was getting. By the time we made it to our room, the sun was starting to set. Like the night before, we sat on my bed and ate dinner. I tried to focus on the TV, so I didn't have to think about today. I wasn't calm enough yet to think about my words to my dead mother or the look in David's eyes.

Once we finished the pizza, I grabbed clean clothes and walked to the bathroom. "I'm going to shower," I called over my shoulder.

I turned on the water and stripped down as it warmed up. Once it was hot enough to burn me, I stepped into the spray. My skin was bright red within seconds, but I didn't care. I was trying to wash the past off of me. I scrubbed my hair until my scalp was screaming at me to stop.

After I rinsed out the shampoo, I grabbed the soap and a washcloth. I started running it over my skin roughly, but I barely noticed the pain. I just wanted a fresh start, and I couldn't do that if I didn't wash away every trace of the past. I wasn't satisfied with the washcloth, so I dropped it to the floor and started running my nails across my skin. I had no idea what was wrong with me, but I couldn't stop.

I just want to be clean.

I looked down to see that my nails had clawed deep enough into my arm that I was bleeding. I screamed and hit my fist against the side of the shower stall. When that didn't help, I slid down the wall and brought my knees up to my chest. I couldn't stop the cries of despair pouring out of me. I just wanted to let it all go, and I wasn't sure if that were even possible.

I looked up when the stream of water stopped. Logan was staring down at me with a horrified expression.

"Oh, Jade." He grabbed a towel and wrapped it around me.

I clung to him as he lifted me from the floor and carried me to my bed.

"I'm sorry," I whispered.

"Don't be sorry. You can't control how you feel right now." He reached for my arm and turned it over, so he could see the scratches I'd made. "These aren't too deep. I can bandage them up if you want."

I shook my head. "They're fine. I don't know what came over me, Logan. I was fine one minute, and then it was like a switch flipped in my head. Am I going crazy?"

"Of course not. Today was nuts. I would have worried if you *didn't* freak out. You can't let your emotions bottle up inside of you. If you do, they'll eat you alive."

"I thought I would feel better once I saw them again. I thought that all the pain and anger I've kept inside would magically disappear. It didn't, and now, I have no idea what I'm supposed to do to make everything better."

"I wish you could make it go away all at once, but there's nothing you can do. You just have to keep living and let yourself heal. You've spent the last six years focusing on the things they did to you instead of the things happening in your life. Look at where you are now, Jade. You're living your dream! You have so many people who care about you. You have to focus on those things and let the past stay where it belongs—behind you. It won't happen in a split second. It'll take time and patience."

I thought about what he'd said. He was right. I had a new family now. I'd even pointed that out to my sister and David. I needed to think about them instead of my past. Logan, Eric, Drake, and even

Adam were my family now. Chloe was, too. *Those* people were the ones I needed to focus on.

"When did you get so smart?" I finally asked.

"I'm not sure. I think it was when I talked to this really hot drummer chick one night. The love of my life had just married another man, and I was pretty down, but the hot drummer chick made me realize a few things." He smiled down at me.

"Hot drummer chick? When can I meet her? I think I have a lot in common with her."

He moved until he was lying beside me on the bed. It was only then when I realized I was wearing nothing but the towel *he'd* put around me.

"You're different from anyone else I've ever met, Jade. You didn't give up on me, even when I'd given up on myself. You have no idea how much that means to me." He stared down at me with a troubled look on his face. "Did you mean what you said at the cemetery?"

"Which part?"

"That I'm part of your future."

I grinned at him, suddenly feeling very vulnerable. "I guess I did. I mean, like I said earlier, I'm not expecting a ring or anything. I don't know how to say this right. I've wanted you for a really long time. Now that we're kind of together, it just feels right. Does that make sense?"

He smiled. "I've spent the last nine months trying to figure out what I wanted when it came to you. You're so different from any other girl I've ever met. You don't need anyone. You're so independent that I wasn't even sure you'd really want to be with me. I wasn't sure how I felt about that, and I still don't know. I want to be with someone who needs me. It kills me to know that you don't."

"You're so wrong, Logan. I do need you. You kept me together more than once today. Just a few minutes ago, you pulled me out of that shower and helped me. I need you so damn much, and that scares me. I've never needed anyone."

He leaned down and kissed me. I kept one hand clasped on my towel, so it stayed in place as my other hand went to his neck. I pulled him toward me until part of his weight was on top of me. Feeling him pressed against me was like nothing else I'd ever experienced. I felt safe, like Logan could shield me from the world.

"I'm falling in love with you. I think I have been for a while," I whispered against his lips.

He stilled for a second before kissing me again. His lips attacked mine with a ferocity that took my breath away. His tongue slipped into my mouth and caressed mine. I moaned and wrapped my other hand around his neck, no longer worried about my towel. His lips moved to my neck, and I tilted my head to the side. He moved up to my ear and bit down gently on my earlobe before slowly kissing his way down to my shoulder.

"Your skin is so soft," he whispered.

I didn't say a word as he kissed lower. When he reached the top of my towel, he gave me a questioning look. I nodded, giving him the permission he was asking for. He slowly pulled the towel away, and then I was completely naked. I felt heat rise to my cheeks as he stared down at me.

"You're so beautiful, Jade."

I practically felt his hunger as his eyes moved down my body.

He stopped his appraisal when he noticed the script on my ribs. "What does your tattoo say?" he asked as he leaned in closer.

I shut my eyes and rolled to my side, so he could read the script. I had the words memorized.

You cannot destroy me. Only I can destroy myself.

"I had it done a few months after I ran away," I said quietly.

"It's true. People can affect your choices, but they can't change the person you are."

"So, I made myself a closed-off, bitter, old cat lady all by myself?" I asked, half-joking, half-serious.

He laughed. "You're too hot to be the little old lady with all the cats. I promise you that."

"You think I'm hot?" I asked innocently.

He leaned down farther and kissed the script on my ribs. "I do."

His lips continued to explore me as he rolled me back over. He kissed a trail to my belly button and dipped his tongue inside. I gasped in shock. He kissed his way back up to my face, making sure to avoid my breasts. Then, he kissed along my neck again. I wasn't sure if he was torturing me on purpose or not.

"I want you to kiss me everywhere," I said.

He shook his head. "I told you last night that I wasn't going to move too fast with you, and I meant it. I'm not going to screw this up with you."

"You won't, I promise. I just really need you tonight, Logan. Please. I want you."

When he shuddered, I knew that I'd won.

He pulled my face to his and kissed me deeply. "Promise me something before we go any further."

"Anything," I said against his lips.

"If you ever decide that you don't want me, you tell me. Don't try to hide it or force yourself to love me, okay?" He pulled away from me enough to look down at me.

The pain in his eyes broke my heart.

"Oh, Logan. I won't do what she—I'll never hurt you, and I won't lie to you. I promise."

Chloe had hurt him so badly. Even now, he was still thinking about what she'd done to him.

"I can't go through that again. I can't give someone my heart and watch as she stomps on it before throwing it away."

I reached up and grabbed the sides of his face, forcing him to stare directly into my eyes. "No matter what happens between us, *I will never hurt you.* I've wanted you for so long. I'd be a fool to cast you aside. Since I met you, you're the only man I've thought about."

He smiled down at me, and I saw relief fill his eyes.

"Thank you, Jade."

I pulled him back down to me, and I kissed him. He didn't hold back this time. Instead, he threw everything he had into that kiss. It was like an invisible wall had been between us, and it was gone now. I knew deep down that he was still scared, but in time, he would see that I meant what I'd said. I would never hurt him. He was all I wanted. I'd spent so much time wanting him that it felt surreal to be lying here with him.

He sat up and pulled his shirt over his head. After tossing it aside, he leaned back down and started kissing me again. I moaned as our naked skin touched. I ran my hands down his chest and ribs. He shivered at my touch, and I smiled. I felt powerful and sexy and so many other emotions that I hadn't felt in a very long time.

I shoved on him gently until he rolled to his back. Before I lost my nerve, I rolled on top of him. He seemed surprised, but he grinned up at me.

"It's been a really long time since I've done this, so bear with me, okay?" I asked.

"Somehow, I doubt you'll disappoint." He rested his hands on my hips.

I leaned down and kissed along his neck and then down to his chest, teasing him like he had teased me earlier. My hands explored every ripple of muscle on his stomach as my tongue darted out and attacked his nipple. His body jerked in response. I slowly kissed my way down his stomach to the top of his jeans. I reached down and undid the top button with shaking hands. Once it was loose, I slowly unzipped his jeans. When I sat up and started tugging on them, he grabbed me and dropped me onto the bed beside him.

I watched with rapt attention as he stood and lowered his jeans. He kicked them off and climbed back onto the bed, never taking his eyes off of me. I couldn't stop my eyes from lowering and taking in all of him. His fingers grazed my cheek, and I raised my eyes up to meet his. He gave me the sweetest smile possible, showing off his dimples, and I felt myself melt.

Dear God, he is so beautiful, and he's mine.

"You're sure?" he asked quietly as he ran his fingertips down my arm.

I nodded, unable to speak.

"Are you on anything?"

It took me a moment to realize what he was talking about. *Birth control. Shit.* I wasn't. I'd had no reason to be. I'd spent the last six years on my own. Babies and pregnancy-scares had been the last things on my mind.

I shook my head. "No, I never had a reason to be."

"It's fine. I have condoms in my wallet."

I raised an eyebrow, and he grinned.

"Hey, I didn't come down here, expecting anything with you. I'd just rather be safe than sorry."

He reached down and grabbed his jeans off the floor. After pulling his wallet out of the back pocket and grabbing a condom from inside, he threw them back down. I watched as he put the condom on the table beside the bed and turned back to me.

"You're the most beautiful girl I've ever seen, Jade." He leaned in and kissed me gently.

As he moved his body over mine, I moaned. I could feel his dick against my thigh, hard and ready.

"I'm nervous," I whispered after I broke the kiss.

139

"Don't be. I won't do anything you don't want to do. If you're unsure, we'll stop now."

I shook my head. "No, I don't want to stop. I don't know why I'm so nervous."

"Let's see if I can distract you."

He started at my neck and slowly kissed his way down my body. When he reached my ankle, he started his way back up. The kisses were gentle and sweet. When he reached my inner thigh, my breathing increased. I felt fire flood my veins when he kissed higher. His breath tickled my skin when he reached the apex of my thighs. He pressed a light kiss where my body needed him the most, and I moaned loudly.

"Is this okay?" he asked.

"Yes." My voice cracked.

He continued to press kisses between my legs. When I felt like I was going to explode from all his teasing, he pulled away. I groaned and opened my mouth to beg him to stop teasing, but his mouth was suddenly against me. My back arched off the bed as he ran his tongue across my clit, and then he sucked on it gently.

"Oh my God!" I gasped as my hands grabbed for the sheets, and I fisted them tightly.

This was new to me. Mikey had never tried anything like this with me.

Logan sucked and bit down gently, never giving me a chance to catch my breath. I felt myself building, and I tensed when I came undone. His mouth never left me as he worked me through my orgasm. When I finally came back down to earth, he pulled away and kissed his way up my body, stopping at both of my breasts to tease them. When he kissed me, I could taste myself on his lips. I wasn't sure if I was disgusted or more turned-on by it.

He grabbed the condom off the table and ripped it open with his teeth. All I could do was lie there as he rolled it on and then moved until his body hovered over mine.

"Are you ready, babe? I can't wait anymore after tasting you. If I don't fuck you, I might die right here and now."

I reached up and pulled his face down to mine. I kissed him viciously, letting him know that he had my permission to do whatever he wanted. He could have tied me to the bed at this point, and I would have let him.

Taking my kiss as a yes, he lowered his hips and pushed into me. It was uncomfortable at first, but he went slow, giving me time to adjust to his size. I relaxed my body, letting him fill me. Once he was in, he stopped. I wiggled my hips, silently begging him to move. I felt totally and completely filled.

"You sure you're okay?" he asked.

"Better than okay," I whispered.

He pulled out and then slammed back into me, over and over. I wrapped my legs around him, allowing him deeper. I closed my eyes, letting the sensations take over my body. Each thrust brought me closer and closer to the edge. I wanted more, needed more, *craved more.*

"Faster, Logan. Please!" I gasped.

He obliged, pumping into me faster. I clung to him, my fingernails digging into his back. I opened my eyes to see him staring down at me. The look in his eyes nearly pushed me over the edge. There was so much hunger and passion in them that I wanted to look away. Instead, I continued to stare at him, watching his face, as he started to lose control. It was the single most erotic thing I'd ever witnessed in my life. Logan in everyday life was beautiful, but at this moment, he was simply breathtaking.

My orgasm crashed over me suddenly, and I cried out his name. As he released into me, his body was taut and slick with sweat, but it was his expression that did me in. Before my eyes slid shut, the last image I had was of him coming with me. The look of pure ecstasy was something I knew I'd remember for the rest of my life.

15

I opened my eyes, and my head was resting on Logan's chest. I could hear the solid *thump, thump, thump* of his heart under my cheek. I tried to move my legs, but they were pinned between his. His arm was wrapped around my back, and his hand rested on my shoulder. Every inch of my body was touching his.

I smiled as I snuggled tighter against him. He sighed in his sleep, and his hand squeezed my shoulder gently. I was exactly where I wanted to be. Despite the disaster of yesterday, I was glad we'd come to Crossville for the simple fact that I was in his arms now. Memories of the night before filled my mind, and I shuddered with desire. It had been perfect. *He'd* been perfect.

I didn't want to leave this bed, but after glancing at the clock, I saw it was almost eleven, and I'd promised to pick up my sister at noon. I slowly started running my fingers back and forth across his stomach and chest, trying to wake him. After a few minutes, he started to stir. He groaned and stretched just before his eyes slowly opened. He stared down at me, and a sleepy smile lifted his lips.

"Morning," I whispered.

He rolled so that I was forced to rest my head on a pillow. Once he was facing me, he leaned in and kissed me gently.

"Morning," he whispered back as he pulled away. "Did I dream last night? Or was it really that good?"

I laughed, unable to stop myself. I felt light and happy. I couldn't remember the last time I'd felt like this. "It wasn't a dream."

"Prove it." He grinned.

I glanced down at our naked bodies. "I'm naked while lying in bed with you. What more do you want?"

His blue eyes darkened with lust. He opened his mouth to speak, but I shook my head.

"I know what you're about to say, and we can't. We have to pick up my sister soon."

"Later?" he asked.

I nodded. "Later."

"Good. Now, I have something to look forward to all day."

I grinned. "Last night was incredible. Now, I know why Adam is always so happy. Sex does that to a person. It's addictive."

He laughed. "Only one time, and you're already addicted to me? Damn, I must be a fucking god in bed."

I raised an eyebrow. "A fucking god? Really?"

He just laughed again as he pinned me to the bed. I could feel him pressed against my thigh, ready to go, and I cursed the fact that we had less than an hour to get ready and pick up Bethaney. My body was craving him. He kissed me long and hard, making my toes curl. When he finally pulled away, I was breathing heavily.

"I'm going to get off of you before we both decide that your sister can wait. I doubt she'd appreciate being stood up after yesterday."

"Good point," I said.

He moved away from me and stood up. I watched him walk, completely naked, across the room. He grabbed clothes out of his bag and headed toward the bathroom.

"I'm going to shower really quick, and then the bathroom is all yours."

I lay in bed and stared up at the ceiling as I heard the water turn on. I couldn't believe that I'd had sex with Logan. I felt like a sixteen-year-old who had just lost her virginity. I grinned as I crawled out of bed and walked to the bathroom. Logan didn't notice me until I opened the shower door and stepped inside with him.

"What are you doing?" he asked as he rinsed his hair.

"I need to shower, too. I thought I'd join you and conserve water."

He laughed as he reached for me and pulled my body tight against his. Water cascaded down around us, soaking my hair and running down my face and body, but I barely noticed. All I saw was Logan, naked and wet. My body practically begged me to attack him, but I held back. We didn't have time.

Later, I promised myself.

Instead of pushing him up against the wall and climbing him like a monkey, I kissed him lightly on the lips and pulled away. I turned away from him and grabbed my soap. Our bodies constantly brushed against each other as we showered together. I wasn't sure which of us was going to lose control first.

When he shut off the water and grabbed a towel, I let out a relieved sigh. He shot me a quick grin before climbing out and wrapping a towel around his waist. I grabbed two towels. I wrapped one around my hair and then dried off with the other. I towel-dried my hair quickly before brushing it straight and grabbing the hairdryer. Once it was dry, I applied a small amount of makeup and hurried back into the room to get dressed.

Logan was lying on his bed, already dressed. His wet hair was hanging over his eyes, driving me wild. We needed to get out of this room and fast before my hormones took over. I dressed quickly, constantly aware of his eyes on me. As soon as I finished tying my neon-green shoelaces, he sat up and pulled me down onto the bed with him.

He kissed me for a few seconds before reluctantly pulling away. "This is going to be the longest day ever."

"Agreed. Now, come on, let's go before my sister thinks I forgot about her." I stood and grabbed his hand, pulling him to his feet.

He kept my hand in his all the way to the car. As soon as we were inside, he pulled my hand back into his where it stayed until we arrived at Lily's.

"Do you think today will go better than yesterday?" I asked as I stared out the window at Lily's house.

"Yeah, I do. Things got a little…intense yesterday. Your sister was upset, but she's had time to cool off now," Logan said as he rubbed the palm of my hand with his thumb.

"What if she's still mad at me and decides that she wants nothing to do with me anymore?"

"Jade, you're her sister. She's been without you for over six years. Now that you're trying to make things right and be a part of her life, she isn't going to just let you walk away again. You're the only real family she has left now."

"She has David."

Logan snorted, and I couldn't help but grin.

"Like I said, you're the only *real* family she has now."

I glanced down at my phone to check the time. It read *12:06*, so I took a deep breath and opened my car door. The last thing I wanted Beth to think was that I'd stood her up. I didn't want to piss her off more than I already had.

Hoping that Marie wasn't around, I knocked on the front door. Only a few seconds later, it opened, and Bethaney stepped out of the house. She closed the door quietly behind her and turned back to me.

"Come on, let's go." She hurried past me to Logan's car.

"Where's the fire?" I called after her as I tried to keep up with her fast pace.

When we reached the car, she jumped into the backseat and quickly closed the door.

What is up with her today? I wondered as I sat down in the front seat.

"Want to tell me what that was all about?" I asked.

Logan pulled back out onto the main road.

She glanced back at the house one last time before turning her attention to me. "Marie wasn't all that excited about my plans to meet with you."

"That doesn't surprise me. She wasn't exactly nice to me yesterday. But that still doesn't explain why you snuck off like a thief."

"I didn't want her to know you were outside or that I was leaving with you. She would have come out and called you a bunch of bad names. In turn, you probably would have punched her and broken her nose, and she would have called the cops on you. Then, I would have to spend my whole summer as a hooker, trying to save up enough money to bail you out and send you to some foreign country with the band so that you could narrowly escape your death sentence. I thought it would be easier to just sneak out instead of going through all of that."

The car was completely silent. Through the rearview mirror, Logan was staring at Bethaney like she'd lost her mind. She tried to keep a straight face, but she finally gave up and started laughing uncontrollably. I lost it, too, as I watched her fall over and clutch her stomach in the backseat.

"Okay..." Logan said, glancing between the road and us. "I think I'm the only sane person in this car."

I finally stopped laughing long enough to speak. "This is just how Beth is—sarcastic, weird, and occasionally funny."

"The looks on your faces were priceless. Oh my God!" She tried to stop laughing at herself.

"Yep, I'm surrounded by crazy people," Logan muttered as we pulled into a Denny's parking lot.

"Oh, by the way, we're stopping here for lunch. I didn't have a chance to eat breakfast, so I'm starving. After this, we can go wherever you want," I said as I looked back at Beth.

"Fine by me. I'm hungry, too." She opened her door and stepped out.

I could still hear her giggling quietly.

"Come on," I told Logan before opening my door and climbing out.

"Actually, I just remembered that I forgot something back at the hotel. I'm going to run back there and grab it really quick." Logan said as I closed my door.

"What did you forget?" I asked, confused.

He grinned at me, and then he backed out of the parking spot. I watched as he left the parking lot and headed back the way we'd come. As soon as he was out of sight, I realized what he'd just done. He was giving me time alone with Beth. I smiled at his thoughtfulness. Logan had to be one of the nicest guys out there.

"Where did he go?" Beth asked.

"He had something to take care of. It's just us."

We walked to the building side-by-side. Once we were inside, we found a table away from everyone else and placed our orders. I wanted alone time with Bethaney, and that would be hard if someone recognized me and came over. Crossville didn't have a huge rock music crowd, but there were a few, and I used to know them all. They would recognize me instantly.

"So, what's up with you and Logan? Are you two a thing or not?" Beth asked. She certainly didn't waste time with small talk.

I couldn't keep the sappy grin off my face. "Yeah, we are, but it's in the early stages."

"Wow. Really? I figured you guys had been together for a long time."

Our waitress appeared with our drinks, halting our conversation.

"Why would you think that?" I asked once we were alone again.

She shrugged. "Just the way you two look at each other. It's kind of gross actually. It's like you're fucking each other and saying wedding vows with just your eyes."

I choked on my soda and started coughing violently. When I could finally breathe again, I frowned at my sister. "We do not eye-fuck, and we certainly aren't getting married. You'd better get your eyes checked."

"Oh, whatever. You two probably go at it like rabbits. You're blushing! I was right!"

I felt my face heat as tingles raced through my body. All I could think about was the way Logan had looked last night while he fucked me. If I died right now, I'd die a happy woman from just thinking about him like that. The thought that I could have had a repeat performance this morning had me wishing that I'd rescheduled with my sister and stayed in the room with Logan all day…or all week.

"So, how's your love life?" I asked before I let my thoughts distract me from why I was here. I wanted to get to know Beth again.

"What love life? Have you seen the guys around here? And college isn't much better. College guys are hot, yeah, but they're dicks. I can't handle their egos long enough to make it to a second date."

"What college do you go to?"

"University of Tennessee. I stay in a dorm during the school year, but I came back with Lily to stay at her mom's house over the summer. I love Marie, but she drives me up the wall. She's so damn bossy that I think she's pretending to be my mom."

"She's just looking out for you, Beth. Does she know what David did to you?"

She nodded. "Yeah, I kind of had to tell her when I showed up on her doorstep with all my stuff. She wanted me to go to the police, but I told her no. I just wanted to forget about it. I was doing a pretty good job until you showed back up."

"I really am sorry that I left you alone with him. If I had known, I never would have left. You're my baby sister, and I want to protect you."

"In case you haven't noticed, I'm not a baby anymore."

I rolled my eyes. "You'll always be my baby sister. So, tell me about college. What are you studying?"

"Ugh, gag. I'm still undecided. I hate college."

"Why? You used to love school."

"Yeah, when I was, like, fourteen. Things change, Jade. What I'd really love to do is go to Hollywood and become a famous actress or a model. I want out of Tennessee so bad that I can taste it."

"Bethaney, I don't think that's a good idea. I mean, how many people go to California with the same dream? You'd be one of thousands. The odds aren't in your favor. You're better off getting a real education."

"Hypocrite much? You went to California with dreams of making it big, and you did it even though thousands of people are out there, trying the same thing all the time."

"That's different. The only reason we went out there was because they called us. We never would have just packed up and moved if Brad hadn't called."

"Brad?"

"Our manager at the label," I clarified.

Bethaney sighed. "You have it all, you know that, right? A band, a record deal, a label, and thousands of fans. You got out of this town and accomplished everything you'd ever dreamed."

"Yeah, I guess so. All I ever wanted was to play my drums. All the other stuff was just an added bonus."

"So, what's it like?"

"What's what like?" I asked.

"Everything—living in L.A., recording music, touring, having fans."

"It's all great. I like L.A., but I miss living in West Virginia. It was my home for so long. The touring is awesome. I get to meet tons of people who love the band's music, but being on the road constantly wears on me, especially when it's just the band and Chloe. You try living in close quarters with three guys for almost a year. You'd pull your hair out."

"Chloe? Isn't she the lead singer's wife?"

"Yep. They're pretty much attached at the hip. It's cute and sickening all at once."

"What about the other two? Do they have girlfriends?"

"Nah. Adam has hookups, and Eric just ignores everyone."

"I've looked at pictures of you guys. The one is super hot, and I'd love to meet him. He's just so...yum."

Panic shot through my body. "Oh no, not a chance on your life. You will *never* meet them, and if you do, you'll stay far away from Adam. I won't allow you to be around him unless you're wearing a turtleneck, pants, and a chastity belt."

The thought of Adam noticing my sister made me want to castrate him. I made a mental note to threaten him the next time I saw him just in case I decided to bring Bethaney around the band.

"Why? He seems so sweet," Bethaney said, looking at me like I was nuts.

"What is it about him that makes him seem sweet? The boy is covered in tattoos and piercings. He has a blue Mohawk, for God's sake!"

"What? No! Not that guy, the other one. I think his name is Eric."

My mouth dropped open. "You think Eric is hot?"

I couldn't even process the fact that Beth thought of Eric like that. To me, he was just Eric—my best friend, my confidant.

"Um...yes! Don't you?"

I shook my head. "He's practically my brother, and you're my sister, so that makes you siblings. You're basically saying your brother is hot."

She looked at me like I'd lost my mind. "Jade, you're seriously weird. Eric isn't related to us, and I sure as hell don't think *brother* when I look at him."

"No. Just no. I refuse to think of you crushing on Eric. New topic."

"Whatever. So, where does Logan fit into all of this? Did you meet him in L.A.?"

"No, I've known him for a long time. We met through Chloe. He's her ex-boyfriend and best friend."

"Awkward much?" Bethaney asked.

"You have no clue. It's a mess. Chloe cheated on him with Drake, and it really fucked Logan up. No one even knows that we're together yet. I'm not sure how everyone in our group of friends will take it."

"Does he live in West Virginia?"

I nodded.

"So, what happens when you go back to L.A.?"

"We haven't really talked about it. Like I said, this is brand-new. I haven't really thought about what will happen after I go back to California."

I had no idea why I hadn't thought about the fact that his life was in West Virginia and mine was in L.A. I couldn't just move back to West Virginia to be with him, and I would never ask him to move to California for me. We didn't have years of history like Drake and Chloe had. He wouldn't give up everything for me. My stomach clenched when I realized that this summer might be all I had with him.

"Hey, stop frowning. I didn't mean to make you sad. I'm sorry," Bethaney said as she looked at me with concern in her eyes.

"You didn't. I'm just now realizing that I'm fucked when it comes to Logan." I dropped my head down onto the table in defeat.

"Don't freak out just yet. You have no idea what the future will bring. Just focus on the time you do have with him this summer and then go from there. Things will work out."

"I hope so," I said as I sat back up.

It was nice to be able to talk to someone again, especially another woman. I loved Eric, but I could never tell him some things, and Logan definitely fell into that category. Chloe had been around, but I would never talk to her about Logan. There were just too many fuck-ups between them for me to feel comfortable discussing my feelings with her. I missed Bethaney more than I'd realized.

"I've missed you so much, Beth. I don't know how I made it the last six years without you."

"I've missed you, too, big sister. So, how long do you plan on staying?"

I shrugged. "That depends on you. If you want me, I can stay for a couple of months. We've been staying at a hotel in town, but I'd like to find something a little more permanent while I'm here."

"Of course I want you, you idiot," Beth said, frowning at me.

"After yesterday, I wasn't sure if you would or not."

"You were a first-class jackass yesterday, but you're still my sister. I definitely want you around."

"Then, I guess Logan and I will start looking for a place to rent."

"Good." She paused before grinning at me. "Now, about Eric…"

16

After we finished up our lunch, Bethaney and I spent the rest of the afternoon walking around Crossville. We talked about the things we'd seen and done over the past six years. She loved listening to my stories of how Adam would get himself in trouble, and one of us would have to bail his dumbass out.

When I'd told her about Drake's cocaine problem, she had been shocked. Apart from our little group of friends, no one knew what he had gone through. The label had been very careful to keep his problems private. I cried when I told her about the night he'd overdosed. I thought I'd lost him then, and reliving the memories of that night nearly brought me to my knees. Even though he seemed truly happy with Chloe, I knew I'd watch him for a long time. I would *never* let him go back to how he had been.

When it was almost dark, I finally called Logan to pick us up. Bethaney and I had ended up at the old playground, and that was where Logan found us, sitting on the swings. Logan dropped Bethaney off at Lily's, and I promised her that we would get together in a few days. I needed to find a place for Logan and me to stay until we were ready to go home. Since we only wanted to rent for two months, I knew we'd have very few places to choose from.

Once we dropped her off, Logan and I stopped at a diner for dinner. It was a small family-run business that I'd only been in a few times before. My goal while I was here was to stay away from all the places where I used to hang out. I didn't want someone from the past to see me. I didn't want to explain why I'd left or what I'd been up to the last few years. I was here to see Bethaney, and that was it. I wasn't interested in seeing old friends. None of them mattered to me anymore.

"So, how did things go with your sister?" Logan asked after we'd placed our orders.

"It was actually good. She wants me to stick around, so I thought you and I could go hunting tomorrow for a place to stay while we're here."

"Works for me. As much as I like our hotel room, it'd be nice to have an actual apartment or house to stay in."

"Agreed. The hotel room is way too tiny. Hopefully, we can find someplace with a washer and dryer. I'm tired of using Laundromats. I hate washing my clothes where a complete stranger's underwear was before."

Logan laughed. "You're so strange. I never noticed before."

"Is that a bad thing?" I asked, suddenly self-conscious.

"Not at all. It's cute and refreshing."

"Oh, okay. Good," I said.

I had no idea where strong, independent Jade had gone, but she needed to get her ass back here pronto. I wasn't used to second-guessing myself the way I did around Logan, and it sucked.

"What are you thinking?" Logan asked.

I looked up, realizing that I'd been staring down at the table in front of me for longer than I should have. "Nothing. Just thinking."

"Jade…"

"Ugh, fine. I was just wondering why I'm always second-guessing myself around you. I'm not usually like this. You make me nervous, and I'm always worried that I'm going to say or do something that's going to make you rethink this whole thing with me."

"Jade, never doubt yourself, especially around me. I like you just the way you are. Nothing you do or say is going to change that, okay? Just be who you are."

Our food arrived, and we ate in silence. I couldn't stop myself from glancing at him every few minutes. He was just…perfect. He was sweet and kind on the inside and sexy as hell on the outside. I never in my wildest dreams thought that I'd be sitting here with him. Men like him were one in a million, and I'd never been the kind of girl who would normally have a chance with a guy like him.

I realized that my stepdad had really fucked with me. That thought angered me. He'd damaged me so long ago, killing my self-esteem, and I was still fighting with myself to get over the things he'd beat into me.

"You ready?" Logan asked once we finished.

"Yeah." I pulled out a few bills and dropped them on the table, ignoring the glare Logan was sending my way.

He wrapped his arm around me as we walked outside to where he'd parked the car. I snuggled into him, loving the feel of his body pressed against mine.

He stopped on my side of the car and kissed me gently. "I missed you today," he said quietly.

"I missed you, too."

He grinned before walking around to his side of the car.

All the way back to the hotel, he kept bringing my hand up to his lips and kissing it. I couldn't help but smile at his sweetness. We were both so different, yet we clicked. I was the hard-ass who would go balls to the wall on everything while he was the quiet, sweet type. We complemented each other's personality perfectly.

When we arrived at the hotel, I stepped out of the car and stretched. I squealed when Logan scooped me up and started carrying me to our room.

"Put me down!" I yelped.

He ignored my protests as he stopped at our door and stuck the key card into the slot. He opened the door and stepped inside. The minute the door closed, he had me pressed up against it, and he began kissing me until I couldn't breathe. His hands cupped my bottom, and I wrapped my legs around his waist, pulling him closer.

"I've been waiting all day to get you alone," he whispered before kissing his way up to my ear.

I moaned softly when he nibbled on my earlobe.

"Is that so?" I asked.

"Mmhmm..." He kissed down my neck.

He turned and carried me to one of the beds. Before he pushed me down, he grabbed my shirt and pulled it over my head. As soon as I was lying down, he climbed on top of me and resumed kissing me. He dropped kisses along my collarbone and then down to the swells of my breasts. His tongue darted out and traced the top of my bra. I arched my back and unsnapped my bra. I tossed it aside as he ripped off his shirt. Then, he was back on top of me, and the rest of the world ceased to exist.

"I wanted to go slow, but I don't think that's going to happen." He sucked my nipple into his mouth.

Everywhere he touched made my skin feel like it was on fire.

"Fuck slow," I muttered as I pressed my body up against his.

He released my nipple and slowly kissed his way down my body. I threw my head back as he ran his tongue across my most sensitive areas. I'd pictured this moment over and over again in my head all day. Now that I was living it, the buildup was more than I could handle.

I grabbed his shoulders and pulled until he finally gave in. He kissed his way up my body. When we were face-to-face, I pushed him until he was lying on his back beside me. I rolled over so that I was on top of him and started kissing his neck.

"I can't wait, Logan." I flicked my tongue across his nipple.

"Condoms are in the drawer," he said.

I reached over and pulled open the drawer. I couldn't hide the laugh escaping me when I saw it was full of condoms. I grabbed one and shoved the drawer shut. Turning back to him, I raised an eyebrow.

"What? I stopped at the store today while you were with your sister. I thought we might need them." He gave me an innocent grin.

I ripped the package with my teeth and pulled out the condom. "Oh, I guarantee we'll need them, all of them." I grabbed him and ran my hand up and down his shaft.

He hissed as his hips came up off the bed. "Jesus, Jade."

I grinned as I slowly rolled on the condom. By the time I finished, he was breathing heavily. I climbed on top and slid down onto his shaft. A moan escaped me as I felt him filling me. Neither of us moved for a minute until I adjusted to his size. Once I was ready, I slowly started moving my hips. I rested my hands on his stomach as I raised and lowered my body over his.

As I increased my pace, my body came alive. Sweat beaded across my forehead, and my arms began to shake, but I never slowed down. Just as I reached the edge, he flipped me over, so he was on top of me. Without a word, he slammed into me. I cried out as my hips rose to meet his thrusts.

"You're so fucking beautiful," he said as he continued to pound into me.

He brought his hand between us and started to rub my clit. That was all it took to send me flying into my orgasm. I cried out his name as my body tightened around him. He moaned as he gave one final thrust, and he followed me into my release.

"Do we really have to get out of bed?" Logan asked as he ran his fingertips back and forth across my arm.

I snuggled closer to him, unwilling to let our morning of bliss end. We'd spent the last few hours tangled up in each other. It was well after noon, and we had yet to drag our tired bodies out of bed to search for a new place to stay.

"Not really. We could just lie in bed all day together, but we do kind of need to look for an apartment or a house," I mumbled.

"I guess we do, but I really don't want to move. Truthfully, I don't think I *can* move at this point."

I laughed quietly. "Why? Did I wear you out or something?"

"Or something." He grinned down at me. His expression turned thoughtful, and he looked away.

"What are you thinking?" I asked.

He hesitated before turning back to me. "I'm not sure if you'll like it or if it'll piss you off."

"I'm too tired to get pissed at this point. Try me."

He sighed. "I was thinking about you and...well, Chloe."

My body tensed. "What about us?"

"It's different being with you compared to how things were with her. When I was with her, I always felt like there was this barrier between us, like she wasn't completely comfortable with me, even when we...even when we had sex. Jesus, I can't believe I'm talking to you about this."

"I told you before that you could talk to me about anything, and I meant it. I know your history with her. Nothing you tell me will take me by surprise. I want you to be honest with me," I whispered.

"You're pretty damn incredible, you know that? Any other girl would have shoved me out the door, still naked, if I'd brought up another girl. I just...I feel closer to you than I ever did with her. That scares the fuck out of me, but it makes me happy at the same time. I thought what I had with her was *it* for me, but I'm starting to realize that it was nothing compared to what I could have."

"I feel the same way when I think about you and Mikey. Sometimes, we have to put things in perspective to realize that they're not perfect. I think that you did love Chloe when you were with her and that it was the happiest you'd ever been. After what happened though, I think you realized that things weren't as good as you'd thought they were."

"I think you're right," he murmured. "I spent almost all my teenage years chasing after her. I'd wanted her for so long that I didn't even stop to think about how things felt once we were together. At that point, I didn't care. Did you know I lost my virginity trying to make her jealous?"

I propped my head up with my arm. "Do tell."

He frowned. "I was dating this chick, Angie, my sophomore year of high school. She asked me out, and I said yes because I was tired of waiting for Chloe to notice me. Angie was the kind of girl who would screw anything that moved. We were together for, like, a week, and then she started trying to convince me to have sex with her. I was sixteen and a guy, so naturally, she didn't have to try very hard. I told Chloe what happened, hoping that she'd get jealous, but instead, she was excited for me. That stung my pride like a bitch."

I couldn't help but laugh at him. "Oh, Logan, you're so fucking cute."

He looked at me like I was nuts. "I tell you a story like that, and you think I'm cute? You might want to get your head checked out."

"I'm trying to picture a sixteen-year-old you. I bet you were even sweeter then than you are now."

He frowned. "I'm not perfect, Jade. I know how you see me. I'm the nice guy, the guy who would do anything for anyone. I'm fucked-up, too, though. I hope you realize that."

It was my turn to frown. "I know that, Logan. We're all fucked-up one way or another. We're human. I never said I thought you were perfect. I don't want perfect. All I want is you."

He leaned forward and pressed his lips against mine. "Same here. I'm not sure how I ended up with you, but I'm not complaining."

I fell back as he continued to kiss me senseless. The feel of his lips on mine made me forget the rest of the world. Apartment hunting could wait.

"Well, this one is definitely better than the last two. The door actually locks," Logan said as he inspected the door in front of us.

Once we'd finally managed to crawl out of bed, we'd started our search for a new place to stay. Since we would only need it for a month or two, our choices were limited. Most places required us to sign a lease for at least six months. While I had the money to pay for it, I didn't really feel like just throwing it away. I guessed spending years living on almost nothing could do that to a girl.

"So far, it's a lot cleaner than the other two," I said as I looked around.

We were standing in a tiny living room. The carpet was a dark brown, not a color I would choose, but it looked clean enough. A worn-out brown leather couch sat against the far wall. Besides a small flat-screen television and a dark brown table sitting in front of the couch, the room was empty.

I turned to the left and walked into a postage stamp–sized kitchen. A few cabinets, an electric stove, a refrigerator, a microwave, and a cheap-looking table and chairs were in the room. Unfortunately, the room was so small that it could barely fit even those things inside it comfortably.

I walked back into the living room and made a left toward two doors. I opened the first one to see a small bathroom. The next door was the one and only bedroom. The queen-sized bed made me like this place a little more. A dresser was sitting in the far corner next to a window. Two nightstands sat on either side of the bed.

Overall, the place was tiny and a little outdated, but it was clean.

"I kind of like it," I told Logan as I watched him walk out of the kitchen.

"It's a hell of a lot better than the others," Logan said as he stopped beside me.

"I don't think we're going to find anything better than this. I say we take it."

Logan fake-sniffled. "It's our first home together. I think I'm going to cry."

I elbowed him in the ribs, trying not to laugh. Then, what he'd just said hit me.

Our first *home together.*

He'd said it like there would be more after this one, like he planned on us being together for a long time. My stomach fluttered in excitement, but I forced myself not to get ahead of myself. I had no idea where Logan and I were going, and I didn't want to think about it. If I did, I would remember that I had to leave him in two months…unless he would want to go to L.A. with me.

"I'll go find the guy and sign the paperwork," I said as I headed for the door.

I closed it softly behind me and walked back down the stairs.

The apartment was in a two-story building across town from where my sister was staying. Crossville really didn't have a bad part of town, but it did have portions that had mostly lower-income families. The apartment was smack dab in the middle of the low-income side.

I reached the main floor and walked to where I'd talked to the owner of the building, Joe, earlier. I knocked on the open door before stepping inside.

He glanced up and smiled at me. "Did you like it?"

"It's perfect and fits what I'm looking for. I wanted to sign for two months." I sat down in the chair across from him.

Joe seemed like a nice enough guy. He was older, probably in his mid-sixties, with a big build. His skin had that leathered look someone gets from being out in the sun for years. His hair was snow white, and his eyes were a pale blue. For some reason, I didn't think he was the type to try to rip me off. He reminded me of someone's nice grandpa. Maybe if I were really nice, he'd give me cookies or some shit like that.

"Great!" He reached down and opened one of his desk drawers. After grabbing a folder out of it, he closed the drawer and pulled papers out of the folder. "This is the lease agreement. I can set you up for two months. If you want to renew after that, just come see me."

I listened as he went over the rules in the building. Most were pretty basic—no pets, no crazy parties, no loud noises after nine, and other things like that. Once he finished explaining everything, I looked over the lease and then signed. Just like that, Logan and I had a place of our own.

I was still grinning when I walked back up to our apartment. When I saw Logan lying on the couch, watching TV, my face nearly split in two. He looked so comfortable and at ease.

He looked up when I closed the door behind me. "Everything set?"

"Yep." I held up our new keys. "We're officially living in sin together."

He laughed as he stood up and walked over to me. I giggled as he lifted me up and spun me around.

"I'm living in sin with a rock star, smack dab in the middle of the Bible Belt. I think I just lost Christian points."

"You make it seem like I'm a bad influence!" I said innocently as he set me back down on my feet.

"Not you. You're an angel." He leaned down and kissed me softly.

I wrapped my arms around his neck and pulled him closer. He pushed me back until I was pressed up against the wall beside the door. His hands gripped my hips before sliding under my shirt. I shuddered as he caressed my stomach and ribs before stopping just below my breasts.

"I don't feel like an angel right now," I whispered against his lips.

He pressed tighter against me, and I felt him growing hard against my thigh. "I think we should christen the new place, don't you?"

I nodded as I ran my hands through his shaggy hair. I loved it longer like this. I hoped that he never cut it. He reached between us and unbuttoned my jeans. I kicked off my shoes and then my jeans and underwear. I pulled off my shirt next and then my bra. I watched as he undressed quickly. He pulled his wallet from his pants and grabbed a condom.

The sight of him standing naked and ready in front of me took my breath away. I ran my hands down his chest and stomach, tracing the lines of muscles under his soft skin. I continued down, following his happy trail, until I reached his cock. He sucked in a breath as I grabbed him and started running my hand across his shaft.

I kept my eyes on his as I knelt down in front of him. He watched me intently, seemingly frozen, as I leaned forward. I ran my tongue along his shaft, and he shuddered in response. I smiled wickedly. I loved how I held so much power over him like this. It made me feel like a goddess. I pulled him into my mouth and rolled my tongue over his head before sucking on him gently.

"Shit, babe," Logan said as he grabbed my hair and tugged gently, egging me on.

I sucked harder, and he moaned out loud. He released my hair and pressed his hands against the wall to steady himself. I bit down gently, and his hips thrust forward involuntarily. I kept up a steady suction as I reached up and started massaging his balls. He gasped as his hips started moving faster.

"Stop!" He tried to pull away.

I ignored him as I continued to suck on him.

"Jade, stop, or I'm going to come."

I finally released him, and he grabbed me, pulling me back up until I was standing again. He ripped the packet and pulled out the condom. After rolling it on faster than I'd thought possible, he grabbed my legs and lifted me off the ground. My back was against the wall, and he plunged into me a second later. I gasped as he filled me completely. He started out slow, torturing me in the best possible way. I wrapped my legs around him, allowing him to go deeper.

"Please, Logan, I need it faster," I said breathlessly. I was going to explode with need if he didn't stop torturing me.

"Shh…I want to savor this," he whispered. "I love the way you look when I'm fucking you. You're so goddamn beautiful that it hurts…but in the best possible way. When I bury myself deep inside you, I don't ever want to stop."

He leaned forward and kissed me, his tongue exploring every crevice of my mouth. Our tongues tangled together as he increased his thrusts. I clung to him as I felt myself building. He plunged into me over and over again, knocking me back into the wall each time. My body exploded as my orgasm rocked through me. I shouted his name as I felt him release with me.

When our breathing returned to normal, he slipped out of me and set me back on the ground. I still clung to him, unwilling to let him go just yet. What I felt with him blew my mind. I wasn't sure that I ever wanted to let him go. It dawned on me that I was more invested in Logan than I'd realized, and that scared the shit out of me. He could hurt me if he wanted to. I just hoped I wasn't a fool for trusting him completely.

"I can't believe you dragged me here," Logan grumbled as he grabbed a shopping cart and pushed it into the store.

I grinned. He'd whined the whole way here. For some unknown reason, he hated to shop, even when it was for food.

It must be a guy thing, I thought to myself, remembering how Eric would refuse to go shopping.

Instead, Eric would shove cash into my hand every week and tell me to get whatever we needed. Even after we'd moved to California, I would still pick up his shit for him and drop it off at his house. Now that I was away, he was paying some chick to do it.

Men.

"Quit whining. We need stuff for the apartment," I said as I walked toward the personal care items. I grabbed a bottle of shampoo, conditioner, body wash, and toothpaste. After I tossed them into the cart, I moved on to the next aisle.

"I don't see why you couldn't come by yourself. I *hate* shopping. Hate it. People are rude as fuck."

"Well, you could have stayed home, but then the next time you needed something like body wash or toilet paper, I would make you beg for it," I teased. "If I shop on my own, everything I buy is mine."

He grumbled under his breath as he threw stuff into the cart. I couldn't help but smile at him. Sure, I could have come on my own, but I wanted him with me. Watching him push around a cart while we shopped made me feel like we were just a normal couple. With everything going on in my life I knew we were anything but, but I ignored that. I just wanted some normalcy after so many months on the road, and Logan was my safe haven.

After we finished in the personal care section of the store, we headed back to where the food was. As we walked from aisle to aisle,

I threw food into the cart, not paying attention to whether or not he was doing the same.

"Please tell me you're buying more than this crap." He pointed down to the vegetables I'd just thrown into the cart.

"Why?" I asked, confused.

"Because I need *real* food—meat, snack cakes, pasta, soda. I can't live off of that green shit."

I raised an eyebrow as I looked at the muscles that were clearly visible under his tight black shirt. Over the past two years, Logan had changed dramatically. He'd always been fit, but he was nothing but pure muscle now.

"There's no way you look like that by eating junk food."

He smirked as he walked up beside me. "I'm good at working off calories."

I sucked in a breath as he ran his hand down my ribs and stopped at my hip. His touch felt like fire against my skin.

"In fact, we should probably get more junk food. That way, I have an excuse to work off more calories."

He released me and stepped back, but he was still staring at me like he wanted to take me right then and there.

I spun on my heel and started walking. "I'll get the cakes!"

I could hear his laughter following me as I turned the corner. *Asshole.*

I couldn't keep the grin off my face. *Yeah, I really fucking like normal.*

Two Months Later

Two months had passed, and it had been two months of pure fucking bliss. I couldn't remember the last time I'd been this happy. Even with the band, I hadn't felt the way I did now. Whether he realized it or not, Logan was changing me. He made me so happy that it scared me. Anytime I'd ever come close to happiness in the past, it had been blown to hell and back.

Living with Logan wasn't at all what I'd expected it to be. I'd expected it to be the same as living with Eric had been back in West Virginia. I had been prepared for all the things that came with living with a man—the mess, forgetting to put the toilet seat down, and other normal things like that. What I hadn't been prepared for was how it felt to wake up with Logan in my bed every damn morning. Not one day had passed when I didn't wake up with my body pressed up against his as his arms were wrapped around my tiny frame. It was like our bodies were drawn to each other as we slept.

The sex was unbelievable. I'd thought we would slow down after the first few weeks, but so far, that hadn't happened. We would be together every chance we got. Just thinking about the way he'd looked this morning as he'd taken me hard and fast had me rubbing my legs together in anticipation of the next time we would be alone. I'd explored every inch of his body, and I still wanted more of him.

My relationship with Bethaney had started out rocky when we first showed up, but after two months of spending nearly every day together, we were best friends once again. It was like the last six years had never happened. Bethaney and Logan had been getting along great. Maybe that was because she was a younger version of me—

hotheaded, opinionated, sarcastic, and funny. Well, I thought I was funny at least. It was obvious that she had missed me just as much as I'd missed her. Logan had told me that both of us would smile constantly when we were around each other. Bethaney and I were making up for lost time and making each other's lives better in the process.

Crossville was starting to feel like home again, but the fact that Logan and I would be leaving soon never left my mind. Logan wouldn't mention it, and me, being the fucking coward that I was, wouldn't be the one to bring it up. We had a week left here before we planned to head back to West Virginia. Once we got there, I had no clue what would happen.

I would have to go back to California to work on the new album. Even though I wanted to stay with Logan, I couldn't. I had responsibilities. I just wasn't sure where that separation would leave us. Logan would be starting classes again in a little less than a month, so it wasn't like he could stay with me in L.A. I had my life, and he had his. I had no clue how we were going to make it work.

A long-distance relationship was the obvious decision, but I wasn't sure how I felt about that. I didn't think I could handle being thousands of miles away from Logan—that was, if he even wanted something more than this summer with me. I had no fucking clue what he wanted, and I wasn't going to ruin what we had right now by asking.

"That was the bloodiest movie ever!" Bethaney said as we walked out of the movie theater together.

"Oh, it wasn't that bad, you big baby," I shot back.

Logan stayed quiet, grinning, as Beth and I bickered. He knew there was no point in trying to make us stop fighting. Once we had gotten started, nothing short of duct tape would make us shut up.

"Logan, tell her it was scary!" Bethaney said as she gave him a pleading look.

"Oh no, my happy ass is staying out of this one. I like you, Bethaney, but I'm not about to piss off Jade."

I smirked until Bethaney muttered, "If she wasn't banging you, you'd totally agree with me."

He full-out laughed as I jabbed Beth in the ribs. The two of us were like little kids when we were together.

"Don't talk like that! You're my baby sister!"

"Oh, whatever. I might be younger, but that doesn't mean I haven't fu—"

I put my hands over my ears. "La-la-la! I can't hear you!" Once her mouth stopped moving, I slowly lowered my hands. "Are you done now?"

She laughed. "I'm done. I promise not to talk about the guys I've fucked."

"Ugh! Bethaney! Damn it. I don't need to know!" I grumbled.

I glanced at Logan, but he was laughing too hard to say anything. *No back up there.*

"Let's get out of here," I said as we walked toward the exit.

"Jade?" someone called out from behind me.

I froze, and Logan bumped into me.

Oh no…please no. Anyone but him.

"Jade?" The voice was louder now.

I turned slowly to see him approaching us.

Mikey.

My eyes widened as I took him in. He still looked exactly the same as he had six years ago. His blond hair brushed his shoulders. His bright blue eyes stared straight at me. When I'd left, he'd only had a nose ring. Now, his lip and eyebrow were pierced as well.

"Holy fuck! It is you!" he said as he reached us.

He grabbed me and pulled me into a tight hug. I let myself relax into him for a split second before I pulled away.

"Mikey," I said, still in shock.

K.A. Robinson

I couldn't believe that he was here. After two months of hiding from everyone, I was running into him right before I would be leaving. My luck was shit.

"I can't believe you're really here. It's been so long, Jade. How have you been?" He laughed. "Never mind. I've watched you on TV, and I've heard you on the radio enough times to know you're doing just fine. Damn, Jade. I never would have guessed you'd end up being in one of the biggest breakout bands in a decade. It's hard to believe my Jade is a big rock star now."

I shrugged and looked away. All I wanted to do was turn and run as far as I could from Mikey. Being around him wasn't something that I'd anticipated, and truthfully, it sucked. I didn't want anything to do with him. He was a nice guy overall, but there was just too much shit between us. That was why I'd left without even so much as a good-bye.

"Well, it was good to see you, Mikey, but we were just leaving," I said as I grabbed Logan's arm and started to turn away.

"What? You're leaving already? I thought you'd want to catch up with me. Don't you want to know how Ryan is?"

That stopped me, just like he had known it would. Ryan was Mikey's little brother, and I loved that little shit to death. He'd followed Mikey and me around as much as he could. The last time I'd seen him, he was twelve.

"How is he?" I asked as I turned back around to face him.

"He's good. Just got out of juvie a few months ago."

"Wait, *what?* Why the hell was he in juvie?"

That didn't sound like Ryan at all. While he could be a little pain in the ass, he'd seldom gotten in trouble. At least, he never used to get in trouble. A person could change a lot in six years.

Mikey frowned and glanced away. "It doesn't matter. What *does* matter is that he's out now. He took your old spot in the band."

I raised an eyebrow. "Ryan plays drums now? What happened to singing and wanting to be like his big brother?"

Mikey laughed. "He decided that I wasn't cool once he hit sixteen. He can't sing for shit anyway. Listen, we're playing a show out at Vince's bar on Friday night. Why don't you stop by and watch us? All of your old friends will be there. I'm sure they'll want to talk to you."

I shook my head. There was no way I was going to go see my old friends. They would want to know why I'd left, and I had no intention of telling them.

"No, thanks. We're leaving Saturday anyway."

"We?" Mikey asked as he glanced at Logan.

I glanced over at Logan and gave him a brief smile, one that he didn't return. Actually, he didn't look happy—at all.

"Mikey, this is my boyfriend, Logan."

Mikey and Logan stared at each other, neither bothering to say hi. They were sizing each other up like they were debating on who would win in a fight.

I wanted to roll my eyes. *Men.*

"Boyfriend, huh? I'm surprised, J. He isn't your normal type," Mikey said as he smirked at Logan.

"And what would her normal type be?" Logan asked, his voice and body both tense.

"Oh, you know, the wild guys, the ones who like to have some fun. You look a little…stiff to me."

Logan grinned. "I haven't heard her complain yet, especially when I'm *stiff.*"

Bethaney busted out laughing behind me. She quickly covered it with a cough. My mouth was hanging open in shock. Logan wasn't the type of guy to say things like that. He was usually laid-back, shy even.

A small smile tipped the corner of my mouth. *He's fighting for me.*

Mikey's nostrils flared in anger as he clenched his hands into fists. I expected him to hit Logan.

Instead, he took a deep breath and turned to me. "So, will you come see us on Friday night? I won't tell anyone that you're there, if that's what you're worried about. I know Ryan would love to see you before you leave again though."

I hesitated. I did *not* want to go to that bar, but I really did want to see Ryan again. It'd been so long, and after Mikey telling me that the little shit had ended up in juvie, I felt the need to check on him. It'd been a long time since I'd even thought of him, and for that, I felt guilt trickling in over me. The kid had worshiped Mikey and me when he was younger.

"Alright, I'll go. *But* no one needs to know I'm there. I'll watch you guys and talk to Ryan, and then I'm leaving."

Mikey grinned. "Ryan will love that, Jade." He glanced down at his phone before turning his attention back to me. "I gotta go, but I'll see you on Friday night."

I nodded as he stepped forward and hugged me again.

"We still have a lot to talk about, Jade. I'll see you Friday," he whispered before pulling away.

Bethaney, Logan, and I watched in silence as Mikey disappeared through the doors. My stomach churned as I thought about what he might want to talk about. After all these years, I had nothing to say to him, but he obviously didn't agree with me on that. Once he was out of sight, I glanced up at Logan. He was obviously pissed, but he was trying to hide it.

"Why did you agree to go watch them play, you idiot?" Bethaney finally asked.

"Because I'd really like to see Ryan. I loved that kid when he was younger."

Beth snorted. "Yeah, well, he sure isn't the same kid you left behind. I can promise you that."

I opened my mouth to ask her what she'd meant by that.

Logan interrupted, "Let's get out of here."

We walked to the car in silence. I knew the minute we dropped off Beth, Logan would start asking me questions.

"You didn't mention how much of a dick Mikey is," Logan said as soon as my sister got out of the car.

I sighed. I'd known this was coming, but I didn't really want to talk about Mikey. He was part of my past, a past I didn't want to visit anytime soon. I just wanted to move on from here.

"He can be a dick. He can also be really nice. It depends on the day."

"Today was obviously a dick day," Logan said as he glanced over at me.

I snorted. "Yeah, I'll say it was. No complaints when you're stiff, huh? What the hell was that?"

He gave me a tiny grin. "What? He pissed me off. I didn't mean to say it. It just slipped out."

"It was stiff, but it slipped out? Sounds like you've got a real problem there," I said as I tried not to laugh.

As soon as he realized what he'd said, he started chuckling. I followed quickly behind. Both of us were dying from laughing so hard. Every time we started to settle down, I'd think about it and lose it all over again.

"Oh my God! We're idiots," I said once I could speak again.

He grinned. "You're the idiot who made me laugh." His expression turned serious. "Look, I'm sorry for saying that to him. I honestly didn't mean to. The way he kept looking at you pissed me off, and I didn't think before I spoke. I knew he was baiting me, but I couldn't help myself. I wanted him to know that you're mine and mine alone."

"Am I?" I asked.

He glanced over at me. "Well, yeah—at least, I thought you were. Am I wrong?"

I couldn't keep the silly grin off my face. "I am. I just wanted to hear you say it. You're kind of hot when you get all possessive and shit."

"He reminds me of Drake—well, the way he used to be when I first met him. Mikey is cocky. The way he looked at you told me what he thought of you, and he thinks he can have you anytime he wants. When Drake looked at Chloe like that, I thought she knew better than to fuck around with him, but I was wrong."

I reached across the console and rested my hand on his thigh. "Mikey can't have me. Even if I wasn't with you, there's no way I'd go back to that. He is cocky and possessive and bossy. I stopped dealing with his shit a long time ago."

"Good. I don't want to worry about him. I trust you, Jade. It's hard as hell to trust someone again, but I do. Don't fuck me over. Please."

Fucking Chloe was messing with his head again. I bit my lip to stop myself from saying something I'd regret later. I liked Chloe a lot. I honestly did. So, I kept my mouth shut. I wouldn't be the friend who talked shit behind someone's back just because I was angry.

"I won't ever hurt you, Logan, I swear. I know what you went through with her, and it means a lot to me that you trust me. I'm not stupid enough to throw it all away."

He grabbed my hand, brought it up to his mouth, and kissed it gently. "Good. Do you want to tell me why you're going to that show Friday night?"

"Ryan," I said. "If it wasn't for him, I wouldn't bother, but that kid meant a lot to me before I left here. He's Mikey's little brother.

He followed Mikey and me around all the time. I watched out for him the way I watched out for Beth. I want to see him before we leave. I want to make sure he's okay, especially after Mikey said Ryan has been in juvie. That doesn't sound like the Ryan I know."

He frowned. "Whatever it takes to make you happy. Just be careful, and don't get mixed up with Mikey too much, okay?"

"I won't. I promise. I'm going to that show to see Ryan, and that's it. I'll see him, and then we'll leave."

"Good."

We were silent the rest of the drive home.

When he parked outside of our apartment building, he turned to look at me again. "Can I say something without you ripping off my head?"

"Sure."

"We're leaving in a few days. I know you think you've done everything you came here to do, but I don't think you have."

"What do you mean?"

"You need to go see your mom again. I know you don't want to, but you'll always regret it if you don't."

"Logan—"

"No, listen to me. When you went to her grave before, you were angry. I have no doubt that you're still angry with her for what happened, but you can't leave it like that. You need to tell her good-bye. You need to find some closure before we leave."

"I have closure. Hitting David in the nuts gave me all the closure I needed," I said stubbornly.

"Jade, I'm serious. Will you at least think about it? We only have a few days left before we leave. With everything happening in your life, who knows when you'll have a chance to come back here?"

I sighed. "Fine, I'll go. Happy?"

"Deliriously happy."

I closed the car door quietly behind me and walked across the crisp green grass of the cemetery. It was a beautiful day, just like the last time I had been here. I focused on my mother's grave as I walked toward it. I hated to admit that Logan had been right about me needing to see her, but he was. Everything else had worked out this summer, except for things with my mom. When I'd come here to see her that first day, I'd been shocked and angry. I had my emotions under control now, and it was time to say good-bye to her. This would be the last time. Once I walked away, I would never come back.

Logan had wanted to come with me, but I'd told him no. I needed to do this on my own. I couldn't let him hold my hand every time I was hurting. I had to face things on my own, or I'd never truly be okay.

I knelt down beside her headstone and brushed the dead grass away. I couldn't help but stare at her name carved into the stone. It still didn't seem real. Everyone would die eventually. I knew that, but it was still hard to believe that the woman who'd brought me into this world was no longer in it.

"Hi, Mom," I whispered once the grass was cleared away.

I stared down at the bright green shoelaces on my Chucks. I had no clue what the fuck I was supposed to say. I'd spent the last two days trying to figure out the right words, but they never came to me. Instead, I was here without a clue as to what to say or do to make myself forgive her.

"I'm still really pissed at you. I'm sure you know that though." I sat down in the grass. "You really screwed me up. I think I'm still screwed-up, no matter how hard I try to ignore it."

I stared around the cemetery. I was mostly alone, except for two other people. An older man and a younger woman were standing in front of a grave, both of them holding fresh flowers.

Probably his wife and her mother, I thought to myself.

That was the way the world was supposed to work. Two people were supposed to love each other. Then, they would have a child together, who they would love as well. When one of them passed, the other would mourn until it was time to go. The child would mourn them as well. The thought made me sad. In the end, everyone would feel the loss of loved ones. No matter how imperfect they were, they still had someone out there who loved them.

But I wasn't sure how much love I had for my mother anymore.

"I still love you even though I hate you, too. I guess I'm fucked-up that way. I've been so angry for so long that I've forgotten that I did love you. I have no idea whether or not you loved me back, but it doesn't really matter anymore. What you did to me was wrong, and we both know it. Then, you let him go after Beth. That's fucked-up, Mom. I get why he hated me and why you let him hate me. But Beth? She was his. She did nothing to deserve his anger. Neither did I, for that matter. The screw-up was yours, and I was the one who had to pay for it over and over again."

I rested my head on my knees, trying to calm my temper. The more I spoke to her, the more pissed-off I was. I hadn't come here to tell her to fuck off again. I'd come to say good-bye.

"For what it's worth, I forgive you. I'm tired of hating you, so I'm letting it go. I hope you rest in peace and all that shit. I love you, Mom. Good-bye."

I stood and walked back to the car. I opened the door and climbed inside. I took one last look at her grave before starting the engine and pulling away for the last time. A calmness washed over me as I turned onto the main road. This time, I was really letting everything go. For some reason, when I'd freed her, I'd freed myself as well.

I smiled as I drove away. I was finally free.

Cigarette smoke was everywhere, making me cough, as Logan and I walked into the bar where Mikey's band was playing tonight. After being away from the bar scene for over a year, I'd forgotten just how nasty some of them were. Playing big shows had obviously spoiled me.

I glanced around and found an empty table off to the side. I made my way over to it, holding on to Logan's hand as I went. It was off to the right of the stage where there were hardly any lights. It would be the perfect place to watch the band perform without being seen myself.

I dropped down into one of the chairs.

Instead of sitting down next to me, Logan motioned toward the bar. "I'm going to get us a couple of beers. I'll be right back."

I nodded as he turned and walked away. I leaned back into my chair and looked around the bar. It was fairly full, but there were still several empty tables. I found that strange since the band would be playing in less than twenty minutes. When Breaking the Hunger played, we would usually have a full house an hour before we went onstage. From what I could remember, Mikey's band had been pretty decent when I was with them. Then again, I remembered how much I'd improved once I started playing with Eric. Maybe they weren't as good as I'd thought.

Red's "Perfect Life" played loudly through the speakers as the band walked onstage and started setting up. I noticed Mikey instantly. Logan had been right. Mikey screamed arrogant and cocky. He walked around like he owned the world. For some reason, I'd forgotten that about him. His arrogance was one of my biggest pet peeves when it came to him.

I didn't recognize any of the other guys in the band. When I had been with their band, it had been Mikey, Scott, Jason, and me. A bad feeling came over me as I realized Mikey was the only original member left. Had he run Scott and Jason off? I hoped not, but I could see Mikey doing it. He was enough of an asshole to do it.

My eyes widened as I noticed the guy setting up his drums. *Ryan? Holy shit!*

The kid I remembered was long gone. In his place stood a man who looked like Mikey's twin. His hair, his features, the tattoos covering his arms—everything about Ryan reminded me of Mikey. The only difference was the fact that he didn't seem to have Mikey's arrogance. That was something at least. I just hoped that he wouldn't be an asshole when I talked to him. Sometimes, looks could be deceiving.

"Here you go, babe," Logan said as he sat down next to me. He handed over one of the beers he was holding.

"Thanks." I took a drink and set it on the table.

I looked around the bar to see a few more people trickling in. That made me feel slightly better. As much as I disliked Mikey, I didn't want him or his band to suck.

"I'm exhausted," Logan said as he leaned back in his chair.

"Me, too. Packing sucks ass," I grumbled.

We'd spent the entire day packing our things. Somehow, we'd managed to accumulate more stuff while living in our apartment. Instead of having just a few bags filled with clothes, we now had a few boxes to add to the car. We'd packed up everything and set it by the door. Neither of us had felt like loading all of it into Logan's car just yet.

I wasn't sure about him, but it made me sad to realize that our summer together was over. I didn't want to leave behind Bethaney or my apartment with Logan. I had no idea what tomorrow would bring for Logan and me, but I knew we needed to talk about it. Once we made it back to West Virginia, I would have to fly back to L.A. within a day or two to meet up with the guys and start recording. Logan and I definitely needed to figure out where we stood. If he were willing, I would be okay with a long-distance relationship. It would suck, but I'd deal with it. I didn't want to lose him.

The music coming from the speakers was cut.

"Are you guys ready for Split Chords? Give 'em a big ole round of applause because they're up!" a booming voice said.

Several people stood and walked toward the stage as the band members took their places. I had to admit that Mikey looked good up there, and several women in the crowd seemed to think so, too, as they shouted his name.

I leaned back in my chair and watched as the band started into their first song. I couldn't help but feel a sense of pride when I heard Ryan playing drums. The little shit was good. It was obvious that he'd paid attention to what I taught him before, but he'd definitely learned a lot more since I left.

The two new guys were good as well, but they weren't as good as Mikey and Ryan. Most of the crowd didn't notice when they messed up, but I could tell instantly. Either these guys hadn't been playing with Mikey and Ryan for very long, or the band wasn't in sync like Breaking the Hunger was. I hoped it was the former and not the latter.

It was strange to be sitting in the crowd instead of onstage. It had been a long time since I watched a show. I leaned into Logan and closed my eyes as I listened to Mikey sing about lost love and pain. His voice was soothing, but he had nothing on Drake. Mikey's voice was mellow, but it lacked the emotion that Drake's voice held. Both men were nice to look at, but Drake's voice was what could pull so many people in. Mikey could be the prettiest guy on earth, but if he didn't show any emotion in his song, he would never make it further than playing at bars.

"They're pretty good, but I like your band better," Logan whispered in my ear.

"Agreed. They're decent, but they definitely need some work."

I turned and kissed him. I forgot about the music as Logan's lips molded against mine. He pulled me to him until I was sitting on his lap, and I forgot not just the music, but also the entire world. The heat from his body seeped into mine, and I sighed from happiness. He ran his hands up and down my back as his mouth devoured mine. I couldn't help but want to kick myself at this moment. If I hadn't suggested coming here tonight, we could have spent our last night alone in our apartment.

"We need to get out of here—soon," I mumbled against his lips after pulling away slightly.

I felt his smile.

"You still need to talk to Ryan. After that, I'll take you home."

I groaned. "I don't want to wait that long."

Logan chuckled. "I'll make it worth your while. Now, watch your friends before I change my mind and drag you into the restroom."

He kissed me one last time before putting me back in my own chair. I frowned in disappointment. I hoped that the band's set wouldn't be that long. I wanted to get out of here.

I looked up to see Mikey watching me with a strange look on his face. I couldn't tell if he was hurt or angry, but I really didn't care. He had no right to care about me after six years of nothing. He should have known that if I were happy when we had been together, I wouldn't have just taken off without telling him.

Forty-five minutes later, the band played their last song. Mikey talked to the crowd as the rest of the band jumped off of the stage and walked through a door leading to what I assumed was a back room. I stood and started to follow, but Mikey's next words froze me mid-step.

"I have one last thing to mention. It's actually a surprise really. My girlfriend, Jade, is here tonight. You might know her for being in a certain band taking the rock world by storm right now—Breaking the Hunger."

"You dirty son of a bitch!" I hissed under my breath as he pointed to me.

Everyone in the crowd turned to look at me. I saw recognition on their faces, and all at once, they started to move toward me. I stumbled back as the group approached me. When my back hit the stage, I felt myself being lifted up. I glanced back to see that Mikey was picking me up. I was going to kill him. No, I was going to tie him up and torture him until he begged for mercy, and then I'd kill him. He'd promised me that no one would know I was here. He was a dirty fucking asshole.

"Settle down, guys. Jade will be happy to take pictures and sign whatever you want, but don't turn into a mob." He grinned out at the crowd. "She's my girl. I can't have any of you hurting her."

His girl?

Fury shot through me. He'd planned to do this the entire time.

What does he think he'll get by claiming me? It's not like I would—

Then, it hit me. People would tell their friends that I had been here with him tonight. They would come to his future shows, hoping that one of my bandmates or I would be there. Instead, they would hear his shitty voice, but he was still hoping to get more fans out of it.

I was going to slaughter him when I got off this stage.

I looked around the bar, trying to spot Logan. He stood off to the side, his face a mask of fury. I tried to tell him how sorry I was with my eyes, but I wasn't sure if he could see me. He was too busy sending death glares at Mikey.

"All right, line up, guys!" Mikey said from beside me.

"I'm going to rip your dick off and feed it to you," I muttered so that only he could hear.

"Aw, come on, babe. You should be excited. All of these people want to meet you. I thought you'd like it."

"You know damn well I didn't want any attention, Mikey. You're an asshole."

The first person in line approached me, and I smiled at him. What else could I do? It wasn't his fault that Mikey was a dick. I spent the next half hour posing for pictures and signing stuff. I tried to find Logan again, but he was nowhere to be seen. I hoped that he wouldn't get to Mikey before I had a chance.

When the last person in line had his picture with me and my signature, I turned to Mikey and glared at him. "Back room. Now."

He smirked. "Whatever you want, baby."

"I'm *not* your baby," I spit out.

I jumped offstage and walked through the door where I'd seen Ryan and the other guys go through earlier. I looked around, expecting to see them there, but the room was empty. I turned when Mikey walked in and closed the door behind us.

"Where's Ryan?"

"He had to leave, but I told him I'd bring you by the house later."

"Not a chance on your life, asshole. I can't believe you pulled that shit on me."

"What did I do? Come on, Jade. Those people were excited to see you! Stop acting like you're too good to sign a few things for them."

"I'm not acting stuck-up! I don't mind signing things, but this summer was supposed to be a vacation for me. Besides, you didn't call me out like that for their benefit. You did it for yourself!"

He rolled his eyes. "I have no idea what you're talking about."

"Bullshit. You knew exactly what you were doing. You wanted the attention. You wanted them to tell their friends that I was here, so they would come to whatever bar *you* were playing at. I'm not stupid."

"Look, it was a win-win for both of us. Yeah, it'll help spread the word about the band, but you also got to meet some of your fans."

"You're a total and complete dick. I hope you know that," I growled.

He smiled as he took a step closer. "I've missed you, you know. I forgot what a turn-on it is to see you all pissed-off and ready to kick ass."

"Don't," I said as I took a step back. I wasn't going to deal with his bullshit.

"Come on, babe. I know you've missed me. I missed you."

"No, Mikey, I *didn't* miss you at all. You're an arrogant dick who only watches out for himself."

"I might be an arrogant dick, but I'm *your* arrogant dick."

He took another step forward and grabbed a strand of my hair. I pushed his hand away and took another step back until I was tight against the wall.

"I'm not kidding, Mikey. I'm really pissed off. If you want to keep your dick attached to your body, you'll take a step back."

He grinned as he leaned forward. "I've missed you, Jade. We used to be so good together. Don't you remember?"

"No. What I remember is you trying to control me and boss me around."

"Give me another chance," he whispered.

"Not going to happen. I'm with Logan now, and even if I weren't, I would *never* go back to you," I growled.

"Bullshit. You know you've missed me. I've changed a lot since you knew me. I'm not as much of an asshole as I used to be."

I snorted. "Yeah, right. I might have believed you if you hadn't pulled that shit out there tonight. No, Mikey, you're still as big of an asshole as you were when we were together."

Anger flashed across his face. "And you think *Logan* is better for you? Come on, Jade, wake up. I've met him once, and I can already tell that he doesn't fit into your world, *our world.* What does he do while you're onstage? Sit in the corner and lift weights? No, he's not what you need."

"And let me guess—you're just what I need."

"I am. Think about it. We could take the rock world by storm. Bring me back to L.A. with you and introduce me to your manager. Help me get my foot in the door. Then, I could tour with you, and we'd never be apart. We're perfect for each other."

I stared at him, trying to comprehend what he was saying. He was a bigger asshole than I'd ever thought possible. He didn't give a damn about me. All he wanted was to use me to boost his own career.

"You've got to be kidding me." I laughed. "You're a real piece of work. Well, let me lay it out for you, *Mikey.* You and I are nothing. *Nothing.* I'm not your girlfriend, and I'm sure as hell not the person who's going to help you make it in the rock industry. Now, get out of my way, or I'm going to hit you so hard that Ryan will wake up with a black eye!"

He stared at me for a moment, his face turning bright red in anger. It was probably the first time a woman had ever told him no. He should have known that he couldn't boss me around or control me the way he used to. I wasn't a naïve teenager anymore.

I waited as he tried to control his anger. I knew he would fail though, and I smiled as I pictured the fit he was sure to have. Instead, he shocked me by grabbing me and pressing my body against his. His mouth slammed down on mine brutally. I shoved at his chest, trying to get him to release me, but it was like hitting a brick wall. I raised my knee to hit him in his jewels, but he blocked me.

"What the fuck?" someone shouted from behind him.

Mikey pulled away from me, grinning, and he turned to face the man who had walked into the room—Logan. If I'd thought Logan was angry earlier when Mikey had announced my presence to the whole bar, it was nothing compared to now. Instead of glaring at Mikey, his fury was now directed at me.

"Logan, it's not—" I started to say.

He cut me off with a glare. "Save it, Jade. I should have known this would happen. Why did I think you'd be any different from Chloe? You're just as much of a whore as she is! I trusted you! I'm such a fucking idiot. You were probably waiting for your chance to get back with Mikey, weren't you? That's why you wanted to come here tonight. It had nothing to do with Ryan. What the fuck is it about guys like Drake and Mikey that make women turn into sluts? I don't get it!"

"No! That's not it! This isn't what it looks like!" I shouted, fear flooding my veins.

He couldn't possibly think that I would choose Mikey over him. There was no competition between the two of them.

"Look, Logan, sorry that you had to find out like this. I know you care about Jade, but she's been mine since before you even knew her," Mikey said calmly as he tried to wrap his arm around my shoulders.

I shoved him away. "Shut up, Mikey! Logan, I would never cheat on you! I care about you. I would never do what Chloe did to you."

"Bullshit. You already did it. Unfortunately, you got caught. I have nothing left to say to you. Just...stay away from me, Jade." He turned and reached for the door. "I hope you're both extremely happy together. God knows you deserve each other."

"Logan, wait!" I shouted as I took off after him.

Mikey grabbed my arm and pulled me back.

"Let me go!"

"No. Calm down, Jade. You're better off without him. Come on, let me take care of you."

I jerked my arm free and slapped him. He stumbled back, looking shocked.

"Stay the fuck away from me, Mikey. If you *ever* come near me, I'll make sure you never walk again. Stay. Away. From. Me!"

I ran from the room and out through the bar. I made it out to the parking lot in time to see the taillights from Logan's car pulling out onto the main road. I cursed as I looked around the lot, trying to find a cab or another way to follow him. Of course, there was nothing.

Tears poured down my face as I watched his car disappear back toward our apartment. *What have I done?*

PART 3   LOGAN

Fool me once, shame on you. Fool me twice, I'm a fucking idiot.

Yeah, that just about summed up my life. I was a fucking idiot, no doubt about it. I glared at the TV for a few more minutes before shutting it off and tossing the remote down onto the table. I stood and walked down the hallway, passing Amber's room and going into my own.

I'd been back in West Virginia for almost a week. I'd been confused when I realized that no one was around, but after a quick call to Amber, I'd found out that she was visiting her parents in Charleston with Chloe and Drake. Normally, I would have loved to have the house to myself. I loved Amber, but sometimes, she didn't know when to shut up. Unfortunately, the one time I needed her nonstop chatter, she wasn't anywhere to be found.

A week alone could kill a guy if he was depressed enough. Since I'd walked out of that bar, I'd spent every second thinking about Jade. I'd replayed the entire summer over and over in my head, trying to figure out when she'd decided she would rather be with Mikey. She'd fooled me as effortlessly as Chloe had—maybe better if I were honest with myself. I'd always felt like something was off with Chloe, but I'd somehow missed the signs with Jade. She had completely wrapped me around her finger.

Seeing her kissing Mikey had been like a kick to the balls. At least with Chloe, I'd never actually had to watch her cheating on me with Drake. I'd just heard about it later. With Jade, I'd had a front row seat. There was nothing quite like walking into a room and seeing the girl I loved wrapped around another guy.

How I'd let Jade fool me for so long was beyond me. She'd lied straight to my face, swearing that she would *never* hurt me the way

Chloe had. Jade had known how hard it was for me to trust again. When I'd finally trusted her, she'd promised me the moon and stars, saying she'd never hurt me.

Bull-fucking-shit.

She'd probably been fucking around with Mikey all summer, just waiting for me to figure out what she was up to. All those days with Bethaney had given her the perfect excuse to be away from me so much.

I just wasn't sure why Jade had even brought me with her to begin with. Maybe she had cared about me at first, but after she'd figured out that she wanted Mikey back, maybe she hadn't been sure how to dump me. She'd probably felt sorry for me.

Poor, pathetic Logan, always choosing the wrong women.

Yeah, I felt pretty fucking sorry for myself. I didn't care if that made me a pussy. There was only so much heartbreak a guy could take before he lost his shit and had a pity party. I'd moved past a pity party though, and I'd dived right into a big bottle of Jack Daniel's. I'd actually gone through a few bottles. I'd spent more than one night drunk off my ass.

Jade had tried to call me several times over the past week. I'd ignored every single call and deleted the voice mails without listening to them. I didn't care what she had to say. Nothing she could say would change my mind or make me forgive her. *Nothing.*

Once a whore, always a whore. That was my new motto for the women in my life.

I grabbed the bottle of Jack off my nightstand and took a swig. *Fuckin' whores.*

"Logan? We're home!"

I cringed when I heard Amber's voice outside my door. My head felt like it was going to explode, and she wasn't talking quietly.

"Great. Go away!" I said loud enough so that she could hear me.

The door cracked open. "Logan? Are you okay?"

"I'm fine. Leave me alone. I'm trying to sleep," I mumbled into my pillow.

Instead of leaving, she walked into my room. "Hey, what's wrong?"

"I'm hungover, Amber. Take a damn hint."

"Oh...okay." She walked back to the door. "You need anything?"

"Some silence would be nice," I muttered.

I could practically see her rolling her eyes as she closed the door behind her. I'd missed her, but if she was here, that meant Chloe and Drake were, too. I really didn't want to deal with seeing them in their marital bliss right now. My stomach couldn't handle it.

Just as I was drifting off, I heard another knock at my door.

"Are you kidding me?" I grumbled. "What does a guy have to do to get some peace around here?"

"Logan, are you okay?" Chloe asked as she cracked the door.

"I'm great. Leave me alone."

I opened my eyes to see her walking in and closing the door behind her.

Does no one listen to me anymore?

"Amber said you had a hangover. What's going on?" She sat down on the edge of my bed.

"What do you mean?" I asked as I sat up.

She pointed to the almost empty bottle of Jack Daniel's on my nightstand. "You rarely drink, and you never get drunk unless something is bothering you. What's up?"

I hated that she knew me so well. She knew me better than anyone. I used to know her better than anyone, too—that was, until Drake had decided that he wanted to be a part of her life. Then, I had been pushed to the side, so they could have their happily ever after.

Go them.

I stared at her, willing myself to be angry with her, but I couldn't. She was still Chloe, my best friend. No matter what happened between us, I could never be mean to her.

I sighed and ran my hand over my face. "I had a rough summer, okay? Let's just leave it at that."

She frowned and patted my leg. "You know you can tell me anything, right?"

No, I can't. "Yeah, I know."

She stared at me, obviously waiting for me to spill my guys. It wasn't going to happen. Finally, she gave up.

"All right then, I'll leave you alone. When you're up to it, I'd like to talk though."

I stayed silent as she stood and walked out of my room. I waited until she closed the door to drop back down onto my bed. She might want me to talk, but it wasn't going to happen.

If my phone rang one more time, I was going to throw it out the window. I looked down to see Jade's name flashing across the screen. I hit Ignore and tossed my phone down onto the couch beside me. Five seconds later, it started ringing again.

"Jesus Christ!" I shouted before hitting Ignore again.

"Who's trying to get a hold of you so bad?" Amber asked as she walked into the living room.

Chloe and Drake followed her.

"No one important," I muttered.

She dropped down onto the couch beside me. Drake sat down in the chair across from me, and Chloe made herself comfortable on his lap.

My phone started ringing again. I grabbed it and hit Ignore, but not before Amber saw Jade's name flashing across the screen.

"Jade? Why aren't you answering her?" Amber asked.

"It doesn't matter. I just don't want to talk to her."

Drake and Chloe both frowned, but Amber shrugged.

"Okay then. Anyway, we're thinking about going out. Do you want to come with us?" Amber asked.

"Where are you going?" I asked.

"To Gold's. Drake promised the owner that he'd perform with the band playing tonight."

I almost rolled my eyes. "I'll pass. My head is still killing me."

Amber, Chloe, and Drake had been home for two days. I'd stopped drinking once they came home, but my headache had refused to leave. I swore to myself that I would never drink again.

"Come on, please?" Amber begged.

I shook my head. "No, th—" My phone started ringing again. "Are you fucking kidding me?"

I pressed Ignore *again*, and then I shut off my phone. I was tired of Jade calling me every five minutes. I would think that she would have taken the hint after I'd been ignoring her for over a week. She was nothing if not persistent.

"Logan, what's going on with you and Jade?" Chloe asked.

"I told you, I just don't want to talk to her."

"I call bullshit. You haven't been acting right since you came back. What happened when you guys went on your road trip?" Chloe asked.

"We didn't go on a road trip. We went back to her hometown. She wanted to reconnect with her little sister and deal with some…issues."

"What? I didn't even know she had a little sister," Chloe said, looking shocked.

"Yeah, there's a lot you don't know about her," I said.

"Is she okay?" Drake asked in a serious tone.

"What do you know?" I asked hesitantly.

While I was pissed at Jade, I wasn't going to tell Drake all of her dirty secrets. Her past was hers and hers alone. If she wanted to tell Drake and the rest of the band, that would be her choice.

"I just know what Eric has told me, which isn't much. Her stepdad was an abusive prick, and her mom wasn't much better."

I nodded. "That about sums it up. She's fine though. She did everything she wanted to do while she was there, including reconnecting with her ex." I couldn't keep the bitterness out of my tone when I mentioned Mikey.

"Mikey? Eric said he was a dick," Drake said.

I laughed humorously. "I thought so, too, but apparently, he's not so bad."

"Logan…were you and Jade together this summer?" Chloe asked hesitantly.

"Yeah, we were together the whole summer, except when she was with her sister," I said, dodging her question.

"No, like together, *together*," Chloe said.

I shrugged. "Yeah, but it doesn't matter now."

"What happened? And don't say *nothing*. Tell us the truth." Chloe frowned at me.

I shrugged again, pretending like I didn't care. "It was the same thing as last time. I was with a girl I really cared about, and she chose a cocky, asshole rock star instead of me. Oh, and she cheated instead of just telling me to get lost. I must have *dumb fuck* stamped across my forehead."

Chloe's mouth dropped open in shock. I'd never spoken to her like that.

"Logan—"

"Save it, Chloe. I'm going to go lie down. My head is killing me." I stood and walked out of the room. "Have fun tonight, guys."

I walked back to my room and closed the door behind me. I sat down at my desk and stared out the window. I couldn't help but feel a sick sense of satisfaction over saying those things to Chloe. Yes, we'd talked about everything, but she'd had no clue how I really felt. She'd had no idea how long it took me to get over her. And I really was over her now—whether I'd realized it or not. Jade had helped me move on...only to fuck me over the exact same way Chloe had. The two of them with their lies were enough to turn a straight man gay. Women weren't worth the time or effort.

My door swung open. I turned to see Chloe walking in before she closed the door behind her. I knew from the determined look on her face that I was in for the biggest ass-chewing of my life.

"We need to talk," she said flatly.

"Nah, we're good. I said what I had to say."

"Bullshit. Talk to me, Logan. I want to know what's going on with you. You always keep your thoughts locked away, and I'm tired of it! Tell me what you're thinking!"

"What do you want me to say? That you ripped out my fucking heart when you cheated on me? Okay, yeah, you did. You changed me. I stopped being the nice guy. Instead, I turned into a tamer version of Drake. I became an asshole, and I started sleeping with anything that looked at me. I used women the way you used me. There. Happy?"

"I didn't use you, Logan," Chloe whispered.

"Yes, you did. You wanted Drake, but you stayed with me. You lied to me about how you felt when it came to him, and then you cheated on me."

"I never meant to hurt you. I know what I did to you was wrong, and I'll regret it for the rest of my life. I was so confused, and I didn't want to hurt you when I realized that I thought of you only as a friend."

"So, you thought cheating on me wouldn't hurt me? Are you fucking dense? I would have rather listened to you tell me that you didn't love me rather than hear how you fucked Drake repeatedly behind my back! Who does that to someone they *love*?"

"I'm so sorry. You have no idea how sorry I am." Her voice cracked as tears ran down her cheeks.

For the first time ever, I didn't feel sorry for her. She'd done this to me, not the other way around.

"Sorry doesn't fix how bad you fucked me over, Chloe. Sorry doesn't fix anything."

"I know," she whispered as she leaned against the wall. "I should have told you. The moment I realized that I loved Drake, I should have told you."

"Why him? What was it about Drake that made you love him instead of me? What did I do wrong? Answer me because I need to know. Whatever it is, I fucked up the same way with Jade."

"You didn't fuck up, Logan, I swear. Drake is just…I clicked with him instantly."

"And you didn't *click* with me? I'm your best friend."

"It was different with him. I don't know how to explain it. I cared about him from the very beginning."

"Is it because he's in a band? I know how much you like music." I really had wondered if that was what had drawn her to him in the beginning.

She gave me a disgusted look. "God, no. I mean, it was cool that he was in a band, but that had nothing to do with it. Truthfully, it made things harder. The groupies still get to me from time to time."

I ran my hand through my hair. "Look, I'm sorry for saying what I did. Let's just forget everything, okay?"

She shook her head. "No, not okay. I messed up, and you were the one who got hurt. I don't want you to look at all women and assume that they'll do the same thing that I did. It isn't fair to them, and it certainly isn't fair to you. You don't deserve to be so jaded. You did nothing wrong."

"I can't just forget, Chloe. It isn't that easy."

"I know. I wish it were though. Will you tell me what happened with Jade?"

"I thought things were going great with her. I was happy, really happy, for the first time since...well, you. Jade made me forget how pissed-off I was. She made me care about her. Just like with you, I thought things were going great. Then, we ran into her ex, Mikey. He reminded me so much of Drake. I hated him instantly. We went to watch his band perform. Jade went backstage after the show, and I followed her. I found her with him. He had her pressed up against the wall, kissing her, and she seemed to be enjoying herself. I should have known that things were too perfect. Nothing ever works out for me."

"Oh, Logan. What did she say to you? Did she try to explain?"

I shook my head. "I didn't give her the chance. I left. I went back to our apartment to grab my stuff, and then I drove home. She's been calling me ever since, but I've ignored all her calls. I don't want to hear her excuses. I know what I saw. Nothing can fix that."

Chloe bit her lip. "I know you don't want to hear this, but maybe you should talk to her. I mean, it might not be what it looked like. At least give her a chance to explain."

"Nope, not happening. I'm done, Chloe. I'm done with you, with her, and with every other female out there. I've had it with the lying and the cheating."

"You don't mean that. You're just upset right now."

"No, I really do mean it. I'm finished. Look, I appreciate you coming in here and apologizing, but I think you should go. I know you're going out with Drake and Amber."

"I can stay in tonight. We can hang out and watch a movie or something."

"Nah, I'd rather be alone. Go have fun."

"Logan—"

201

"*Go.* I mean it," I said.

She hesitated before she finally nodded. "All right. But if you need me, call me, okay?"

"Yeah, I will. I'll see you later, Chloe."

She nodded before walking to the door and opening it. As soon as she disappeared, I stood and walked over to my bed. I dropped down onto it and willed myself to fall asleep. I didn't want to deal with reality anymore today. Reality sucked.

I'd spent all my adult life going after the wrong women. Hell, I'd spent my entire adult and most of my teenage years going after the wrong women. What was it about me that had made Chloe and Jade run, screaming, to the assholes in their lives? If it had just been Chloe, I wouldn't blame myself. But when both of them had done the exact same thing, it was proof that something was definitely wrong with me. After everything that had happened, I had no doubt that I would be alone for the rest of my life. There was no way that I would ever trust a woman again.

I'll die alone. That was the last thought that had run through my mind before I drifted off to sleep.

20

I grabbed a pair of jeans and pulled them on before walking to my closet and grabbing a shirt. As I pulled it over my head, someone knocked on my door.

"Come in!" I yelled as I grabbed a pair of socks.

I pulled them on as Chloe and Drake walked into my room.

"Hey, where are you going?" Chloe asked.

"To the shop to talk to my boss. He gave me the summer off, but I need to get back to work. I'm running low on cash, and I need to buy books. Classes start in a couple of weeks."

Truthfully, I had enough money to cover books and a few more months of rent, but I couldn't stand to stay cooped up in this house anymore. I was driving myself nuts by staring at the walls all day.

"I can loan you some money if you need it, Logan," Chloe said, frowning.

Since she was married to a rock star now, I had no doubt that she had extra cash lying around. Plus, she'd inherited a lot of money after her aunt passed away. It was strange to think that the poor girl I'd once known now had a house in L.A. and a full bank account.

"I'm good. What's up?" I asked.

"I talked to Jade last night after my show," Drake said.

I tensed. "That's great. Now, if you'll excuse me, I need to head out."

"She's a mess, Logan," Chloe said sadly.

"I really couldn't care less," I spit out.

"Well, you should. You need to listen to Drake. What you think you saw isn't what happened," Chloe said.

"I need to listen to *Drake?* Really? No offense, bro, but why the fuck would I want to listen to anything you have to say? We're not exactly best buddies."

Drake glared at me.

Good. I wanted to piss him off.

"Look, I know you don't like me. That's fine. Whatever. But this has nothing to do with me. This is about Jade. She's hurting, so you're going to drop the fucking attitude and listen to what I have to say."

I saw red. After everything he'd done, he had no right to come into my house and demand that I listen to him.

"You can go fuck yourself, asshole. I'm out of here." I walked past him and headed toward the door.

He grabbed me and pulled me back.

That was the last straw. I snapped. I spun around and punched him as hard as I could. I heard Chloe shouting as he stumbled back. I expected him to fall, but instead, he caught himself on my desk and then dived for me. We fell to the ground with him on top of me. I waited for him to punch me back, but he just held me down.

"Now that I have your attention, let's talk!" he shouted down at me.

"Fuck off," I said as I struggled.

It was no use. I was a big guy, but he was, too, and he had me pinned down.

"If I let you up, will you listen? Or are you going to try to hit me again?"

"I'll listen. Get off of me."

Drake rolled off of me and stood. "Thank God. No offense, but I never want to be pressed up against a dude like that again."

I slowly stood and walked over to my bed. I sat down, ignoring Chloe's glare.

"All right, now that we're done with punching and cuddling, maybe you'll let me tell you about Jade. She's hurting right now. For as long as I've known her, I've never seen her like this. What you think you saw isn't what happened. Mikey forced himself on her."

"It didn't look like he had to force her very hard," I muttered.

"He did force himself on her right after he tried to convince her to take him back to L.A., so she could introduce him to our label. When she told him to fuck off, he got pissed and tried to kiss her. That's when you walked in. He doesn't care about her. All he wanted was to use her. She hates him, and she's losing her mind because you won't talk to her, so she can explain."

"Do you really expect me to believe that?" I laughed. "She can say anything she wants. It doesn't change what I *saw*. Just because she told you her version doesn't mean it's true."

"And just because I cheated on you doesn't mean you should assume that she would, too. Jade doesn't lie, Logan. She cares about you. If she didn't, she wouldn't be this upset over everything," Chloe said as she walked over to me. "What Drake and I did was wrong. We never meant to hurt you, but we did. Please, don't make Jade suffer for something we did to you. She wouldn't hurt you like that."

"I've known Jade for years. I've *never* seen her with a guy. She doesn't ever get close to anyone. It took her a long time to warm up to me when I joined the band. It's just not in her nature to trust people or put herself out there. With you, she did. You have to give her a chance, Logan," Drake said quietly. "If you don't, you'll regret it for the rest of your life. Don't let what happened with Chloe and me cause you to make the biggest mistake of your life."

I looked back and forth between the two of them, unable to say anything.

What did they want me to say? That I'd go call Jade right now and tell her she was forgiven? It didn't work that way. Just because they thought she cared about me didn't mean that she did.

But what if they were telling the truth? What if Mikey had tried to use her, and I'd just walked in at the wrong time? I wanted that to be the truth, but I was so afraid to let myself hope. If she had lied to them and I went back to her, only to find out that she was with Mikey, it would kill me.

The fact that I was even debating on giving her a chance to explain herself made me realize that I cared about her. This summer with her had been amazing. She'd made me happy, and she'd shown me that I was capable of caring after what Chloe had done to me.

"I need to get out of here," I said as I stood and walked toward the door.

"Where are you going?" Chloe asked, her voice full of hope.

"I have a lot of shit to think about. I'm going for a drive. I don't know where I'm going or if I'll even be back today."

Instead of going out the door, I turned and walked over to my closet. I pulled out a bag, and after throwing some of my clothes inside, I walked back toward the door. "I'll see you guys later."

"Take all the time you need, Logan. Just so you know, we're leaving for L.A. in three days. You're more than welcome to come with us," Chloe said as she walked over to me. She gave me a quick hug. "I love you, Logan. I hope you know that."

I kissed her forehead. "Yeah, I know." I glanced over at Drake. "Sorry I hit you."

He grinned. "It wasn't the first time, and I'm sure it won't be the last. Just get things figured out before Jade loses her mind, okay?"

I nodded, and I walked out the door. I didn't look back as I made my way down the hallway and out the front door. Once I reached my car, I threw my bag in the passenger's seat and climbed behind the steering wheel. After backing out of my driveway, I turned onto the main road.

I had no idea where I was going. All I wanted to do was drive.

When I'd started driving, I never in my wildest dreams thought I would end up here. I stared at the tiny trailer I'd called home throughout most of my high school years. I hadn't come home since I left for college, not even for Christmases. My mom and I weren't close. We certainly didn't hate each other, but we never really got along either. I'd resented her for moving me around so much when I was a kid, and she'd been so busy working that she didn't have time to soothe my anger.

It'd taken me over two hours to drive here, but it'd felt like minutes. One minute, I had been merging onto the interstate, and the next, I had been pulling up to my old driveway. I'd spent most of the drive down thinking about Jade and whether or not she had been telling the truth. I'd left my phone off. I'd been afraid that if she called again, I would cave and answer. I wasn't ready to talk to her yet. I was still processing the fact that Mikey might have forced himself on her, and instead of beating his face in, I'd called Jade names and walked away. Yeah, if she had been telling the truth, I owed her one hell of an apology.

I shut off my car and stepped out. My mom's old Chevy was parked a few feet away, so I knew she was home. I walked across the yard and climbed the steps to her front porch. After taking a deep breath to calm myself, I knocked.

A minute later, the front door opened. My mom stood in the doorway, looking shocked. She looked younger than she actually was. She always had. When I had been in high school, some of my guy friends had made me want to vomit when they would talk about how hot she was. Her blonde hair and blue eyes were exactly like mine. She was thirty-seven, but she could pass for twenty-seven if she wanted to. She was tiny anyway, but she looked like a midget when she stood next to me. It was obvious I'd inherited my height from my dad—whoever the hell he was.

"Logan?"

"Hey, Mom," I said quietly as we stared at each other.

She held the door open, welcoming me inside. "Come in. I have to say, this is a surprise."

I shrugged. "I was in the neighborhood."

She raised an eyebrow. "What are you doing in Charleston?"

"I just needed to get away. I thought I'd stop by."

We stood across from each other, both of us clearly uncomfortable.

What was I supposed to say to someone I'd barely spoken to over the last few years? Apart from a phone call here and there, we weren't even in each other's lives.

"Do you want something to drink or eat?" my mom asked finally.

"Nah, I'm good. I was hoping I could crash here for the night though, if it's okay with you."

"Of course. Your room is still exactly how you left it. I wasn't sure if you'd come back, but I didn't want to change it in case you did."

That surprised me. I'd assumed that she boxed up everything I'd left behind the minute I walked out the front door to go to college.

"Thanks."

"Is everything okay, Logan? I mean, I'm glad to see you, but you don't normally visit."

"I just needed to get away for a few days."

"All right then, I'll leave you to get settled in. I just got home from work a few minutes ago. I'm working on dinner now."

"Cool, thanks," I said as I turned to walk back to my car.

After grabbing my bag from the car, I carried it into the house and back to my room. Opening my bedroom door was like walking into my past. My mom hadn't been kidding when she said she'd left it exactly how it was when I moved out. I dropped my bag onto my old twin-sized bed and looked around. I smiled when I saw the photo album sitting on my nightstand. I'd forgotten it when I left.

I picked it up and sat down on my bed next to my bag. I flipped through the first few pages, looking but not really paying attention. All these photos were from before I'd moved to West Virginia. I wasn't even sure why I'd kept them. It sucked to look at the faces of people I'd called my friends, only to leave them a few months later and start all over.

Once I hit my high school pictures, I slowed down and actually looked. Page after page was filled with Amber, Chloe, and me. They'd taken me in the day I started at their school, and we'd been inseparable ever since. I laughed at some of their ridiculous poses in a few of the photos.

A few photos made me wince. I could see bruises on Chloe. Most of those were from our freshman and sophomore years. After that, her mother had pretty much disappeared, and Chloe had unofficially moved in with Amber and her parents. She looked so much happier after her mom had left. I hated that I'd let things go without telling someone, but the past was the past, and I couldn't do a thing to change it.

"How are they?" my mom asked from my doorway.

I looked up to see her watching me. "They?"

She motioned toward the photo album. "Chloe and Amber. Are you guys still attached at the hip?"

I shook my head. My mom knew nothing about what had happened between Chloe and me.

"Not really. Amber and I live together off-campus, but Chloe is in California now. She's married, too."

My mom's mouth dropped open in shock. "Since when?"

"Last year. He's in a band. A label signed them, and he moved out there, so Chloe followed him."

She frowned. "I always thought you two would end up together."

"So did I, but it wasn't meant to be."

"I'm sorry. I know how much she meant to you."

I shrugged. "It's fine. She's happy with Drake, and we're still friends. That's all that matters."

"I guess. So, are you and Amber—"

I laughed. "No, definitely not. We would kill each other. We're still just friends."

"Oh, I thought since you were living with her that something might be going on."

"Nope."

My mom hesitated for a second. "So, are you with anyone?"

I raised an eyebrow. "Is this the part where you ask me if I'm having sex, and when I tell you yes, you hand me a box of condoms?"

Her face instantly turned red, and she let out a shaky laugh. "No. Just no. I don't want to know if you're...you know. I was just wondering if you were with anyone. I don't really know how you've been doing since you left for college."

"College has been...different. I've changed a lot since I moved to Morgantown. As for whether or not I have a girlfriend, it's complicated."

"And that's my cue to shut up, isn't it? I can take a hint." She smiled at me. "I won't pry, I promise."

"Thanks, Mom. My life is kind of messed-up right now. I'm not sure how I could explain it even if I wanted to."

"Gotcha. Well, if you do decide to talk about it, I'll listen. I know we're not exactly close, but you can always talk to me."

I opened my mouth to tell her no but thanks, and then I stopped myself. Maybe talking to her would help. She wasn't loyal to any of my friends or the band. She wouldn't sugarcoat anything or try to convince me to give Jade the benefit of the doubt—unless my mom thought Jade deserved it.

"When I went to college, I started dating this girl. I loved her more than anything. I really thought that I would end up with her, but she cheated on me. She came clean and told me the truth, but the damage was done. I turned bitter and started acting like an asshole. I was hurt, so I took it out on everyone but her. Then, this other girl started coming around. For years, she was just my friend. She made me realize what a dick I was being. Nothing happened between us until recently. She finally kind of admitted that she had feelings for me. It made me see that I cared about her, too, so we went for it. Things were perfect for two months. I could talk to her about what the other girl had done to me, and she'd listen. She also had problems of her own, and I helped her deal with them. Then, I walked in on her and her ex one night. They were kissing. I took off before she could say anything, but some of our mutual friends have told me that he forced himself on her and that she's really upset. After what happened before, I don't know whether to believe them or not. It's all so fucked-up at this point."

My mom walked into the room and sat down in my old computer chair. "I'm really sorry that you had to go through all of that with both of them. Sometimes, we're so blinded by love that we don't really see what's happening. By the time we do, it's too late to save ourselves." She paused, her face clouded with doubt and uncertainty. "I know I've never really told you about your father, but maybe now is a good time."

I gave her a questioning look. "How will that help me?"

She gave me a sad smile. "Maybe it'll help you, or maybe it won't. You can decide. Regardless, I think you need to hear it. I know you've always had questions about what happened and why we lived our lives the way we did."

"Yeah, I did, but you never seemed to want to talk about him, so I finally just gave up and left it alone."

"I know, and I'm sorry for that." She smiled sadly. "When I was sixteen, I met your father. He was twenty at the time. My parents would have had a fit if they knew I was with him, so we kept our relationship a secret for over a year. Then, you decided to surprise us, and I had to tell them the truth. They were furious with me for messing around with someone so much older and for wanting to keep you. When they realized that they couldn't change my mind about having an abortion, they kicked me out.

"I moved in with your father, and things were good for a while. Randy always had a drinking problem, but things didn't get bad until around the time you turned two. I don't know what had set him off, but he turned into a completely different man. He started hitting me, but I was young and dumb, so I didn't leave him. Then, one night, I came home from work early. You were screaming in your room, and your dad was passed out in the chair. After I took care of you, I woke him up to yell at him. I *never* yelled at him, ever, but enough was enough. You were my baby, and God only knows how long you had been crying like that. When I started yelling at him, he came after me. He nearly beat me to death that night. He took off, and after I was able to move, I packed up everything you and I owned, and I took off. He searched for me for a long time, and he nearly caught up to us once or twice, but I always managed to stay one step ahead of him. I was terrified. I had no family, no friends, and no money. I worked crappy jobs, and we lived in crappy houses in every town we moved to, but we were mostly safe. I lived in terror for almost twelve years, just waiting for the day when he would finally find us."

"Why didn't you tell me any of this?" I asked, shocked by what my mother had kept from me.

"Because it was my problem, not yours. I wanted you to be happy, and you were. You didn't look over your shoulder every day, terrified of whether or not he'd find us. Right after we moved to West Virginia, I got a call from a lawyer out of Louisiana, which is where we're from originally. How he found me, I have no clue, but he did. He said that he represented your father and that he'd passed away. He was in a car accident that he caused in Missouri. He had gone the wrong way and driven down an exit ramp, hitting another car head-on. He killed the people inside the other car as well. I know it makes me a horrible person, but when the lawyer told me that your father had died, all I felt was relief. I was *finally* free, Logan. After years of running, I was finally free."

"I don't even know what to say. Why the hell didn't he give up on us?"

"I don't know. Your father had a lot of anger problems, and I think he was pissed that I'd escaped. I never filed for divorce because I didn't want him to have an address to track me, so maybe he thought I was still his. Regardless, the reason doesn't matter. What does matter is that I let my fear control me. It still controls me. Haven't you ever wondered why I never dated? I was too afraid that I'd find someone just like him. I'm still too afraid to try. My point is, don't do what I did. Don't let the past control you. If this girl says that she didn't cheat on you, give her a chance to explain herself."

"But what if she really did cheat on me?"

"Then, talk to her, and walk away. It doesn't matter what the outcome is. You deserve to know what really happened. Do you care a lot about this girl?"

"Yeah, I do. If I didn't, it wouldn't hurt this damn bad," I admitted.

"Then, give her a chance. If you don't talk to her, you'll always wonder if she was telling the truth or not. You deserve to be happy, Logan. I know that you weren't very happy with me when you were growing up because I wasn't around as much as I would have liked, but I've always loved you."

"We have a screwed-up relationship, don't we?" I asked.

She laughed. "Yeah, we do. I admit that most of it was my fault, but I hope you realize that everything I did was to protect you."

"I know. I was butt-hurt because you were never around and because we moved constantly, but I need to get over it. I'm sorry I haven't called very often or visited at all since I left."

"It's all right, but I wouldn't mind a visit every now and then," she teased.

"I'll see what I can do."

"Good. Now, let's go eat. I'm sure dinner is just about ready now."

I stood and followed my mom from my room. Surprisingly, talking with her had helped me more than I'd ever thought it would.

21

I ended up staying with my mom for two days before heading back to Morgantown. Now that I knew exactly what had happened between her and my father, I didn't feel as resentful toward her for moving us around so much. I hated how my dad had made her suffer for years just because she chose to protect us from him. I didn't feel any loss knowing my dad was dead. It was probably a blessing that I'd never known the bastard.

I promised my mom that I would come back to visit her again sometime soon, and I meant it. I wasn't sure when, but I would make it down to Charleston even if it was just for the weekend.

On the drive home, I couldn't help but wonder if I was doing the right thing. I'd thought about what Chloe, Drake, and my mom had told me, and I knew they were right. If I didn't talk to Jade, I would always wonder what had really happened that night. I had to know the truth.

As I pulled into the driveway of my house, I saw Chloe and Drake walking to their rental car. I parked my car beside theirs and climbed out. Chloe gave me a tentative smile as I walked over to her.

"Hey, Logan," Chloe said.

"Hi. You guys leaving?"

"Yeah, we're heading to the airport now. I was hoping you'd make it back before we left. I didn't feel right leaving without telling you bye."

"I'm glad I caught you guys. I was wondering if you had room for one more on the flight back to L.A." I grinned down at her.

Her eyes widened in surprise before she gave me a huge grin. "Of course we do!"

"Okay, give me a few minutes to pack up some of my stuff."

"Yay! That's fine. Whenever you're ready," Chloe said excitedly.

I glanced over at Drake as I passed by him. He gave me a silent nod before turning his attention to Chloe. I walked inside and straight back to my room. I grabbed one of my old luggage bags, dropped it onto the bed, and unzipped it. After grabbing my clothes out of the closet and dresser, I tossed them inside and walked across the hall to the bathroom to grab some of my stuff.

"What are you doing?" Amber asked, stopping mid-step at the bathroom.

"I'm going to L.A. with Chloe and Drake, so I can talk to Jade."

"Are you kidding me? Everyone is going to California, and I'm stuck here without any of you!"

"I'll be back, Amber. Classes start soon."

"Yeah, right. You'll make up with Jade, and then you'll move to L.A. with her and have five kids, abandoning me in the process."

I snorted. "Really, Amber?"

"Yes, really! You just wait! And when I turn out to be right, I expect an apology and some flowers."

"Amber, I will be back. For starters, I can't just drop out of school. Also, half the rent on this place is mine to pay, remember? I'm not just going to abandon you."

"Like Chloe did? *She* also had school and rent to pay, but that didn't stop her."

I rolled my eyes as I walked past her and back into my room. I threw the rest of my stuff into my bag, zipped it, and turned back to Amber. "I'll see you in a week or so, okay? No wild parties while I'm gone."

"Yeah, whatever. Out of the three of us, I never thought that I'd be the one left behind while you two go off and do whatever your hearts' desire."

I grabbed my bag and walked over to her. "I'll miss you, too, Amber."

I kissed her forehead before walking past her and down the hall.

"Logan?" she called after me.

I glanced back. "Yeah?"

"Will you let me know how Adam is? I didn't want to ask Chloe because it would be awkward since she's around him so much."

I grinned. "Yeah, if I see him, I'll let you know. You could always call him and see for yourself."

She shook her head. "Nah, it's been almost a year since we talked. No going back now."

I opened my mouth to tell her to stop being so damn stubborn and just call him, but I stopped myself. Who was I to give relationship advice?

"Behave yourself while I'm gone," I teased before walking out the door.

Chloe and Drake were sitting in their rental car, waiting for me. Drake popped the trunk with the lever inside as I walked over. I threw my bag inside and then climbed into the backseat.

"That didn't take very long," Chloe remarked as I fastened my seat belt.

"I'm not a girl. It doesn't take me two days to pack."

"Oh, whatever. I don't pack that much."

Drake snorted as he started backing out of the driveway. "Bullshit. The back of this car says you're full of shit."

"That's different! We were gone for a whole summer! Of course I needed a lot of stuff."

Drake glanced back at me in the rearview mirror and shook his head, but he said nothing. Chloe stuck her tongue out at him as he drove away from the house and toward the interstate.

"So, what changed your mind?" Chloe asked as we approached the Pittsburgh airport.

"My mom," I said.

She turned in her seat to stare at me. "Your mom? Seriously? That's where you went?"

I shrugged. "I didn't intend to go there, but that's where I ended up. We talked a little bit. She even told me about my dad. She said some stuff that made a lot of sense."

"I'm glad that you were able to talk with her. I know you guys have an awkward relationship."

"Yeah. I mean, we won't be calling each other daily or anything, but I promised that I'd visit again soon. She seemed happy about that."

"Well, like I said, I'm glad. I always liked your mom even though she wasn't around much."

The car was silent for a few minutes.

Drake spoke up, "So, what are your plans once we get to L.A.?"

I shrugged. "I don't know. If it's okay with you guys, I'll crash at your place. I'll find Jade tomorrow and talk to her, and then I'll go home the following day."

"What if things work out? You won't go home then, will you?" Chloe asked.

"I have to. I'm paying half the rent on the house Amber and I are living in. Plus, I have school. *If* Jade and I work things out, we'll just have to deal with living apart."

"You could always transfer schools, you know. There are colleges in California, or you can do what I did and take online courses. I'm sure Amber's mom and dad will help her with the rent until she finds someone new to room with," Chloe said.

I raised an eyebrow. "Why are you so determined to make sure that Jade and I end up together?"

"Because I want you both to be happy, and after all of this sorted out, I think you two could be really happy with each other. You both care a lot about each other. I've never seen Jade act the way she did when Drake called her. She was really upset. And you've been Mopey McMoperpants since you came home. It's obvious that you're both miserable without one another."

"Do you really think that we'd be happy together? Honestly, I'm not so sure. I don't exactly fit in with the rest of her world."

"Why do you think that?"

"She's a rock star, Chloe, and I'm just...I'm not into that scene. I don't like the same things you guys do. I don't look like any of the other guys she hangs out with. I'm not pierced or tattooed. I'm not...I don't know what the fuck I'm trying to say here."

Chloe started to say something, but Drake cut her off, "Look, Logan, I've known Jade for a long time. I've watched her get hit on by tons of guys, and she's never paid attention to any of them. She didn't care that they were part of our *scene*. Truthfully, most of the guys we hang out with are womanizing assholes."

"True story," Chloe cut in, giving Drake a dirty look.

"Hey, I haven't been that way in a long time. Don't glare at me like that. Anyway, my point is, just because she lives a certain way and has a certain profession doesn't mean that she's going to want a certain type of guy. She obviously likes you, so just go with it."

"He's right. Don't doubt yourself because you two have different lives. You're a good-looking guy, Logan. You don't need tattoos or piercings for girls to notice you. Jade obviously likes you just the way you are."

"I feel like I should pull the car over, so we can all hug. This is getting awkward," Drake muttered.

Chloe laughed. "Don't be jealous, Drake. I think you're a good-looking guy, too."

He rolled his eyes. "Thanks. I feel much more secure about our marriage now that you've admitted you're attracted to me."

I grinned, unable to stop myself. Being around Chloe and Drake was eye-opening. The way the two of them were around each other made me realize just how much they cared about each other. I hated that their beginning had been the end for me, but I was glad that Chloe was happy.

Maybe I would find the same kind of happiness she had with Drake. Jade's face came to mind. Maybe she could be the one.

I just hoped that I wasn't flying toward more heartache.

I slept on and off as we flew to L.A. I'd flown once or twice before, but it was nothing compared to flying in Drake's label's private plane. Instead of sitting in a cramped seat with screaming kids and annoyingly loud passengers surrounding me, I'd been sprawled out on a leather couch for most of the trip. I hated moving back to my seat when the pilot announced that we would be landing soon.

As soon as we landed, I followed Drake and Chloe to where a massive SUV was waiting for us. The Mercedes SUV had black tinted windows, so no one could see who was inside. I climbed into the very back row of seats as Chloe and Drake sat down in the row in front of me. Once our luggage was loaded into the back, a driver took us to Drake's house.

"Nice setup you have going on here," I said as we drove along the crowded streets of L.A.

"I don't think I'll ever get used to it," Chloe said as she looked over her shoulder at me.

"I don't think I could either. I'm almost afraid to see your house," I joked.

"Don't worry. Our home is just a normal house. The label owns this car and the plane. That's why it looks so expensive," Chloe assured me.

It was taking forever to get to Drake and Chloe's house. The traffic in L.A. was like nothing I'd ever seen before. I couldn't imagine trying to drive in it daily. Nope, I'd stick to West Virginia's two-lane roads and four-lane interstates. This was a nightmare. We finally managed to escape the bumper-to-bumper cars when we hit another interstate. It was still packed, but at least the traffic was flowing here.

When we pulled up to their house twenty minutes later, I was surprised. Chloe hadn't been kidding. While the house was large, it was simple. There was nothing flashy about it. It looked like every other house on this street. It was a two-story white house with a black roof. It had a small front porch with a high privacy fence extending all the way around the house. The only hint that someone famous lived here was the keypad on the gate and the huge privacy fence.

"Home, sweet home," Drake said before climbing out of the car. He walked over to the gate. After punching a combination into the keypad, he swung the gate open.

The driver and the rest of us each grabbed a few bags and carried them up to the house. Drake unlocked the door, disabled the alarm, and continued inside. We followed and sat all the luggage next to the door.

I smirked at Chloe as I watched her separate her blue bags from Drake's. "And you said you didn't have that much luggage."

"Oh, bite me, asshole. We were gone for *months*!"

I laughed as I grabbed a few of her bags and carried them up the stairs. I followed her into the first bedroom on the second floor. I glanced around the room before putting her bags down and walking down the steps to carry more up for her. I passed Drake on the stairs as he carried two of his own bags up. He only had two left by the door while Chloe still had four. Yeah, she definitely hadn't packed light. Once all of her bags were in her room, I grabbed my bag and followed Chloe down the second-floor hallway to one of the guest rooms.

"Is this one okay?" she asked as she opened the door.

We walked into the room. It was much larger than the one I had back in West Virginia. The walls and carpet were a cream color. A queen-sized bed sat against the far wall. Other than that and a closet, the room was completely empty.

"Yeah, it's fine. Thank you for letting me stay with you. I shouldn't be here for more than a few days."

"You're welcome to stay as long as you want."

"I also owe you and Drake for convincing me to come out here, especially after I said all those things to you and after hitting Drake."

"Don't apologize for what you said to me. I deserved it. And you felt better after you got everything out, didn't you?"

"Yeah, I guess. I still shouldn't have said what I did though."

She shook her head. "Logan, you and Amber have always been my best friends. We've been through the good, the bad, and the horrible together. You've never kept things from me, and I don't expect you to now. No matter what happens, we'll always be friends."

"Even if I join the circus and Amber runs off to be a hooker in Las Vegas?" I joked.

"Even then. Besides, if you joined the circus, I'd come to watch you perform. And we both know we'd go after Amber if she followed her hooker dreams."

"True." I grinned at her. "Can I ask you something?"

"Sure."

"Are you really happy with Drake? I mean, is being with him everything you thought it would be?"

She gave me a hesitant smile. "It really is. He's everything I've ever hoped for. I can't even begin to explain how he makes me feel.

222

It's like my whole world became clear once we finally found each other again. Because of everything Drake and I have been through, I now believe in fate. I mean, there's no way we would have ended up together if it wasn't for fate. There were just too many things in our way."

I pulled her to me and hugged her tightly. "I love you, Chloe, and I'm truly happy for you. You deserve some happiness after everything you've had to endure."

"I love you, too. And, Logan?"

"Yeah?"

"Like I said, I believe in fate. I think you and Jade found each other for a reason. Don't let obstacles get in your way if you really love her. If it's meant to be, it will happen."

I released her and stepped back. "I hope you're right. The way I felt when Jade and I were together…Jade is special, just like you are."

"Then, don't let her get away, no matter what."

"After I talk to her, I'm hoping that things will work out for us."

"When do you plan to talk to her?" Chloe asked.

"As soon as I can. Classes are starting soon, so I can't stay long. I want things resolved before I go back to West Virginia."

She frowned. "Why are you so determined to go back to West Virginia?"

"What do you mean?"

"Well, it's not like you have anything to keep you there. You could transfer schools and stay here. Your job isn't a big deal. There are plenty of places that would hire you here."

"I can't just leave everything and move."

"I did." Chloe grinned at me.

"Yeah, but it's just Amber and me on the rent now. I can't just abandon her."

She laughed. "I told you earlier. Her parents will help her. Don't let trivial things hold you back if you really want to be here with Jade."

"Amber is trivial?" I asked, surprised that Chloe would refer to Amber that way.

"No, that's not what I meant. What I'm trying to say is that you keep finding insignificant things, like rent, to hold you back. If you want to stay with Jade, then stay. Things have a way of working themselves out."

I shrugged. "I don't know what I'll do. We'll have to wait and see."

"You'll make the right choice. Of that, I have no doubt. I'll leave you alone, so you can get settled in. I'm going to order something for dinner. Does Chinese sound good?"

"Yeah, just order what I normally get."

"All right. I'll come find you when it gets here," Chloe said as she walked to the door.

I sat down on my bed and stared out the window. I couldn't help but wonder what tomorrow would bring.

22

I pulled my phone out of my pocket and unlocked it. I dialed Jade's number, but I couldn't bring myself to press Call. I groaned at how idiotic I was being. I'd come all this way to talk to her, yet I couldn't bring myself to even call her. I wasn't sure why this was so hard for me. All I had to do was pick up the fucking phone and call her, tell her I want to meet, and then go meet her. It wasn't that hard. I was acting like a thirteen-year-old girl.

Pull your head out of your ass and call her. I hit the Call button before I could really think about what I was doing. It rang three times, just long enough for me to think she wasn't going to pick up, before she finally answered.

"Logan?" she asked, surprise flooding her voice.

The sound of her voice was like a punch in the gut. Goddamn, I'd missed hearing her more than I thought.

"Yeah, it's me," I finally said after several seconds of silence.

"I...I didn't expect to hear from you."

"I didn't think I'd call you either. Listen, I think we need to talk."

"Yeah, I do, too."

"Can we meet somewhere?" I asked, forgetting the fact that she didn't know I was in L.A.

"Um...I don't know. I don't really think I can leave L.A. for a while. We're starting on the new album later today."

"Oh, yeah. No, I'm actually in L.A. right now."

"What? Why are you here?" she asked, sounding shocked.

"I came out with Chloe and Drake. I wanted to talk with you face-to-face. I didn't want to talk about everything over the phone."

"Shit, yeah, I definitely want to talk with you. I'm at my apartment right now, but I can come over to Drake's place if you want."

"Why don't I come to you? I don't really want an audience while we sort everything out."

"Good point. I can pick you up if you want," she said nervously.

"Nah, I'll take a cab or have Chloe drop me off."

"Okay. So, I'll see you in a few?"

"Yeah," I said, "I'll be there soon."

I started to hang up, but she called my name, "Logan?"

"Yeah?"

"I'm glad you're here."

"Thanks for driving me here, Chloe," I said an hour later as we pulled up in front of Jade's apartment.

"No problem. Her building is locked. You'll need a code to get in." She grabbed an old receipt and a pen out of the car console and wrote down five numbers. "Just put this code in at the door, and it'll unlock. She's on the sixth floor, apartment 603."

I opened the car door and stepped out. "Thanks."

"Do you want me to hang around for a bit?"

"Nah, I'll call you if I need a ride."

"Okay. And Logan? Good luck."

I gave her one last smile before walking over to the door of Jade's apartment building. After punching in the code Chloe had given me, I opened the door and stepped inside. Two elevators sat to the left. I walked over to them and pressed the button to go up. A second later, the door of one slid open, and I stepped into it. I took a deep breath as I pressed the button for the sixth floor. It seemed like the ride up to Jade's floor was taking forever.

Once the doors opened, I stepped out of the elevator and started down the hallway. Her door was the second on the right. I knocked softly and waited. I glanced around the hallway. The building had looked simple enough on the outside, but I could tell from the hallway alone that I would never be able to afford an apartment in this building. While it didn't scream money, it definitely wasn't a dump or even close to it.

The apartment door opened, and I tensed, preparing myself to see her again. Finally, I looked up. Jade and I stared at each other, neither of us moving or speaking. She was still as beautiful as always, but she looked tired. Dark circles were under her eyes, and I felt guilty because I knew I had probably caused them.

"Hey," she finally said quietly.

"Hey."

Neither of us spoke again, and I couldn't help but grin. "This is awkward as hell."

She laughed. "Yeah, it kind of is. Do you want to come in?"

"Sure," I said.

She stepped aside, and I walked by her and into the apartment.

I glanced around, taking in her home. It was totally her. The living room had dark gray walls with a hardwood floor. The couch and chair were both black leather. A glass coffee table and two glass side tables were in front of the couch. A flat-screen television was mounted on the wall across from the couch. To my right was a kitchen. The floor was black-and-white linoleum. The walls were the same dark gray color as the living room.

"Would you like something to drink?" she asked.

"No thanks, I'm good." I motioned toward the couch. "Why don't we sit down and talk? I think we need to get this over with."

She nodded and walked over to the couch. I followed behind her and sat down on the opposite side from her.

"Do you want me to start? Or do you want to?" she asked. "I'm sure you have a lot to say."

"I do. When I saw you with Mikey, I lost it. It was like I was back in Chloe's dorm room, listening to her tell me how she cheated on me repeatedly with Drake. Only this time, I saw it for myself. I couldn't believe that I'd trusted another woman, only to be lied to and cheated on again. I was angry. No, I was furious, but I was also hurt, too. You didn't seem like the type of person who would do something like that to me, but I saw it with my own eyes. So, I took off without giving you a chance to explain. I shouldn't have, but I wasn't thinking clearly. All I wanted to do was get the hell away from you and hope that I never had to see you again."

"I understand why you left the way you did. I probably would have done the same thing. You've had to deal with a lot of bullshit over the past few years, Logan. I just want you to know that nothing happened with Mikey. I feel absolutely nothing, except revulsion, for him. What you saw was him trying to convince me to bring him here, so I could introduce him to our label. He thought I was his ticket to making it big, and when I turned him down, he got pissed and kissed me. I was trying to get him off of me when you walked in."

I looked at her, trying to judge whether or not she was being completely honest with me. She didn't look away, and her expression was open and humbled. I believed her, and that made me want to kick myself for running in the first place. If I'd just stayed and listened, things would be completely different with us right now.

"I'm sorry for leaving you and for not answering your calls. I really fucked up, Jade."

"It's okay. Like I said, I understand why you did what you did."

"So, where does that leave us?" I asked. Honestly, I wasn't sure what would happen from here.

"That's entirely up to you. I was hurt that you'd assumed the worst of me, but I'm not mad. I still care about you, Logan. Nothing will change that."

"This summer was incredible. For once, I wasn't wallowing in pity or wondering what could have been if Chloe had never met Drake. I was living again. But we both know that a couple of months aren't enough to solidify a relationship, not really. If it were, I wouldn't have run the way I did. I'm not like the guys you usually hang out with, Jade. I'm not the bad boy or the rocker. I'm not wild or crazy. I'm the normal guy who's insecure. I'm just…average. You have to know that."

She frowned. "I don't expect you to be like my friends. I've been around my bandmates for a long time, and I've never felt anything more than friendship for any of them, even Eric, who's been there for me through a lot of tough situations. I like the fact that you're sensitive and sweet and *normal*. If you were arrogant and cocky, I wouldn't want to be around you at all. What I'm trying to say is that I want to be with you, if you still think we have a chance. Besides what happened with Mikey, I think we were both really happy being together this summer."

I nodded. "I was happy with you. You're a great person, Jade. The thing is, we never really talked about what would happen once you went back to L.A. and I went back to West Virginia. I'm not sure if it's because neither of us expected anything after the summer or what."

"I wanted to talk to you about it, but I didn't want to ruin what we had. You have a life in West Virginia, and I have a life here. I would never ask you to give up everything, and I know you wouldn't ask that of me either."

"No, I wouldn't."

I reached up and cupped her face, preparing myself for what I was about to say. It could break us. I knew that, but it didn't change my decision.

"I've spent the last three years of my life loving someone I couldn't have. I haven't really lived a life of my own. Instead, I let my feelings control me. I think what I need right now is to live my life. I have a year left of college. That's it. I need to go out, enjoy myself, and stop letting relationships control me. You're really good for me, Jade, but you're also really bad for me. When I went back to West Virginia, I wasn't living. Instead, I was right back where I'd started when I found out what Chloe had done to me. I need to figure out how to be happy on my own. Once I figure out how to do that, I'll be ready to try to have a relationship. I'm not asking you to wait around for me until I figure things out. I would never expect you to do that. I just…I can't be with you right now. If we start this up again before I'm ready, we'll end up right back where we are right now. That isn't fair to either of us."

She gave me a weak grin. "Logan, you're the first guy I've cared about in years. Do you really think I'm going to just forget you and find someone else? I'll wait for you. It doesn't matter how long I have to wait. When you're ready, find me, and we'll make this work. I faced my demons this summer, and now it's time for you to face yours."

"You're kind of awesome. You know that, right?" I said as I finally let my hand fall away from her face.

She laughed. "Yeah, I know. If it's okay with you, I'd like to keep in touch while we're apart—as friends, of course."

"I'd like that. Just give me this last year of college to sort everything out, and then we'll see what happens. I don't want to lose you, but I need this."

"Logan, you won't lose me. I'll always be yours."

I walked back into Chloe and Drake's house almost an hour later. Chloe was sitting on the couch, but when she saw me, she jumped up and followed me up the stairs.

"How did it go?" she asked when we reached my room.

"I believe her about what happened with Mikey. I think I believed it as soon as Drake told me what had happened," I said as I sat down on the bed.

"So, you two worked everything out?" She sat down next to me.

"Yeah, we did."

Chloe grinned. "I'm so happy for you, Logan! You and Jade are going to be really happy together. Are you going to move in with her or try to find a place of your own? Oh! And as for school, I can show you the online college that I enrolled in. They're awesome, and it's completely online. That was great while we were touring. It would have been hard to attend classes while I was in Europe with the band."

"I'm going home, Chloe," I said.

Her eyes widened in surprise. "Wait, what? Why? I thought you said you two worked things out?"

"We did, but seeing how I was after the Mikey situation made me realize that I'm not ready to have a relationship right now. I've spent the last few years not really living. Instead, I moped around after I lost you. Then, I did the same with Jade. I just want to focus on school and try to get my life in order right now. After I graduate, we'll see how things stand between Jade and me. If we're both willing to give it another shot, we will."

"I don't know what to say, Logan," Chloe said, her eyes filled with sadness. "I feel like this is my fault. You wouldn't have to do this if it wasn't for what I did to you."

"You don't have to say anything, Chloe. I'm going to go home, go to school, and figure things out. If Jade and I are meant to be together, then we'll be fine. If not, then we'll move on. I really do hope that things work out between us, but I'm not going to worry about it right now."

"Do you want to stay with us for a few days to make sure before you go all the way back home?"

"Nah. I'm going to book my ticket and head back tomorrow if I can. I'm sure Amber will pick me up from the airport."

Chloe frowned but nodded. "I'll support you with whatever decision makes you happy."

"I know you will. I'm going to book my flight and go ahead and get packed up," I said, hinting for her to leave. I had a lot going through my head, and I wanted to be alone to try to process all of it.

Despite my words, deep down, I was worried that this would ruin any chance for Jade and me, but I knew I needed to figure everything out if I ever wanted to be truly happy.

"I'll let you be then. I'm going to start dinner since Drake will be home soon. You'll eat with us, won't you?"

I smiled. "Of course. Just yell when it's ready."

She closed the door behind her when she left. I pulled my phone out of my pocket and booked a flight for first thing in the morning. After that was done, I packed up the few clothes I had out and tossed my bag on the floor.

My phone beeped just as I was about to open my door and walk downstairs.

Jade: I miss you already, friend.

I grinned as I typed my reply.

Me: I miss you, too, friend. We'll talk soon.

"I can't believe you came back. I seriously thought you were joking last night when you texted and asked me to come pick you up from the airport," Amber said.

She pulled away from the airport and hit the interstate.

"I told you I'd be back. When have I ever lied to you?" I asked.

"Well, never, but still…I thought for sure you'd move out there and shack up with Jade."

I grinned. "Nah, I like shacking up with you too much."

"Aw, you have such a way with words, Logan. My panties just melted."

I snorted. "Since when do you wear panties?"

She giggled. "Shut up, and tell me what happened. I thought you'd be all whiny and shit since you came home, but you're not. Did you talk to Jade or what?"

"Yeah, I talked to her. She was innocent, just like Chloe and Drake had said."

"So, why aren't you with her now? And don't tell me it's because you enjoy my company so much." Amber changed lanes to pass a car.

"Because I need some time to myself. I need to stop focusing every part of my life on whether or not I'm in a relationship, and I need to just start living. I have a year left at WVU, and then I'll be out in the real world. I want to take this last year to just enjoy myself."

"I get that. I do. I spent so much time focusing on one guy that I forgot how to have fun. Now, I do what I want, and I love it," Amber said.

I shot her a look. "I don't plan to go out and party like you do, Amber. I just want to have fun and relax."

"Hey! I don't party that much!" She gave me an indignant look.

233

"Bullshit. Ever since the band left, you've changed. You're out partying almost every night. I know why, Amber. I'm not stupid."

"Let's just drop it before we end up pissed-off at each other, okay?" she finally said after a moment of silence.

"Fine, but you know you need to face Adam at some point."

She sighed. "Yeah, I know. Did you…did you see him while you were out there?"

"I didn't. Why don't you just call and talk to him, Amber?"

"*No.* I'm not calling him. We're done. We really weren't anything to begin with. I was just another easy-lay groupie to him."

"Have you asked him how he feels?"

She shook her head. "Why would I? If he really cared, he would have asked me to be with him. Drake took Chloe with him to L.A. once everything was settled between them. If Adam wanted me out there, he would have said something. Instead, he told me, 'later,' and walked out of my life."

"Yeah, but—"

"Logan, drop it. Please."

"All right, I'll shut up."

"Thanks. And Logan?"

"Yeah?"

"I'm really happy you're home. I think you're stupid for leaving Jade out there, but I'm still glad you're here with me."

23

I'd made it four months. That was it. I'd handled the rest of August and even part of September fairly well, but then I caved. I missed Jade. It was that simple. I missed her. I had gone through my daily routine of school, work, and homework, but that was as far as I'd made it. My plans to go out and explore life had crashed and burned before I'd even realized what was happening.

Unfortunately for me, I still had to finish my semester. I had a full academic scholarship, and I couldn't just give it up and walk away. Even though I was stuck, that didn't keep me from planning ahead.

By the end of October, I was signed up for the same online college where Chloe was enrolled. I would start classes online in January. I had enough money saved up from working at the shop that I was able to afford the semester's tuition. My web design and graphics major made it a lot easier to take online classes. Learning to build websites could literally be done from anywhere.

My finals would be over a week before Christmas, and my plane ticket out to L.A. was booked for the following day.

Amber figured out what I had been up to a few weeks before I would be leaving. She didn't seem surprised when she cornered me, and I admitted that I was going to L.A. If anything, she seemed relieved.

"It's about damn time you found some happiness, Logan."

I took that as her blessing.

I spent Thanksgiving with my mom, and it was awkward as hell, but she was really trying to make up for how my life had been as a kid. I thought she expected me to spend Christmas with her as well, so I let her know of my plans. She didn't seem happy that I was going all the way to L.A., but she wished me luck.

I called Chloe a few days before I was scheduled to fly out, letting her know what my plans were. While I had every intention of running to Jade's apartment as soon as I could, I wanted to make sure that I had a place to stay in case she decided that she didn't want me. Even though she'd told me she would wait for me, I knew that life happened. If she'd moved on already, that would be my fault, and I'd have to deal with the consequences of my idiotic decisions. I just hoped that she hadn't forgotten me. I doubted if Chloe would mind if I moved in with her and Drake, but I wasn't sure how well Drake would take it. I wasn't sure if I would be able to stand living with him.

Chloe was ecstatic when I told her my plans. Just like before, she was the one who was hoping I'd end up with Jade. I'd kept in touch with Chloe a lot over the last few months, and the awkwardness from before was gone. We were right back where we used to be—best friends. I'd expected to feel disappointment over that, but I didn't. I really was over Chloe. It'd only taken me three years to pull my head out of my ass.

Go figure.

When I walked out of LAX airport and climbed into a taxi, I didn't feel nervous like last time. I knew what I wanted. It was time that I stopped letting my past get in the way and just go for it. If Jade wasn't ready to be with me again, I'd stay with Chloe or find a place of my own until she was or until I was ready to move on. One way or another, I would make this work.

The taxi dropped me off at Jade's apartment just as the sun was setting. I punched in the code Chloe had given me and rode the elevator up to her floor. I knocked on the door and waited.

When Jade opened the door, her eyes widened. "Logan? What are you doing here?" You didn't mention anything about coming out over break," she said, still looking shocked.

We'd talked on the phone and texted a few times each week. It had been enough to let me know how she was doing, but it hadn't been enough to keep me from going nuts. I wanted to be where she was.

"I wanted to surprise you." I grinned at her. "We have a lot to talk about, but before we do…"

I pushed past her into the apartment and dropped my luggage on the floor. I turned back to her and pulled her close. She opened her mouth to say something, but I silenced her with a kiss. She gasped in shock as I pressed her against the wall and ground my body against hers. I thrust my tongue into her mouth, and I felt fire flood my veins when she responded back.

I cursed myself for being stupid and for making us both wait for this. Being with Jade was what I wanted. She was everything.

I bit down on her lip gently before finally pulling away. "I've thought about doing that for way too long."

"I…wow. I don't even know what to say, Logan," she whispered as she looked up at me.

"I do. I'm a fucking idiot. I never should have left you last time. I thought that I could figure everything out if I was on my own. Instead, all I did was realize what an idiot I've been when it comes to you. I won't walk away from you again. Twice was too many times. I should have kicked Mikey's ass and moved here to be with you this summer. When I came here before, I was too worried about my own feelings to care about yours. That's the dumbest thing I've ever done. I hope you'll forgive me."

She wrapped her arms around my neck and kissed me gently. "Of course I do. No one is perfect, Logan. You're not, and I'm certainly not. I've watched you go through hell since I met you. I understand why you did the things you did. It wasn't because you didn't care. It's because you cared too much, and you had too many lessons in pain to deal with any of it. I think I fell for you the minute I saw you even though I never thought we'd have a chance. You're a good soul, Logan, and there aren't enough of those in this world. You wear your heart on your sleeve. You don't hide your emotions. You're strong and proud and brave. I couldn't ask for a better man to fall in love with."

She grabbed my face and pulled my lips down to hers. Instead of me kissing her, she took control. Her lips explored mine with a hungry need that left me gasping for air. I picked her up and carried her through the living room. She wrapped her legs around my waist, pressing her center against my dick.

"Where's your bedroom?" I asked, my voice rough from emotion as I ended our kiss.

"Straight back, second door on the left," she mumbled before attacking my lips again.

I carried her through the apartment, bumping into walls and furniture as I went. Her bedroom door was open.

Thank God.

I walked in and fell onto the bed with her underneath me.

"You're okay with this?" I asked, wanting to be sure.

I would stop now if she wanted. It might kill me, and my cock would probably explode in my pants, but I would stop.

"Yeah," she said before kissing me greedily.

Neither of us spoke after that. She grabbed my shirt and pulled it off. As she worked to unbutton my pants, I grabbed her shirt and pulled it over her head. She helped me remove it before attacking my pants again. As soon as they were loose, I stood and pulled them off. My boxers went next. I grabbed her shorts and yanked them off with her underwear. She unclasped her bra and tossed it to the floor.

I climbed back onto the bed and started kissing her again. I ran my tongue along the soft skin of her neck and down to her collarbone. I kissed down her chest, between her breasts, and down to her belly button. As I made my way back up, I ran my tongue across one of her nipples and then the other. I blew on the wet tips, making her shudder.

"I've missed you so much," I whispered before capturing her mouth with mine.

When I broke the kiss, she said, "Shh…just love me, Logan."

I smiled as I kissed back down her stomach. I ran my tongue along the apex of her thighs, making her moan with need. Her body arched off the bed when I found her clit and circled it with my tongue. Her whimpers were driving me mad as I pushed two fingers inside her.

"Oh my God! Please don't stop!"

Her hips rocked up, pushing her wet fold up against my face. I continued to devour her as I increased the speed of my fingers. I felt her tighten around them as she came. My tongue replaced my fingers, and I prolonged her orgasm.

When her body finally quieted, I stood and grabbed my jeans.

"What are you doing?" she asked breathlessly.

"Condom," I muttered. My body was literally aching with need, and I wasn't sure I could get more than one word out.

"Don't. I'm on the pill now."

"Thank God." I grinned as I dropped my jeans and climbed back onto the bed. "I'm not going to last very long this first time. I need you too much."

"I don't care. We have all night," she said as I positioned myself at her entrance.

"We have forever."

I slammed into her, making her cry out. She wrapped her legs around my waist, so I could go deeper.

"Jesus fucking Christ, woman. You feel so good."

Being with her before had been incredible, but now, without a condom, was life-changing. I pumped my hips fast and hard, her cries of pleasure driving me to move faster. I braced myself on my arms and used her footboard as leverage.

"Come with me, baby," I said as I felt myself reaching my limit.

I rocked into her once more before the world exploded around me. I roared as I released into her. If I died right now, I would be okay. I doubted if I would have another moment in my life as good as this one.

"So, I take it you're here to stay?" Jade asked a few hours later.

"Yeah, I'm here to stay, if you'll have me." I pulled her tighter against me.

She rested her head on my chest, and I started running my hands through her hair.

"Of course I'll have you. I've already *had* you three times tonight. I might not be able to walk tomorrow."

"I don't care. That's a good excuse for me to keep you in bed," I teased.

She laughed. "How did we end up here? When you left, I thought you were really gone despite what you'd said. Seeing you at my door was…I don't know. I never thought I'd see you again."

"I realized that you were too important to waste time waiting. I finished up the semester at WVU, and then I transferred to an online college. I only have one semester until I get my degree. Once I'm finished, I can work from anywhere."

"I'm so happy right now. You have no idea. I don't think I'll ever let you out of my sight." She kissed right above my heart. "I love you so much, Logan."

"I love you, too. And you'll never have to let me out of your sight. I'm here to stay."

"What about when I go on tour again? Will you come with me?"

I nodded. "Yeah, I'll be there. Someone has to keep the crazy male fans away. I've seen pictures of you in your stage outfits. I'll be lucky if I don't end up in jail."

She laughed. "Have you been stalking me online?"

"Yep." I laughed. "Since I couldn't be around you just yet, I had to find a way to pass the time."

She sat up and turned to face me. "One more question, and then I swear, I'll stop looking for things that will ruin the moment."

"What?" I asked.

"Chloe—are you really over her? I want you to be honest with me. If you're not, we'll deal with it."

I grinned as I sat up and pulled her against me. "I'm over her. I have been for a long time. I don't want anyone but you, Jade. You have nothing to worry about when it comes to her."

"I trust you." She kissed me. "I'm done with the past. All I want to do is focus on the future."

"Me, too, babe. Me, too."

EPILOGUE

SEVEN YEARS LATER

"Are you nervous?" I asked Jade as I turned into Chloe and Drake's driveway.

"Not really. I think they'll be excited," she said as she looked over at me.

I grinned as I grabbed her hand and brought it to my lips. I kissed her palm before turning it over and kissing the wedding band I'd placed on her finger three years ago. It still didn't seem like we'd been married that long. Waking up next to her every morning was a gift that I still couldn't wrap my head around. It didn't seem real. How I'd ended up with her after everything that had happened made me realize that sometimes, things were just meant to be.

Things had changed so much for us over the past few years. As soon as I'd graduated, I'd started a web design business. I would travel with Jade and the rest of Breaking the Hunger, but my business was based in L.A. It had taken me a while to build up a client base, but after a couple of years, I'd finally managed to make a decent living off of it—not that Jade and I needed my income. Breaking the Hunger was one of the biggest rock bands in the world, and Jade's paychecks were more than I could wrap my head around. Most of my clients were other bands that I'd met through Breaking the Hunger. In the past two years, I'd expanded so much that I employed two designers to help me handle all the clients.

I parked my car next to Chloe's and shut off the engine. I climbed out and then grabbed the box filled with presents out of the backseat. As we walked up the steps to their home, I kept my other arm around Jade's waist.

She knocked on the door since both of my hands were tied up, and a few seconds later, Chloe peeked through the glass window in the door.

Chloe opened the door and smiled at both of us. "We were starting to wonder if you two were going to make it on time."

I grinned over at Jade. We'd stopped by the house we kept in West Virginia to grab the presents we stashed there, and we'd gotten distracted for a while.

"Sorry. Something came up."

Chloe laughed. "I'm sure it did." She held the door open so that we could walk in.

I kissed her on the cheek as I walked by. As soon as Jade and I rounded the corner, a hyper two-year-old tackled me.

"Uncle Loogahn!" Michael shouted.

I dropped the box filled with presents and lifted Michael off the floor. "Hey, little guy! How's it going?"

He grinned at me, and my heart melted. His eyes were the exact same shade of dazzling blue as Chloe's, but the rest of him was Drake. No doubt about it, he was Drake's mini-me, right down to the dimples and coal black hair.

"Santa brought me presents!" He grabbed my shirt in his tiny hands.

"Did he now? What all did you get?" I asked.

"I show you!" He wiggled to get down.

I set him on the ground.

He grabbed my hand to drag me across the living room to the tree. "Sit down!"

I sat down on the floor as Michael went to the tree and started grabbing toys out from underneath it. He picked up a toy guitar first and brought it over to me. I almost laughed.

Like father, like son.

"Lookie." He shoved the guitar in my lap and darted back to the tree.

Jade walked into the room and sat down on the couch, grinning from ear to ear. We both knew that Michael was my little buddy. Anytime we were around, he clung to me.

I glanced up when Chloe and Drake walked into the room. Chloe's eyes were glued to Michael as he carried over several tiny dinosaurs so that I could see them. Drake caught my eye and nodded.

Things had been calm between Drake and me for a long time. While we would never be best friends, we respected each other, and that was enough for both of us.

"Where's Amber?" I asked Chloe.

I knew that Eric and Adam had stayed back in L.A. this year, but I thought that Amber would be here.

"She's with her mom this year," Chloe said, giving me a sad smile as she and Drake sat down.

"Oh," I said, frowning.

"Look, Uncle Loogahn, dino!" Michael said as he held the plastic toys in front of my face.

"Awesome, little man." I took one from him and started poking him with it.

He giggled and dropped to the floor in front of me.

"Hey, Michael. Why don't you go over to that box and grab a few of the presents? I bet some are for you." Jade grinned at him.

She didn't have to tell him twice. He was up and running before she finished speaking. I laughed as he tugged on the box and pulled it over to me. I grabbed a few with Michael's name on them and tossed them to him.

"Open up, little man," I said.

He ripped the paper to shreds and pulled out his toys.

"Woooooow," he said as he looked at the massive bag of jumbo Legos.

"Ugh, my feet are already cursing you both." Chloe mock-glared between Jade and me.

"It gets better," I assured her as Michael went for the next present.

He squealed at the same time as Chloe groaned in defeat. Michael stared at the jumbo carton of tiny cars.

"I think I officially hate you," Chloe muttered.

Drake laughed.

I grabbed two packages out of the box and tossed one to her and one to Drake. "Nah, you love us."

Drake raised an eyebrow as he slowly unwrapped his gift. He laughed when he pulled a pair of Converse out of the box. "You know just what to get me. Thanks, guys."

Jade glanced at Chloe. "Aren't you going to open yours?"

Chloe gave Jade a smile as she opened hers. Her eyes widened in shock, and then she looked at first me and then Jade. "Seriously?" she gasped.

Drake leaned closer to her to see her present. He grinned before looking at me. "I think congrats are in order then."

Chloe pulled a tiny white onesie out of the box that had *I Love My Auntie* written across the front. "Oh my God! I don't know what to say! Just...ah!"

She jumped from the couch and tackled me. I laughed as she wrapped her arms around me.

"Logan, I'm so happy for you!"

"Thanks," I said as she released me.

She ran over to Jade. Both women hugged each other tightly.

"How far along are you?" Chloe asked.

"We go to the doctor next week to see. I just got the positive test last week. You two are our closest friends, so we wanted to tell you first."

"I'm really happy for both of you," Drake said as he stood and scooped Michael up off the floor.

Michael clung to his dad as he grinned at all of us. He was excited because everyone else was even though he didn't understand why.

I felt the breath leave me as Chloe stood and wrapped her arms around Drake and Michael. They looked like the perfect family. I glanced at Jade, knowing that the scene in front of us would be *us* in just a few months.

I stood and pulled Jade up off the couch. She wrapped her arms around me.

"I love you."

"I love you, too," she said.

"I'm starving. Can we eat yet?" Drake asked, breaking our moment.

I released Jade, but I grabbed her hand as we followed Chloe, Drake, and Michael into the kitchen. Michael laughed as Drake tossed him into the air. Jade and I sat down, and Drake tried to get Michael settled into his high chair.

"I gots your nose!" Michael shouted as he grabbed Drake's nose.

"Oh no! Not my nose!" Drake said before pretending to cry.

Michael lost it giggling and finally let Drake sit him in his chair.

Chloe put a plate of food in front of Michael, and Drake cut the turkey into tiny pieces for him. Michael ignored it as he grabbed his spoon and started shoveling mashed potatoes in his mouth.

Jade grabbed my hand under the table and squeezed. I glanced over at her to see her smiling at me.

"That'll be us soon," she whispered.

I leaned in and kissed her softly. "I know. I can't wait."

Jade and I were the perfect example of fate. After the way she'd grown up and the things I'd gone through with Chloe, neither of us had expected to end up happy.

Sometimes, fate steps in though. Sometimes, we're meant to have our happily ever after even if it's not with who we expected. Sometimes the most toxic events and emotions can lead us to where we belong.

I ran my hand against Jade's still flat stomach and smiled. *Yeah, I'd found my happily ever after.*

THE END

deception

Coming Fall 2014

Chapter One

My feet were killing me. All I wanted to do was go home, take a shower, and crawl into bed. Work had been brutal tonight.

I'd worked at the same diner for almost two years, but up until last week, I'd only been part-time. The day after I'd graduated from Morgantown High School, I'd switched to full-time.

I didn't mind waitressing, not really, but my body was still getting used to being on the move constantly. The diner, a small family-owned business, was always busy with the same customers. Most of them knew me by now and usually tipped well. We had a few college kids come in from time to time, but they usually went to one of the more popular spots in Morgantown. I didn't mind because they were normally the ones who would leave crappy tips.

I pulled into the driveway of my foster parents' house and yawned. I hoped they were asleep. My foster dad, Rick, was an asshole to me most of the time. The only reason he kept me and the other foster kids around was because of the nice checks he would receive for taking care of us. I knew my time here would be up soon. Today was my eighteenth birthday. Hopefully, my foster dad wouldn't remember. I didn't feel like getting kicked out of the only place I had to go tonight. My foster mom, Tammy, wasn't as bad as Rick. She was even nice at times, but her fear of Rick's temper would keep her from defending any of the kids. Rick wasn't abusive physically, but when his temper got the best of him, he would go on a rampage that rivaled a three-year-old's. Tammy had learned long ago to lock up anything breakable.

I'd been in twelve different foster homes since I was three. Tammy and Rick's house wasn't the best, but it definitely wasn't the worst. I shuddered as I thought about my last two houses. Yeah, I could deal with Rick's asshole ways. I didn't give a gigglefuck about Rick's temper as long as he didn't try to touch me.

I climbed out of my piece-of-shit car and headed for the house. My car was the only thing I truly owned. I'd saved every penny I could and purchased it two months ago. I'd paid six-hundred dollars for it, and I'd definitely gotten what I paid for. It was a 1989 Chevy Impala. The body was rusted out in several places. The rear fender was an ugly green color while the rest of the car was a faded red. It was the ugliest Christmas-themed car I'd ever seen. It was the ugliest car I'd ever seen, period. But it would get me from point A to point B most of the time. Sadly, it wasn't even legal, and I didn't have the extra cash to get everything I needed to make it so.

Once I reached the house, I stuck my key in the lock and turned it. I frowned when the door didn't unlock. I pulled the key out, thinking that maybe I'd shoved it in backward, so I tried again. Realization hit me when the lock still wouldn't turn over. Rick had changed the lock while I was at work.

I sighed in defeat before knocking loudly on the door. Lights turned on in the living room, and then I heard the door unlocking.

Rick opened the door and frowned at me. "Yes?" he asked.

"Um…the door wouldn't open for me," I said.

"Probably not. I changed the lock."

"Why would you do that?" I asked even though I knew the answer.

"You're eighteen now, Claire. You're no longer my problem."

I laughed humorlessly. "Seriously? You're kicking me out on my birthday?"

"Yeah, I guess I am," he said without remorse.

"Can I at least get my clothes and stuff?"

He shrugged. "Make it quick."

He moved out of the way, and I hurried past him toward the room I shared with Shelly. She was a foster kid, too. She'd been here when I arrived. She was only ten, but I'd found myself gravitating toward her from the beginning. We would look out for each other. I hated to think about her being here alone. I was pretty sure I was the only person in this house who cared about her. I passed by the boys' bedroom on the way to my room. There were four foster kids here total—Shelly, me, and two boys. Kevin was thirteen, and Jerimiah was eight. I wasn't as close to them as I was to Shelly, but I would still miss them as well.

I opened the door to my room and flipped on the light switch. Shelly was sound asleep in the bottom bunk. I moved around the room quietly, shoving my clothes and personal items into the suitcase I'd carried around since I was first put into foster care. It didn't take me long to pack. I had very few clothes and even less personal items. My eyes misted as I picked up the only thing I had left of my mom— a locket. I opened it up to see the tiny picture of her and me. I was only a few months old in the photo.

My mom had been killed in a car accident right before I turned three. Her parents were also dead, and no one knew who my father was. With no family to take me in, I had been thrown into the foster system.

I closed my eyes and tried to remember my mother. As always, nothing came to me, except the way she had smelled. That was all I knew about her—that she'd smelled like strawberries. I closed the locket and slipped it into my jeans pocket. Once it was tucked safely away, I closed my suitcase and glanced down at Shelly. I hated to wake her up, but I couldn't leave without saying good-bye.

I crouched down next to her and poked her gently a few times.

Her eyes slowly opened, and she stared up at me. "Claire? What's wrong?" she asked as she sat up.

"I have to leave, kiddo. My time is up." I tried to smile at her.

"What? Why?" she asked, panic filling her voice.

"Rick is giving me the boot. I gotta go."

"He can't do that!" she cried angrily.

"I'm eighteen, so technically, he can."

Her eyes filled with tears as she sprung off the bed. She wrapped her tiny arms around me. "I'm going to miss you so much."

I hugged her back tightly. "I'll miss you, too. Take care of yourself, and keep out of trouble, okay?"

"You know I will. Will I see you again?"

I pulled away and cupped her cheek. "I don't know. Maybe someday."

She nodded as her shoulders sagged in defeat. "Please be careful."

"Always. I love you."

"Love you, too," she whispered.

I pushed her back into bed and tucked her in. I kissed her forehead before pulling away. I stood and grabbed my suitcase off the floor. I gave her one last smile before I opened the door and slipped silently into the hallway.

Rick was still standing by the front door when I walked into the living room.

"Did you get everything?" he asked.

"Yeah."

"Good, because you're not welcome back here. Got me?" he asked.

"Yeah, I got you." I shoved past him.

I didn't look back as I walked to my car. I tossed my suitcase into the backseat before climbing behind the wheel. I backed out of the driveway and headed back toward the main part of town. I couldn't stop the tears from falling as I realized just how screwed I was. I had fifty bucks to my name until I would get paid next week. There was no way I'd be able to afford an apartment, even a shitty one. I just hoped that I could make decent tips until then, or I'd be living on air. I had no money, no friends, no credit. I had nothing. I was completely alone. The only thing I did have was my car.

I patted the dashboard gently. "Looks like it's just you and me now, ugly Christmas car."

I drove back to work and parked behind the building. There was no way I was parking on the street. With my luck, a cop would come by and notice that every sticker on my car was expired. I didn't need a tow bill that I couldn't pay for. I shut off the engine and reclined the seat back so that I was looking up at the roof of the car.

At least it's not cold out, I thought to myself as I closed my eyes.

My entire body went limp as I tried to control the emotions raging inside me. I tried to find the positives, but aside from the fact that I didn't have to deal with Rick anymore, there were none. I tried to shut off my mind, so I could sleep. I was working the morning shift tomorrow. I needed the money too much to oversleep and miss my shift. Plus, I didn't want to do that to my boss, Rob. He was a really nice guy, too nice for his own good sometimes.

I vowed to myself that I would figure things out when I woke up the next morning. I had no other choice. I had to make a plan, or I'd never survive.

Two days had passed since Rick kicked me out of his house. I'd accomplished nothing—unless I counted the tips I'd made. I was living off of dollar cheeseburgers and washing in the restroom sink at work. There was a Laundromat nearby, so I at least had clean clothes.

The first day, I'd left after my shift ended. I'd waited until the diner closed and everyone was gone before driving back and parking behind the building again. I'd made sure that I was up and gone before the diner opened up the next morning since I was on the night shift. The second day had gone much the same way, except I worked the night shift. I'd hidden at the local library all day, losing myself in the pages of not one, but two books.

It was the third day, and I was working the morning shift again. I was taking my daily sink bath in the restroom, and one of my coworkers, Junie, walked in on me while I was naked. Apparently, I had forgotten to lock the door, and now, I was caught.

"Oh my God!" I screamed as I tried to cover myself.

Junie looked like she wanted to die as she quickly mumbled an apology and slammed the door shut. After I dried off with paper towels, I walked back into the main part of the diner. I walked to the coffee pots and started making both decaf and regular, praying that Junie wouldn't mention what had happened. Naturally, she cornered me while I was dumping coffee grinds into the filter.

"Claire, why were you taking a bath in the restroom?" she asked.

I glanced up to see concern in her brown eyes. Junie was older than me, probably in her late twenties or early thirties. Her hair was light brown. She was pretty but plain. She'd recently gone through a nasty divorce, and she had lost a lot of weight. I knew the stress from her divorce and trying to raise her two boys on her own was taking its toll on her.

"I didn't get a chance to shower at my house this morning," I lied.

"Cut the crap, Claire. What is going on?" she asked.

I debated on lying again, but I couldn't do it. Junie had always been nice to me, and I couldn't lie right to her face.

"Rick kicked me out of the house the other night," I said as I looked away from her.

"He what? That asshole! I'm so sorry, Claire," Junie said.

I looked up to see her brown eyes had filled with anger.

"Don't apologize. There's nothing you or anyone could have done to stop him. We both knew it was coming."

"You could call in and report him though. I mean, he's still getting paid for this month even though you're eighteen."

"And then what happens if Child Protective Services decide Tammy and Rick aren't suitable foster parents? Shelly, Kevin, and Jerimiah would be pulled and possibly put into a house that could be ten times worse. Rick's an ass, but he'd never hurt them. I won't be the reason they're sent to a horrible home," I said as I stared at her.

She sighed. "Fine, I see your point, but it's still not right. What are you going to do?"

I shrugged. "I have no clue. I guess I'll just keep saving my tips until I can afford a place to stay. My car is fine for now since it's summer, but I'll have to find somewhere to stay before winter hits."

"I wish you could stay with me, but I have no room," she said, clearly upset over the fact that she couldn't help me.

"Don't worry about it, Junie. I'll be fine. I just need you to promise me that this doesn't leave the two of us. I don't want anyone to know what's going on with me. It's embarrassing."

"Claire…" She bit her lip.

"Junie, *please*," I begged.

"Fine. I won't say anything. I just wish I could help you somehow."

"Don't worry about it. Just focus on taking caring of your kiddos. They need you more than I do."

She gave me a weak smile before walking over to a family that had just walked in. I watched as she led them to a table and handed them menus. I smiled as I watched the mom pick her baby up out of the portable car seat and cradle the baby in her arms. A wave of sadness swept over me as I thought of all the things I'd missed out on with my own mother. I just hoped that this baby would have a better life than I had.

The rest of the morning went by quickly. By the end of my shift, I was dragging. Once my last table was cleared, I walked into the back room and grabbed my purse. I headed out to the front and waved at Sarah, the waitress taking over my tables. She waved back before turning her attention to the two guys she was waiting on.

Rob came barreling out of his office and headed straight for me. "Claire, I need a favor," he said when he stopped in front of me.

"Sure. What's up?" I asked.

"I hate to ask you this, but Stacey just called off. Can you work the evening shift, too? I'd ask Junie, but I know she has to pick up her boys from the sitter."

My feet screamed at me to run away, but I couldn't do that to Rob. Plus, I needed the extra money.

"Of course I'll stay." I smiled at him.

"Thank you. I owe you one, Claire. Don't think that I haven't noticed how hard you've been working lately."

I nodded. "I try. I'd better go put my purse away and head back out onto the floor before Sarah gets overrun."

He nodded before turning and walking back into his office. I hurried to the back room, and I shoved my purse in my locker. After making a quick stop in the restroom, I walked out onto the floor. Sarah was running back and forth, trying to take care of her tables as well as mine. I gave her an apologetic smile before heading to my side.

By the time my second shift was over, I could barely walk. It was a Friday night, and we'd been especially busy. The diner didn't serve alcohol, which I knew kept away several potential customers, but we were constantly busy with families. Most of them had tipped well, and I ended the day with almost one-hundred dollars in tips. I smiled when I realized I would be eating something besides artery-clogging hamburgers when I left. I might even splurge on a salad.

"I'm beat," Sarah said as we wiped down all the tables. "I don't know how you're still standing. You've been here since we opened."

"Sheer will and determination. Plus, I made a ton of tips today."

She high-fived me as she walked by. "Nice. Go buy yourself something pretty."

I laughed and smacked her on the butt with my towel.

The tables were clean, the condiments and shakers were filled up, and the floor was mopped, so I walked to the back room and grabbed my purse. After shoving my cash inside, I told everyone good night and headed out to my car.

I drove across town to Denny's and ordered the salad I'd been desperately craving. I even ordered a Coke instead of water. I was a splurging fool tonight.

When I glanced up from my salad, I noticed two guys watching me from a few tables over. Both of them were good-looking from what I could tell. They were around my age, so they were probably students at West Virginia University. Morgantown was a college town through and through, and the streets were crawling with kids. I assumed that these two were local since most of the students had packed up and headed home for summer vacation.

One of them noticed me staring, and he gave me a smile that sent my heart racing into overdrive. Suddenly embarrassed by my gawking, I looked away and used my blonde hair as a shield between them and me. I'd had a few dates in high school, but they had been nothing to get excited over. I wasn't a virgin. I'd lost that to Scott Marks my junior year, but I definitely wasn't skilled when it came to the opposite sex.

I ate my food quickly and paid my bill without looking over at the guys' table again. My life was a disaster as it was. Adding a guy would only complicate things more. I walked out to my car and quickly unlocked the door before climbing inside. Once the doors were locked, I started the engine and pulled away from the lot.

I couldn't help but grin as I remembered the guy's smile. He'd been cute from what I could tell. His dark brown hair had been shaggy, but it hadn't been so long that it looked messy. His arms had looked toned, probably from playing football or basketball. Those were the only two sports, especially football, that people really cared about around here. Once football season hit, that was what everyone would talk about. I wasn't a big fan of sports, but even I cheered for the Mountaineers.

I drove back to the restaurant and parked, trying not to think about the cute guy or his smile. I yawned and reclined my seat. Yeah, there was no way in hell I could think about boys right now.

EXCERPT FOR

BREAKING ALEXANDRIA

CHAPTER ONE

I groaned and rolled over to escape the sun shining through the window of Joel's bedroom. My body tensed as I realized for there to be sunlight, then it must be day. My eyes opened, and I grabbed my cell phone from the table beside the bed to check the time. *Shit.* It was almost three o'clock in the afternoon, and I had a ton of voice mails and missed calls. I couldn't believe that I'd slept this late. I was so fucked.

I sat up and pulled the blanket up to cover my naked body. I had snuck out of my parents' house last night after they grounded me for fighting in school again. I'd thought I could sneak back in this morning before they woke up, but that obviously wasn't going to happen now.

My eyes traveled to Joel as he snored lightly beside me. The sun was directly on his back, showing off the skull and crossbones tattoo that covered most of the area. His normally guarded expression was gone while he slept. Joel looked like the typical badass, but he was so much more. His body was covered in tattoos—and when I say covered, I mean, covered. There was barely an inch of him that didn't have ink with the exception of his face. His hair was a dark brown color, and he kept it just a bit shaggy. His eyes were a startling green color that made people stop and look twice. His cheekbones and overall face structure would make any male model jealous.

I smiled dreamily as I thought about our night together. At twenty-two, he was five years older than me, but our age gap never seemed to bother him. We'd been together for almost a year now, and I couldn't be happier. I'd met him at my cousin's graduation party two years ago, and I'd instantly developed a crush on him. He hadn't paid any attention to me, but when I'd started hanging out with some of his younger friends who were in high school with me, I'd finally gotten him to notice me.

I'd been drunk at a party one night and braver than usual. Girls much older than me had surrounded him, but I had shoved through them when I saw him and walked straight up to him. He'd raised an eyebrow when I stopped in front of him, but I'd simply hopped on his lap and kissed him until I couldn't breathe. After I had finished, I'd stood up and walked away.

We'd been together ever since that night.

My parents weren't happy that I was dating someone who was so much older and more experienced. The fact that he was covered in tattoos from head to toe hadn't helped my case any either, but I'd sworn to them over and over that Joel and I weren't having sex. Obviously, that was a lie, considering where I'd woken up just now, but they didn't need to know that.

Joel was trouble. I'd known that before I got with him, but I'd still taken a chance, and I was glad that I had. Everyone knew he was the son of the town drunk, and it showed. Joel had one hell of a mean streak. Even when he had been in high school, everyone had been terrified of him. He had been kicked out for fighting more times than I could count. On top of that, everyone knew he was the go-to guy if someone needed a fix. He'd later explained to me that he'd started selling drugs to help pay the bills that his dad never worried about. Joel was good at dealing though, and he'd stuck with it even when he could have left this town and started fresh.

He had already been living on his own by the time we met, and I was glad. I wasn't sure how I would have handled seeing the man who had abused Joel for years. I wanted to cause Joel's father as much pain as he had done to Joel. I knew it had been years since Joel had talked to his father, but it still bothered me.

"Joel, wake up. I need to leave," I said as I nudged his shoulder.

He groaned in his sleep and rolled over, but he refused to open his eyes. I sighed as I hit his shoulder harder. His eyes finally opened when I started smacking him on the stomach. He shielded his eyes as he rolled over to look at me.

"What?" he grumbled.

"I need to go home, like, right now. We slept in." I stood up and started looking for my clothes.

"You're already in trouble. Why hurry home to be yelled at?" he asked as he sat up.

He didn't bother to cover himself, and I couldn't bring myself to look away from his naked body. I loved the trail of dark hair leading down his stomach…to other places. His nose was a bit crooked from being broken more than once, but it didn't take away from his appearance. If anything, it made him look sexier and dangerous. His eyes were his best feature by far though. They held a vulnerability in them that made me want to crawl into his arms and try to make everything better.

He was in great shape. I guessed he had to be when he dealt with strangers who were high and desperate for their next fix on a daily basis. The muscles in his arms were well-defined, and his chest was as hard as a rock. I loved curling up in his arms. I always felt like he could protect me from anything.

"I don't want to make it worse," I said as I located my clothes.

They were next to the door, making it obvious as to how they had come off. We'd barely made it to his room before he started stripping me.

"Your parents suck. Why do they care so much about you fighting? At least they know their kid can defend herself. Personally, I'd be proud," he said as he stretched.

"They're sick of me getting kicked out of school. They said something about college and doing something with my life."

"I fought, and look at me. I'm living the high life." He grinned at me.

I rolled my eyes even though I knew he had a point. He used drugs occasionally, but he sold more than anything, and he'd made quite a lot of money doing it.

"I'm sure they'd be so proud of me if I decided dealing drugs was going to be my career choice in life. I might even get the Daughter of the Year award."

I still couldn't find my underwear, so I decided to skip them. He grinned as he watched me pull on my shorts.

"Looking for these?" he asked as he held up my underwear.

I walked over to the bed and held out my hand. "Come on, I need to hurry. Give them to me."

"Make me," he taunted.

I grumbled as I went to grab them, but he held them just out of my reach.

"Damn it, Joel."

He reached up and pulled me back onto the bed. "Maybe I don't want you to go home. Maybe I should hold your underwear for ransom, so you'll stay."

"Keep them. I'll get them another time."

I tried to sit up, but he kept me pinned against him.

"Stay for a little while longer. We can light up and have some fun."

"I can't go home stoned. That's just asking for trouble."

"But you could go home thoroughly fucked," he said as he ran his fingers down my back.

I shivered. "I could, but I need to leave."

"I'll make it quick." He started pulling my shorts down my legs.

"Joel…"

"Shh…you know you want to."

Of course I wanted to, but I was already in so much trouble.

He silenced my protests as he rolled me onto my back. His naked body was tight against mine, and I could feel just how much he wanted me. He tweaked both of my nipples with his fingers, making me moan.

Fuck it. Going home will have to wait.

"Oh fuck," I said as he nudged my opening with his dick.

He leaned down and ran his tongue across my throat and then across my breasts. I arched my back, trying to get as close to him as possible. His hand traveled down my body to my core, and he started rubbing my clit. His dick was still teasing me at my entrance. I tried to adjust my body, so he would enter.

"I thought you had to go home," he taunted.

"I do, but I thought you said you wanted to fuck me."

"Oh, I do. Grab the bedposts."

I did as he'd said, preparing myself for his entry. He didn't disappoint. He slammed into me hard enough that I had to hold on to the bedposts to keep myself from moving up the bed. I gasped out his name as he pulled out and ran his thumb along my clit.

God, I'm going to kill him for torturing me.

"Again," I said as I shifted, trying to force him to enter me.

"You like it rough, don't you, baby?" he teased.

"You know I do," I groaned.

He ran his hands over my body before grabbing my hips and thrusting into me again. Over and over, he slammed into me until I was gasping for breath. He wasn't gentle, and I hadn't expected him to be. It was just the way we were. He liked rough sex, and I was happy to oblige.

I wrapped my legs around his waist to allow him to go deeper as I met him thrust for thrust. His grip on me tightened as he came closer to his release. I couldn't hold out much longer either. I was *so* close. He continued to pound into me as he reached between us. He flicked my clit and sent me screaming into my orgasm. My legs clamped tighter around him as I came. His thrusts became harder and more erratic as he came with me.

TOXIC

My body went limp. Once my orgasm left me, I could see again. Joel was panting above me with his forehead resting against mine. After his breathing returned to normal, he slipped out and rolled over to his side.

"I told you I'd make it quick," he said as he grinned over at me.

"Yay for you." I stuck my tongue out at him.

He continued to grin as he leaned over, and then he kissed me. "Come on, let's get you home."

We both dressed quickly, trying to hurry. Now that I wasn't staring at Joel's naked body, the need to get home was strong. I knew I was in trouble, but I just couldn't bring myself to care at the moment. I was tired of spending all my time trying to figure out ways to get around my parents' rules.

I knew fighting didn't solve anything, but it sure as hell made me feel better. Since Joel and I had become a couple, I'd made quite a few enemies, especially from the female population, but I didn't really give a fuck. He was mine, and if people tried to come between us, I'd take care of them.

I wasn't the sweet and innocent girl I'd been before I met Joel. He'd changed me—but for the better. Before him, I'd rarely partied, and I'd never gotten into trouble. Now, I did what I wanted, and I didn't care what anyone thought of me. I had no friends of my own. I only hung out with his. It didn't bother me though. I hated girls. My solitude and bad attitude usually led to rumors that I was on drugs or helping him sell them. And both rumors were true, so they didn't bother me either because it made most people leave me alone.

But there was always some dumb skank who thought she could talk about me or try to push me around. I knew how to take care of myself. The girls who tried to start fights with me always ended up with blood dripping down their faces as they cowered on the floor.

Joel had taught me how to fight since he would bring me along to deals. He would even send me out to do them on my own if he was

267

busy. Most people who were aware of the fact that I was helping Joel deal thought I was nuts, but I considered it a normal part of our relationship. Besides, he never sent me out on deals that were dangerous. He always handled those on his own. I would try to help him as much as possible. I knew that if I got caught, I wouldn't end up in as bad of a situation as he would since I was under eighteen.

I didn't use drugs often —with the exception of weed. While I had no problem dealing, I didn't want to end up like one of the addicts who I supplied. They were gross and pathetic. Joel smoked weed a lot, but as far as I knew, that was the only thing he did. We both knew that if he started using, his profits would disappear.

We walked down the steps from his house to where his Harley was parked outside. He was the only guy I knew who was confident enough in his badass reputation to leave his bike out on the street all night. I grabbed my helmet and put it on before climbing on the bike behind him. I wrapped my arms around him as it came to life, and we tore down the street.

I loved being on his bike more than anything else. I'd made him promise me that we would go on a road trip the summer I turned eighteen. I wanted out of this town and away from my parents. I just wanted to be free.

The ride was short but exhilarating. We arrived in front of my house faster than I would have liked. While I had been in a hurry to get home, I hadn't taken the time to mentally prepare myself for the fight that was sure to ensue. Sure enough, the front door flew open as soon as Joel parked and shut off his motorcycle. My mother stomped down the sidewalk to where we were sitting before I even had the chance to take off my helmet.

"Get. Inside. Right. Now!" she shouted.

I sighed as I pulled off my helmet. *This should be fun.* "I can explain—" I started.

She held up her hand to stop me. "I don't want to hear it. Inside the house—now."

I kissed Joel's helmet and hopped off the bike. He started it back up and left, leaving me to deal with my mother alone.

Asshole.

"Mom, let me explain," I started again, hoping that she would let me talk. "I just wanted to see him for a little bit. I planned to stay with him for only an hour or two, but then I fell asleep when we were watching a movie. I woke up and started freaking out."

"You never should have gone to him in the first place. You're grounded."

"You can't keep us apart. I love him, and he loves me!" I shouted.

"You have no idea what love even is, Alexandria! You're still a child."

"Yeah, I do. I know what I feel for him is love, and there is nothing you can do to change that."

I stomped past her, focusing on the front door in front of me. Once I made it inside, I hurried upstairs to my room. She followed, obviously not finished with me.

"You are not to leave this house for a week. You were kicked out of school for the rest of the week, and since you don't need to be there, you don't need to be anywhere."

"What does it even matter? This is the last week of school anyway. If I hadn't been suspended, I would have skipped anyway."

My mother shook her head. "I will never understand you, Alexandria. You're not my baby girl anymore, and I have no idea what happened to you. I'd blame Joel, but this attitude of yours started long before him. If things don't change, I'll—"

"You'll what? You might as well figure out what you'll do to me because this is me, and I won't change who I am to make you happy."

"You're destroying yourself, Alexandria. Look at you—you're as thin as a twig. You've dyed your beautiful blonde hair black and put red through it. You won't listen, and you have no respect for your father or me." She glared at me. "And don't even get me started on those piercings in your lip and nose. They look horrible."

Currently, I was rocking a septum piercing, a piercing in my nose, and looped snakebite piercings. I really wasn't sure why she was still so angry over it. I came home with new body modifications all the time. I would think she'd be used to it by now.

"Don't forget about my tattoo. I know how much you love it," I said sarcastically.

Almost three months ago, I'd come home with a tattoo on my left arm. I wasn't eighteen yet, but Joel's friend was a tattoo artist, so he had done it for me. I'd wanted a tattoo forever, so I'd jumped at the opportunity to get one. I had drawn the design myself. It covered most of my inner arm from my elbow to my wrist. At the top was a skull that ended with partial butterfly wings. Below that was a blue rose. I loved it even though I'd ended up being grounded for a month when my mother saw it.

"I'm tired of your attitude, Alexandria. Enough is enough."

"I love you and Dad, but I'm tired of you both looking down at me. This is my life, and I'll live it however I want to. I don't have an attitude. I just can't handle how you freak out over every little thing."

My mother's nostrils flared as she tried to control her temper. She closed her eyes, and I watched as she counted to ten under her breath. Her entire body sagged the second she hit ten. It was like someone had dropped a ton of bricks on her shoulders.

"I don't know what you expect from me, Alexandria. I refuse to just sit here and watch you self-destruct."

I stared at my mother as she spoke. She looked tired, the kind of tired that came from worrying. Her blonde hair was hanging limply around her face, and there were lines around her mouth and eyes that I hadn't noticed before. Her hazel eyes that were identical to mine had fear in them. I felt a twinge of guilt for causing her any worry, but I pushed it away.

"I don't expect a damn thing from you."

Acknowledgments

For me, this is the hardest part of my books to write. I need to thank so many people, and I know I'm going to miss a few of you!

First, I want to thank my husband. He's stuck with me since the beginning. If it wasn't for him, I would never finish a book. His support means more to me than he knows. I love you.

To my son—You make me smile when I have absolutely nothing to smile about. Your giggles, silly games, and sarcasm (I wonder where you get that from!) make every single day brighter.

To my author friends—I love you all so much. Without your constant support, I'd be a raging lunatic by now. I love tossing ideas back and forth with you ladies. You rock my socks. A special thanks to Tijan for being my rock. I swear, I'd marry you if you lived closer. Please never stop answering my 3 a.m. Facebook messages. If you do, I'll hop on a plane and hunt you down.

To my blogger friends—GAH! You guys are so incredible. Seriously. Several of you have been with me since the beginning, and I don't know what I'd do without you. Your dedication to everything *book* constantly amazes me. Nicole, Kristy, Amanda, and Amber—please never stop Snapchatting me.

To my assistant, Amber—This is my seventh book, and I'm just now mentioning you. How horrible am I? Don't answer that. I just want to thank you for everything you do. I would be lost without you! Also, you make traveling to signings so much more fun! If you ever tell me no, I'm going to force you onto an airplane. You know I'll do it. I can't survive airports without you.

To my parents—I love you guys. That about sums it up. You're always there for me, no matter what.

Chasity—You were Logan's very first fan. Thank you so much for beta-reading this book for me. I hope his story was everything you hoped for. Love you, chica.

And last but not least, to my readers—Your dedication constantly blows my mind. I owe you guys everything, and I love all of you so much! I couldn't ask for better readers. YOU make all of this totally worth it. If it wasn't for you, I would have given up long ago.

About the Author

K.A. Robinson is twenty-three years old and lives in a small town in West Virginia with her husband and toddler son. She is the *New York Times* and *USA Today* bestselling author of The Torn Series, The Ties Series, and Breaking Alexandria. When she's not writing, she loves to read books that usually have zombies in them. She is addicted to rock music and coffee, mainly Starbucks and Caribou Coffee.

For more information on K.A., please check out the following pages:

Facebook: www.facebook.com/karobinson13

Twitter: @karobinsonautho

Blog: www.authorkarobinson.blogspot.com

22014031R00164

Made in the USA
Middletown, DE
17 July 2015